Lynne Francis grew up in Yorkshire but studied, lived and worked in London for many years. She draws inspiration for her novels from a fascination with family history, landscapes and the countryside.

Her first saga series was set in west Yorkshire but a move to east Kent, and the discovery of previously unknown family links to the area, gave her the idea for a Georgian-era trilogy. Lynne's exploration of her new surroundings provided the historical background for the novels, as well as allowing her to indulge another key interest: checking out the local teashops and judging the cake.

When she's not at her desk, writing, Lynne can be found in the garden or walking through the countryside or beside the sea.

By Lynne Francis

THE MARGATE MAID

A Maid's Ruin
The Secret Child
The Lost Sister

THE MILL VALLEY GIRLS

A Family Secret
A Daughter's Hope
A Country Scandal

THE LOST SISTER

Lynne Francis

PIATKUS

PIATKUS

First published in Great Britain in 2022 by Piatkus
This paperback edition published in 2022 by Piatkus

1 3 5 7 9 10 8 6 4 2

A CIP catalogue record for this book is
available from the British Library.

ISBN 978-0-349-42465-1

Typeset in Caslon by Hewer Text UK Ltd, Edinburgh
Printed and bound in Great Britain by Clays Ltd, Elcograf S.p.A.

Papers used by Piatkus are from well-managed
forests and other responsible sources.

MIX
Paper from
responsible sources
FSC® C104740

Piatkus
An imprint of
Little, Brown Book Group
Carmelite House
50 Victoria Embankment
London EC4Y 0DZ

An Hachette UK Company
www.hachette.co.uk

www.littlebrown.co.uk

THE LOST SISTER

PROLOGUE

I have been through more than one hard time in my life. As I sit here thinking, I suppose I can account for at least four. But then I fall to wondering whether, in fact, these are all part of the same whole, one a consequence of the other. It is true that they all result from the same thing — believing myself to be in love with a man who spurned me, leaving me with child and with no alternative but to flee to London. My first hard time.

Then I come to the second, when I had to abandon my baby. And then another, when I thought I might reclaim him, only to discover I had been duped in my hopes for the future; then, again, I fell into a pit of despair. So — three sets of hard times in as many years, followed by a long period when I found my way back to happiness, with a husband and three grown daughters of my own. The rediscovery of the son I thought lost should have been a happy time but I was blamed, and rightly so, for keeping the child a secret; blamed by my husband, by my family, by the lost child himself.

Somehow, we found our way back to a new balance, a new happiness, one I had every hope that I would enjoy for the rest of my life. But then came the fourth hard time, in the form of Harriet, my half-sister, whom I had loved and cared for from when she was born until I had to leave home (due to my own folly) when she was small.

I was glad to hear that she had returned to the area again, some twenty years after her mother had moved away on the death of our father. But I didn't know then what I know now.

Undated, in Molly Dawson's hand, on a piece of paper folded into the back of her housekeeping accounts.

PART ONE

HARRIET

CHAPTER ONE

I'd recently fallen into the habit of stopping to gaze out of the window when I should have been attending to the patients. The changing face of the sea – the way it could be a mysterious green in colour and flat calm one day or churning and brown when the wind was driving directly against the windows – was more interesting to me than the men and women I was supposed to be tending.

Their humours tended not to vary. On the whole, they were full of complaints – usually about their doctors' insistence that they must be exposed to the maximum amount of sea air each day. Or about the charity cases – impoverished Londoners suffering from scrofula, an affliction affecting their glands, joints and bones – for whom the hospital was originally founded. I was, on occasion, forced to remind my patients that at least they didn't have to spend each night sleeping in the open air, as the charity cases did. To my surprise, though, they rarely complained about the sea bathing, the cornerstone of their treatment programme. One and all, they were impatient for improvement in their condition and hoping for relief from their damaged lungs.

Throughout my time working at the Royal Sea Bathing Hospital in Westbrook, I had my doubts as to the efficacy of the treatment but, since it kept me and others in employment, you would never catch me saying anything other than soothing words to the patients. I had regular work, and although the money wasn't very good and the lodgings even worse, I needed to stay there for as long as I could – or so I thought then.

I had become used to having only myself to look after, since my mother had remarried and my brother John had been incarcerated in Maidstone gaol. I had, I thought, resigned myself to a life of hard work with but a few simple pleasures – a new frock every now and then, ribbons for my bonnet, the loan of a novel from the lending library in Hawley Square. I might long for a gown of Indian silk, but such finery would be wasted. Since I had moved to the edge of Margate, from Eastlands Farm, I had had no cause to travel further afield.

I had family in the area but we had lost touch more than twenty years earlier and I did not seek them out. They would enquire after John and I was hard-pressed to come up with a convincing lie. Years of petty crime and brawling had culminated in his latest sentence of five years. I could have invented a new life for him somewhere distant – London, Scotland, Australia perhaps. Although the latter was too close to where he would inevitably be sent if he transgressed again. That or the gallows. Meanwhile, the risk of his reappearing once his sentence was over, in search of whatever money I might give him to go away again, meant his existence was best kept quiet.

I had taken a different name, in an attempt to distance myself from my brother's notoriety. I had been Harriet Goodchild when I moved to Eastlands Farm. Now, having adopted my mother's maiden name, I was Harriet Dixon. It was a gesture of rejection of my father's family too, I suppose. They had abandoned me, after all.

I have taken care to acquire a small nest-egg, built up in the course of my work but not necessarily as a result of my own efforts. It was the decision by the hospital trustees to fund the charitable patients by taking private ones that played into my hands. Not all of these private patients were careful about where they kept their jewellery or small amounts of cash. It was hardly my fault if rings discarded thoughtlessly on bedside tables apparently slipped down between the floorboards. I was always meticulous in warning the patients of such hazards; even so, several items of jewellery vanished in this way.

Gentlemen, I noticed, were equally careless of how they emptied change from their pockets before divesting themselves of their clothing in preparation for immersion in the sea. They rarely, if ever, noticed the absence of one or two coins and it soothed me to see how quickly small amounts added up to something more appreciable. Soothed me because, it has to be said, I was not always sanguine about where my life had taken me. Like the sea that I watched with increasing frequency from the windows, I had been buffeted by life – dragged under and flung out to a place not of my choosing.

CHAPTER TWO

It was neither the sea nor the hospital treatments that led me back to my half-sister, Molly, after more than twenty years. It was the hospital garden – which I'm sure Dr Lettsom, who ran the hospital, saw as his greatest accomplishment when I started work there in 1815. By then, the hospital had been open under his guidance for nearly ten years and the garden was well-established. On the days when Dr Lettsom was at the hospital he was as likely to be found out there, clipping and watering alongside the head gardener, as he was to be in his office. He said the garden was for the benefit of the patients, although few seemed inclined to take advantage of it.

I discovered later that it was on his London estate that Dr Lettsom had first met Charlie Dawson, who was to play such a key part in my story. Charlie made regular plant-finding trips for the Powells at Woodchurch Manor; one to Dr Lettsom's beloved garden. Dr Lettsom was delighted to discover a plantsman living so close to his hospital in Kent – no more than a couple of miles away as the crow flies – and he invited Charlie to Westbrook. He'd been visiting the garden for a little while when I first had cause to speak to him, and that was only because I was in search of Dr Lettsom.

It was a hurried enquiry, driven by the need to find the doctor: one of the patients had become particularly quarrelsome and declared his intention to return to London. The doctor was nowhere to be found within the building so the overseer, Mrs Murray, sent me to look outside in the gardens.

Finding a man at work in the borders, I asked him whether he had seen the doctor. My query was initially impatient, conscious as I was that Mrs Murray was waiting. But I barely heard the man's response, 'The doctor has gone to Margate with a promise to be back before too long,' for I was so arrested by his appearance. When he straightened, I saw that he was a good deal taller than me, with a well-tanned face and hands. The smile he gave as he replied crinkled the skin around his dark brown eyes. I judged him to be about a decade older than I was, for his hair had a few threads of silver, but his slender, wiry build could easily have been that of a much younger man.

I found myself blushing as I thanked him and hurried back inside, knowing I would have to appease Mrs Murray for returning without the doctor. For the next hour or so, I caught myself glancing out at the garden whenever the opportunity arose, hoping for further glimpses of this man at work. Of course, I didn't know his name at this point, but it was easy enough to find out from Dr Lettsom. I saw the doctor return from Margate, walking in his usual brisk way despite the warmth of the day, and hurried down from the room where I was folding laundry to meet him in the hall.

I told him that I had been in search of him earlier, but that the man in the garden – here I paused, hoping he would supply the name – had told me he had gone on an errand to Margate.

'Ah, Charlie. Charlie Dawson – the head gardener from Woodchurch Manor. I do hope he is still with us and hasn't

9

had to return. It took me longer than I thought to see to business in town.' Dr Lettsom looked flustered. 'But first I had better attend to the problem with Mr Conway.'

I would have offered to take a message out to the garden but Dr Lettsom clearly expected me to be at his side while we went in search of Mrs Murray. I was distracted while the issue with Mr Conway was resolved, for the name the doctor had given me had stirred an elusive memory. I felt sure it was familiar to me from my childhood, too far back to remember it with any clarity. I resolved there and then to meet Charlie Dawson again to find out more.

It was, perhaps, no coincidence that I began to pay more attention to my appearance at work each day. My uniform was surely pressed with a little more care and my dark hair pulled back a little less severely under my cap, although still neat enough to satisfy Mrs Murray. I may also have tried out some different expressions before the glass in my room, aware from the frown lines on my brow that I was in danger of looking like an old maid.

For old maid I surely was – twenty-nine years old, with no husband and no prospect of one, unless I was prepared to take on one of the pot-bellied men of the so-called genteel class in Margate; one of those somewhat older than myself whose wife had departed this life, worn down by the toil of looking after the household and the children and listening to her husband's complaints. Is it my fault if I began to wonder whether there might be another way to achieve the sort of life I surely deserved after the hardships I had endured?

CHAPTER THREE

Ibegan to make it a habit to take one of the patients, old Mr Walters, out into the garden each day, judging him the least able to demur. I'd told Mrs Murray that I had reason to believe Mr Walters missed his own garden and that he took pleasure in our daily perambulations, with me pushing the heavy and somewhat creaky Bath chair along the gravel paths. My efforts had been rewarded by a growing acquaintance with Charlie, whom I had discovered would call by the garden at regular intervals. He would arrive bearing cuttings or recommendations of plants that Dr Lettsom might try, to see if they would withstand the salt-laden breezes that the doctor declared plagued his attempts to replicate his London garden.

I had progressed from nodding polite greetings to Charlie to stopping to ask him about various plants as he worked in the borders, relaying the information received loudly to Mr Walters. My patient appeared somewhat bewildered by this but so far hadn't given voice to his confusion. In any case, his deafness meant that many other members of staff at Westbrook assumed his other faculties were affected, too.

'And have you always lived around here?' I was hoping that Charlie's answer to my apparently casual enquiry would reveal where our paths had originally crossed and I wasn't disappointed.

'I've lived and worked at Woodchurch Manor for more than twenty-five years now, but before that I was at Prospect House in Margate.' Charlie's expression clouded and he frowned as he bent over his spade. 'That's the poorhouse. I lived there and I was apprenticed to the head gardener, Mr Fleming. He's dead now.' Charlie sighed. 'He was very good to me. He set me on the right path and I owe everything to him. I wish I'd made more of his company. It's too late now.'

'I'm sorry to hear that,' I said. 'It's so often the way. We think we will have plenty of time to spend with our friends and family at some point in the future. Then, before we know it, they've gone.' I made my voice as sympathetic as possible and adjusted my expression to suit, but inside I was jubilant. I knew at once who he was and our paths had indeed crossed when I was very young. I wasn't sure, though, whether to reveal this now or save it for a later date.

I was spared that decision by a call from the house, asking me to bring Mr Walters back as he was due his sea immersion. It was to be several days before I came across Charlie in the gardens again, but by then I had planned what I needed to say to him. I was out with Mr Walters in the Bath chair once more – by now Dr Lettsom was completely convinced that the gardens were beneficial to him – and I wasted no time in speaking to Charlie.

'I'm so pleased to meet you again, Mr Dawson,' I said, with no preamble whatsoever. 'It came to me after we last spoke that we have met before, although I don't remember a great deal about it. My half-sister used to take me to the Prospect House gardens when I was very small, along with my brother

John. I'm afraid my main memory is that there was cake, and lemonade too.'

Charlie frowned. 'Your half-sister – do you mean Molly? Why then you must be . . .' He paused, and I could see he was searching his memory. 'Harriet?' He stopped what he was doing and stared at me. 'You were a little scrap of a thing back then. Molly will be so pleased to hear that I've come across you. I know she wondered what became of you.' He paused again. 'We're married, you know, Molly and me.'

I nodded vaguely, although he was too caught up in shaking his head in wonder to notice. Of course I knew they were married – my mother had told me. I also knew that none of my half-sisters – Molly, Lizzie or Mary – had made any efforts to find out what had happened to me when our father died. They knew what my mother was like, yet they let her take me and John away from the family and all I had ever known to that God-forsaken farm of her father's in Eastlands.

John was always her favourite, the one she indulged, while she set me to work helping around the house. I was only seven or eight and could barely see over the copper, but she'd have me pounding the family washing when I wasn't peeling vegetables or feeding the pigs. Not that she stayed there for long. Before a year had passed she'd married again: a neighbouring farmer with two sons of his own. She said it was more convenient for John and me to stay where we were, on her father's farm. No other members of the family ever thought to look for us.

I didn't say any of this to Charlie. What I said was, 'Oh, I do so hope I can meet Molly again. She took good care of me when I was small and it's been such a long time since I last set eyes on her.'

13

'Well, we must remedy that,' Charlie said. 'I'll speak to her tonight. I'm sure she will want to arrange a meeting very soon. Imagine coming across you here, like this.' He was still shaking his head in astonishment as I excused myself, saying I should take Mr Walters back inside.

To begin with, I was mainly curious. Why had the family given me no thought once I was gone? It was because of Ann, my mother, I expect. I saw how people were around her. Men were eager to do her bidding but a little frightened of her. Even her own father.

'She's a difficult woman,' I heard him say to John, when he demanded to know why she'd left us. 'She does what she thinks is best.'

Were the women of the family scared of her, too? It was something I wanted to know. My mother was cold and indifferent to me, so perhaps I had got off lightly. I could shrug off her moods when we first moved to Eastlands Farm, and later I tried to ignore her desertion of us.

I could, in fact, remember more of my early years in Margate than I let Charlie think. Lizzie and Mary had looked out for me as I grew, but before then it was Molly who made sure I was well cared for. She lived next door at the time – a result of her not getting on with my mother, I think. Molly made sure to take John and me out regularly – most often to the gardens at Prospect House. When one of my mother's black moods came upon her, it was Molly who made sure I had a clean pinafore and my hair was brushed, and that we'd at least dined on bread and jam if there was nothing more to be had.

Now those days in Margate appear to me as if they were bathed in a golden glow. By contrast, the days at Eastlands were cold and damp, summer and winter, in a farmhouse that was tumbling down through lack of care. Our grandfather fell ill shortly after we arrived, which was probably when our mother decided it was time to move on. She didn't intend to play nursemaid to anyone. That role fell to the cook and, as I got older, increasingly to me. I suppose the best you can say about caring for my grandfather is that it helped me to get the job I have now. There was no need to lie in that respect.

I'd changed my mind about not wishing to see my family. I was curious to meet Molly again and discover why John and I had been abandoned. At that point, I don't think there was anything more to it. But the meeting I had begun to look forward to was unaccountably delayed: as summer came to an end, I hadn't encountered Charlie again and all too soon the hospital closed in the autumn, as it did every year.

Chapter Four

Dr Lettsom's death late in 1815 came as a shock to us all. It meant that none of us knew whether we would have jobs to return to in the spring of the following year. At that time, the hospital shut between October and March because the sea was too rough for the immersions, and the weather too chilly to spend all the hours outside that the doctor recommended. Sleeping outside in those months would have been the death of many of the patients – not necessarily a bad thing, in my view.

I was relieved on two counts when I received word that the hospital was saved: I would have a steady income to rely on once more, and there was the prospect of seeing Charlie again. I was worried, of course, that with Dr Lettsom gone, Charlie had no reason to continue visiting the hospital gardens. I passed a few anxious days looking out for him and I had just decided that I would have to ask the head gardener about him when, through the windows, I spotted him. Mr Walters's treatment had finished and he had returned to Bermondsey at the end of the previous September. I needed another excuse to be outside.

In fact, it proved easy enough. The patients, encouraged to take the air as often as possible, were usually to be found on the terrace overlooking the sea, as the breezes there were considered so beneficial. That week in March there was still a chill in the air and I noticed Mrs Pearce shivering, despite the blanket wrapped around her legs.

'Can't I be moved out of this wretched wind?' she complained.

'I could take you for a turn around the gardens,' I suggested, and she agreed at once.

The gardens were on the more sheltered side of the building and Mrs Pearce, unlike Mr Walters, was fit enough to walk. We spent some time examining the new shoots appearing in the borders and the leaves beginning to unfurl on the trees, before she professed herself a little breathless. I settled her on a bench in the sun, to rest and listen to the birds singing, for I'd spied Charlie just leaving the glasshouse at the end of the garden. I excused myself to Mrs Pearce and hurried to catch him before he departed.

'I'm so pleased to see you here,' I said. 'I feared that with the sad loss of Dr Lettsom you might not visit again and I didn't want to lose touch.'

'A sad loss, indeed.' Charlie looked grave. 'I will miss my discussions with Dr Lettsom, and it is true that I will be here a good deal less frequently now. But I'm glad to see you at last, Harriet. I had hoped to come across you before the closure last autumn, as I had an invitation for you. Molly wanted me to ask whether your work allowed you a free afternoon and, if so, whether you might be persuaded to come out to our cottage at Woodchurch Manor?'

I told him that I had every second Sunday afternoon free and would be delighted to visit them, if that wasn't an inconvenient day.

'I'm sure it will suit well,' Charlie said. 'You must come on your next free Sunday,' and so it was arranged for the following week and their address committed to heart.

I dare say Mrs Pearce had barely noticed my absence, for she had fallen into a doze and was none too happy when I suggested it was time to return to the seaward side of the hospital. I had accomplished what I needed and had no great interest in spending any more time in the garden.

I took some care when dressing for my first visit to Molly and Charlie, choosing my plainest frock but taking delight in being able to wear my hair in a freer style than usual, with only my bonnet to confine it. I thought of my hair as my crowning glory. Almost black in hue and luxuriant in its growth, it tended to fall in natural waves. I must have inherited it from my father, for my mother's hair was fair. I think she disliked me for it, for whenever she brushed it when I was young she tugged on the hairbrush, yanking my head back, and complained about knots and tangles. Thinking about it now, I realise that she never once paid me a compliment.

I walked over to the Woodchurch Manor estate, taking pleasure in the spring sunshine. It felt good to escape the confines of the hospital, even though I had only recently returned to it. I'd spent the autumn and winter caring for the elderly father of a London family, a post that Dr Lettsom had found for me. They'd tried to persuade me to stay and if it hadn't been for my wish to reacquaint myself with Charlie, and Molly, I might well have done so. But I was glad now to be back in the fresh air of the countryside and my heartbeat quickened with anticipation at the thought of seeing Charlie and Molly again.

Charlie had provided good directions to the cottage and I caught but a glimpse of the splendid house that had to be

Woodchurch Manor, before I turned off on a quiet lane leading directly to their front door.

Molly must have been watching me walk up the garden path for she answered my knock almost immediately.

'Harriet!' she exclaimed, stepping back to usher me in. 'Let me take a good look at you. Why, I don't think I would have recognised you.'

She led me through to the parlour, glancing back and smiling over her shoulder as we went. 'How well you look,' she said, encouraging me to take a seat by the fireplace.

I would have been hard-pressed to say the same of her. She had aged a good deal since I'd last seen her – hardly surprising, I suppose, given the amount of time that had passed. I was shocked to see her chestnut hair now faded, and her face more lined than I remembered it. But she was talking and I needed to pay attention.

'I've often wondered what became of you, Harriet, and wished that we could see you again. But Ann spirited you away to her father's farm and here we are – all those years behind us.'

I thought she looked a little uncomfortable at her own words but she moved on swiftly. 'And how is your mother?'

'Well, as far as I know,' I said. 'She married again, shortly after we moved to Eastlands, and I saw her only rarely after that.'

Molly looked shocked. 'Oh, Harriet, I had no idea. That must have been very difficult for you. And for little John. How is he?'

'Hardly worthy of the name "little" any more,' I said, 'for he is as broad as he is tall.'

'And does he live close by? Do you see him often?'

Molly was hovering by the door and I knew she was eager to go and set the kettle on the range and attend to the tea.

'He's in Maidstone gaol,' I said, taking delight in the effect that my words had on her.

'Oh, my goodness.' She sat down suddenly in the nearest chair, her previous intention to depart to the kitchen now forgotten.

At that moment Charlie came in and looked between us, sensing something amiss. He went to stand by Molly and put his hand on her shoulder. She reached up to cover it with her own.

'Is all well?' he asked.

'Oh, Charlie. Harriet has just told me that little John – I mean, John – is in Maidstone gaol.'

I thought Charlie seemed less surprised than Molly, but he politely enquired as to the background to this sorry state of affairs.

I filled them in as briefly as possible, then Molly departed at last for the kitchen, leaving me alone with Charlie.

'You have a beautiful cottage,' I said, looking around the room at the polished wooden furniture, the grandfather clock ticking in the corner, the samplers hung on the wall by the fireplace. 'Have you lived on the estate for long?'

'Aye. I've been here since I was seventeen, straight from Prospect House back in 1788. Molly joined me here three years later. It suits us well. Mr Powell and his sons are a good family to work for.'

I delayed enquiring about his own family until Molly returned, asking him instead about the nature of his work on the estate. I was listening as he spoke but barely took in a word of what he said. Instead, I watched his hands move, fascinated by his long, strong fingers, which he used to emphasise a point.

Once Molly had returned and set the tea things on the table, politely declining any offer of help, I asked her whether she and Charlie had any children.

'Oh, heavens, yes! And grandchildren, too.' She told me about their four children: George, Sally, Agnes and Catherine, and their grandchildren – Grace, Simon and Eleanor.

'And George and Judith married last summer so we'll have another on the way before long.'

From the fond look that passed between Charlie and Molly, I could see what a strong bond they had and how important their family was to them.

I'd never had anything like that. It cut me right to the core.

CHAPTER FIVE

By the time I began my walk back to the hospital later that afternoon, I had recovered. I told myself that, after such a length of time, my first encounter with Molly had gone well. I'd expressed an interest in renewing my acquaintance with the rest of the family, as well as my other half-sisters, Lizzie and Mary. I felt I had been quite respectful, being careful not to push for such a meeting too soon. There was plenty of time to get to know them, and for them to get to know me – or, at any rate, the Harriet that I was prepared to let them see.

The wind was coming directly off the sea and, as I left the fields behind and passed the cottages on the edge of Westbrook, I could feel the chill in the air. I breathed in deeply, taking in the distinctive salty scent carried on the wind. I was looking forward to shutting myself into my room to think about my next steps, although, of course, these were entirely dependent on Molly and Charlie. It felt good, though, to know that I had made the first contact with my family. I felt sure it wouldn't be the last.

I didn't see Charlie in the gardens for quite some time after that and my initial euphoria began to give way to unrest. I vowed to myself that if I had had no word from Molly, or sight of Charlie, by the time May came, I would get in touch with them instead. In the last week of April, though, I was distracted from my worries in an entirely unexpected way. Summoned by Dr Harwood, our new doctor in charge of the hospital, I found him in his office with a slender figure, wearing our drab brown working garb, standing in front of his desk. He introduced her as Margaret Roberts and said she was the new assistant, engaged to work alongside me with the private patients. She was the replacement for Mrs Norwood who had recently left under a cloud, accused of improper relations with an elderly gentleman in her care. (I'm convinced she had an eye on his money, and her married title was, I suspect, one of convenience.)

I was so startled by Margaret Roberts's appearance that I was unable to utter a word after Dr Harwood had made the introductions. To give him credit, Dr Harwood filled the awkward silence that threatened to develop by telling Margaret Roberts he had full confidence in me and she was to ask me anything at all that troubled her during her work.

Her eyes had been downcast when I first entered but when she raised her head and turned her gaze full upon me, I declare it was the first time I had seen a dark-skinned person at close quarters. There were such fellows at work along the jetty in Margate, of course, unloading cargo that must have travelled a great distance over the seas. But I had no reason to concern myself with them: they were just a familiar part of the scene. Margaret Roberts was a good deal lighter in hue than the sailors, but I could hardly examine her in great detail without causing offence. I could see, though, that she was dressed neatly enough, and her hair was pinned up, out of sight beneath her cap.

23

Dr Harwood was speaking again. 'Margaret looked after her father in his later years, caring for him through a long-drawn-out and unpleasant illness. I'm sure you will find that she has all the necessary skills for her work here.'

He had lost interest in us now, returning to his desk and beginning to shuffle through the papers there, so I knew we were dismissed.

'This way,' I said to Margaret, gesturing to her to follow. I walked ahead of her down the corridor, mind racing.

As we began to ascend the staircase leading up to the seaward terrace, I felt I must make some sort of conversation.

'Where have you come from, Margaret?' I asked.

'From my lodgings in Margate,' she replied. There was a pause and then she relented. 'But perhaps you mean where was I born?'

It was a shock, both to hear her speak and to be teased by her in this way. She spoke as well as I did, if not better, but with an accent I couldn't place.

'I was born in Jamaica,' she continued, 'but my mother is from Martinique. That's where I lived from when I was twelve until just before I came here.'

I was curious to learn more, not least as to where Martinique was, although of course I had heard of Jamaica. But there was no time to question Margaret further for we had arrived on the seaward terrace. Here, I was outdone in my reaction to Margaret's appearance. Some of the patients regarded her with outright hostility and I overheard remarks that would have made my blood boil, had I been Margaret.

She acted as though she hadn't heard and embarked on her duties with serenity and dignity. I couldn't help but keep watching her throughout that first day, although I told myself I had an excuse: I had been tasked with keeping an eye on her. I wanted to dislike her – in fact, I'm ashamed to admit now that when I was introduced to her in Dr Harwood's office, my first reaction had been indignation that we were expected to work together. But she was good with the patients, tolerating their complaints and happy to resettle any who would submit to her touch. Some seemed to believe that the colour of her skin would rub off on them and I noticed them shy away from her. I confess that over the next few days I took some pleasure in asking her to attend most particularly to those patients who showed the greatest aversion to her. She never once demurred, even if they did.

Mr Franklin took particular exception to her. I heard him talking to some of the other private patients, boasting about his knowledge of 'her type' as he put it. 'She's a mulatto. Daughter of a slave and a plantation owner, I'll be bound. Common enough out in the West Indies. My brother is in the sugar trade out there, you know. It may be all right in those parts but I can't see why we should be forced to put up with this sort of thing.'

On the first day, he had quite a circle around him, nodding in agreement, but by the end of the week it amused me to see that nearly all of the patients, apart from him, had fallen under Margaret's spell. She never showed any awareness of what was being said about her and she was undoubtedly skilful in her work.

Margaret kept herself to herself but, after I'd been forced to express my grudging admiration about the way she had handled a particularly unpleasant encounter with Mr Franklin, she told me that she was no stranger to difficult Englishmen.

'My father, after all, could be described as such, although not out of disrespect for my mother. His ire was all directed at the Royal Navy, at how they had treated him.'

She turned away after that, as if annoyed that she had revealed something of herself, leaving me intrigued. A father in the Navy: this was worth knowing more about.

CHAPTER SIX

In fact, it was to be a while before I learnt more of Margaret's story. She proved to be a private person – so private that I began to wonder what she had to hide. Turning my mind to uncovering more about her situation diverted me, at least, from worrying about why I had heard nothing further from Molly or Charlie. My working day was long but the hours were, on the whole, tedious, filled with small tasks that didn't fully occupy my brain. I had too much time to think about my situation and ponder how to improve it, gazing out to sea even as I encouraged the patients to fill their lungs with the beneficial air, or while I turned beds and folded linen.

Working alongside Margaret, I took the chance to probe her for a little more information whenever I could. The obvious place to start was how she had arrived in Margate from this place called Martinique.

The answer was both more straightforward and more complicated than I had imagined. It turned out that Dr Lettsom had family connections with the West Indies, where he was born, his father having been a planter out there. Margaret told me that he was well known among the islanders for freeing his slaves when he inherited the estate from his father. This was a surprise to me. I'd had no idea that the doctor had been anything other than a London man, who had set up the hospital here by the sea to treat the poor in accordance with his Quaker beliefs.

Margaret gave me a look when I voiced this. 'He was a wealthy man, wasn't he?' she asked.

'Why, yes,' I replied. I knew that he'd had a large estate south of the city, which was where his passion for gardens came from.

'And where do most of the rich men in London and other great cities get their wealth from?' she demanded.

I confess I was puzzled. 'He was a doctor?' I ventured. 'And I suppose the other great men have professions or businesses that have made them wealthy.'

'Indeed,' she said, as we conducted the little dance between us, required to fold the sheets that had been drying outside in the sun. 'And what sort of businesses?'

'I don't know,' I said. I was becoming impatient now with her questions. 'Sugar, tea, tobacco, cotton.' I ran out of ideas.

'There you have it,' she said. 'All the product of plantations. And plantations are worked by slaves.'

I frowned. I was in danger of losing the thread of the conversation now. 'So you're saying Dr Lettsom's wealth came from slavery?' I knew enough to realise that this was a touchy topic, one that led to a great deal of debate in Parliament. I never felt it had much relevance to me.

'Yes, but the doctor had no wish to have his estate worked under these conditions, so he freed his slaves. He was much admired locally for it.'

'I still don't see how this relates to your arrival here,' I said, keenly aware that our linen-folding was almost at an end and Mrs Murray would move us on to something else, doubtless with less chance to continue the conversation.

'When my father died, my mother and I decided that we must move to Jamaica, thinking it more likely we could get work there. I applied to the hospital in Kingston, and the overseer there told me she had recently been approached by a doctor from England, in search of women to work in his sea-bathing hospital. He had already returned home but she urged me to write to him, thinking I would be a suitable candidate because of my command of English.'

'But why was Dr Lettsom in Jamaica?' I wondered aloud.

'His son and his brother live there. I gather he visited them every few years.' Margaret smoothed the last pillow slip and laid it on the pile. 'We are done here. We had better inform Mrs Murray.'

'But you haven't finished your story,' I protested. 'What happened next?'

'Why, Dr Lettsom wrote back and asked me to come here as soon as possible, which I did. But it is a long sea journey from Jamaica and when I arrived I was very sorry to discover that he had died. I would have liked the opportunity to meet him and thank him. Dr Harwood was happy to honour my offer of employment, though.'

'Did you come alone? What about your mother?' I thought I could hear Mrs Murray's footsteps echoing along the corridor.

Margaret turned away from me, pretending to straighten the stack of linen. 'She wasn't well enough to come with me so I had to leave her behind. She told me she would get work as a dressmaker there. I will send her money whenever I can. It takes so long for letters to find their way to and from Jamaica, though. Nearly two months in either direction.'

Mrs Murray was upon us now. 'I asked you to fold the bed linen, not waste time in idle chatter. The patients are waiting for their soup to be served. Go and attend to them in the dining room.'

We bobbed our heads in recognition of her orders and set off along the corridor and up the stairs in silence. I kept glancing at Margaret as we ladled out the soup and handed out the bread, sure that I had seen the gleam of tears, but she steadfastly refused to catch my eye.

She must have thought she had overdone the confidences for it was at least two weeks before I got anything else out of her other than the normal day-to-day information regarding the patients.

In the meantime, I'd thought about her words and grown used to the idea of Dr Lettsom having had another life, one that had taken place a great distance away in another country. I wanted to know more about this strange land, about plantations and slaves. I had never travelled above fifteen or twenty miles from the place I was born in all my twenty-nine years. Margaret, who was a few years younger, had already travelled far across a sea such as the one I gazed upon every day as I went about my work. I tried hard to imagine what her life had been like, but it was already clear to me that she came from a place most unlike Westbrook or Margate or even Canterbury.

CHAPTER SEVEN

The arrival of a letter from Molly, inviting me to join them at a family christening, diverted me from trying to discover more of Margaret's history.

> *I must apologise for the delay in writing to you but we have a new grandchild and I do not know where the time has gone. George, my son, and his wife Judith have had a son of their own and the christening is planned for the first Sunday in May. We would be delighted if you could join us. The service will take place at the church on the estate and there will be a gathering afterwards, here at the cottage. It will be a chance for you to reacquaint yourself with my sisters, Lizzie and Mary, along with other members of the family, and also to meet my three daughters. I know a full day away from the hospital might be difficult to arrange but I hope your overseer can be prevailed upon.*
> *Your loving sister,*
> *Molly*

I stared at the letter for some time, struck most of all by the words 'your loving sister'. It had given me a jolt of pleasure to read them but, on reflection, how true were they? I wondered whether Molly had hesitated before writing them or if they had come naturally. I rather thought the former to be true.

Then I turned my attention to the invitation. On Sunday mornings we were required to attend the church service held in the hospital chapel, along with our patients. After that, if we were due a half-day, we were free to leave. It would be hard to secure a full day away, as Molly had anticipated, in addition to which the date did not coincide with my free half-day: I would have to arrange to swap with someone.

I worried over this through the course of the day, knowing that few among the staff would wish to change their half-day with mine. Most had families nearby and they would be unwilling to postpone their visit to them. There was one exception, of course: Margaret. As far as I knew, she had no one.

By the end of the day, I had made up my mind. I asked Margaret whether I could have a word with her in private before she left and, although she looked surprised, she agreed readily enough.

I put it to her straight away. 'Margaret, I've received an invitation to join my family at a christening on Sunday week. I've been separated from them for years and I would dearly love to be able to go. It isn't my free Sunday afternoon but I believe it is yours – would you be prepared to exchange?'

'Of course,' Margaret replied, without hesitation. 'But if it is a christening, won't you be expected in the morning? How can that be managed?'

I shrugged. 'I'm not sure. But I'll find a way.'

I had no plan, other than failing to appear for work that morning. I would be in trouble, without a doubt, but I didn't think Mrs Murray would seek my dismissal. I was confident of my own value to the hospital. I put aside the thought and turned instead to making plans for how to look my best for the christening, only ten days hence.

I had few good dresses, since my daywear consisted of the drab hospital garb. In my room that night I took down each one from its hanger and subjected it to hard scrutiny. I settled on a striped muslin, praying that the weather would be kind. I was pleased that I had recently invested in new ribbons for my bonnet.

It was early on that May Sunday morning when I slipped away from my room, hoping I wouldn't encounter either patients or staff. I had decided that I would far rather have time on my hands away from the hospital than run the risk of Mrs Murray stopping me. I walked along the coast for a while, enjoying the sparkle of the sun on the water, before the coolness of the breeze drove me inland to seek the sheltered lanes between the hedgerows. My spencer was adequate but the fine muslin gown provided little protection against the wind.

The hedgerows, newly leaved, were full of birds darting hither and thither, nest-building or already feeding their young. The sun provided much more warmth there and I found myself all of a sudden too hot and forced to remove my spencer to carry it over my arm. It was as I walked along the lane towards Woodchurch Manor that I heard a cart coming up behind me. I stood back to let it pass, surprised that a carter would be at work on a Sunday. I saw the driver was Charlie in the same instant that he recognised me and slowed the horse to a walk, before bringing it to a halt.

'Climb up,' he said. 'I can save your legs the last mile.'

I hesitated a moment, fearful of soiling my pale muslin but not wanting to lose the chance of sitting up beside Charlie.

Once I'd scrambled onto the seat, he explained himself. 'I was despatched to fetch the ale for the party. The brewery should have delivered it yesterday but their horse took lame. It seemed easier to borrow the estate's cart and do the job myself.'

We set off again with a bit of a lurch that threw my legs against Charlie's. I suspected he was more skilled as a gardener than as a carter, but I kept my counsel. Instead, I nodded as he cheerfully described the confusion he had left at home as Molly attempted to prepare for the party while helping her son and his wife get the baby ready for his big day. I noticed at once that he'd said 'her son' and not 'our son', saving the thought to be pondered later.

'I fear they'll be taking the baby to church with butter in his hair and a gown full of breadcrumbs,' Charlie said, smiling to himself at the idea.

'Perhaps I can help,' I offered, rather hoping that I wouldn't be called upon to do so. I wanted to look my best for my first meeting with the family after all these years.

'Oh, I'm sure you can be excused,' Charlie said. 'You're our guest of honour today.' We bowled along for a minute or two in silence before he added hastily, 'But it was good of you to offer.'

We had left the lane behind, joining the road from Margate, and in another minute or two we turned off towards Woodchurch Manor. A short time later, I was climbing down from the cart outside Molly and Charlie's cottage, surreptitiously brushing the back of my gown, while Charlie unloaded the barrel of ale and rolled it along the path.

'Come along in,' he said over his shoulder, seeing me loitering by the gate. 'I'll take the horse and cart back to the stables and then I'll be with you in time for the walk to the church.'

He was hardly dressed for church, I noticed, but his hand was on my arm and he was ushering me through the door, into a kitchen filled with warmth and noise and containing at least two more new members of my family, whom I had never met before.

Chapter Eight

In my eagerness to rediscover my family, I hadn't antici-pated how exhausting I would find the experience. I had led a solitary life for several years, caring for the sick by day with little in the way of socialising. Now I found myself thrust into the heart of an extended family, all intent on introducing themselves to me, all with questions to be answered. Before we even set off for the church I had met George and his wife, Judith, and cooed as expected over baby Joseph.

Agnes, Molly's only unmarried daughter, came to join us in the kitchen and I learnt that she was an artist, staying overnight at the cottage, although she was more usually to be found in Ramsgate or London. I suppose her occupation accounted for her attire, which I felt to be rather shabby for a formal church occasion. She was petite, like her mother, and wearing a plain dark green serge dress – quite severe, I thought – noticeably worn around the cuffs. Her brown hair was also in disarray, but her mother didn't chastise her. Although probably not long in her majority she was, admit-tedly, old enough to know her own mind. Molly gave her daughter a hug and declared that as soon as Charlie returned from the stables she would chivvy him to change and then we must set off for the church at once.

Within fifteen minutes, we were walking along the lane from the cottage, Molly – arm-in-arm with Agnes – taking the lead, while George, Judith and Joseph followed. Charlie and I brought up the rear.

As we walked, Charlie was still smoothing his hair and checking that his shirt was properly buttoned and tucked in, such was the haste of his preparations after his return from the stables. I hardly knew how to make conversation with him at first but settled on, 'It's unusual, is it not, to have a daughter who is an artist, Mr Dawson?'

'You must call me Charlie, please,' he said. 'Well, I can't say I've thought about it. She's always had talent and what with Mr Powell, my employer, seeing something in her – along with Molly's friend, William Turner, of course – it seemed only natural to let her have her head.'

'William Turner?' I asked. 'The artist William Turner?'

'Why, yes.' Charlie turned to me with a smile. 'Molly knew him when he studied in Margate as a youth. She met him again in London and again when he came to stay with the Powells some years ago.'

His smile turned to a frown. 'I can't say that I took to him but he's been good to Agnes and she sees him every now and then. He still comes to Margate – seems to have a liking for the place.'

Far too soon, for I was enjoying the sensation of walking at Charlie's side, we arrived at the gate of the church where yet more family members had congregated. I had to break off from my conversation with him to be introduced to their other two daughters, Sally and Catherine, with their husbands and children – the latter too numerous for me to recollect their names. I could see that Catherine had done well for herself in marrying into the Powell family, taking as her husband Francis, the youngest son of the Woodchurch estate. The manner in which she and her husband were dressed showed me at once that they had money, but they were as relaxed in the company of Molly and Charlie as everyone else.

'Aunt Lizzie and Aunt Mary are already in the church,' Catherine said to Molly, taking Agnes's place at her mother's side. 'They said the sun was too warm for them out here.'

'Very wise,' Molly said, smiling. 'We'll all be getting unseemly colour in our cheeks.' Then she turned to me. 'Come inside, Harriet, and see my sisters. Or, rather, see them again. They are your sisters too, you know. And I will introduce you to their families.'

Molly took my arm and I had a moment's flashback to a time in the past, when I was very young and Molly would take me to Prospect House gardens, always holding my hand on the way to make sure I didn't stray. Lizzie and Mary would join us on those trips, too, and now here they were once more, standing up in their pew to greet me as we took the row in front of theirs. We embraced awkwardly across the pew's wooden back and I wondered whether I would have recognised them if I'd come across them by chance in the street. They were young girls back then. Now they were matrons with three grown children between them. Their husbands looked ill at ease in their Sunday best, tugging at their cravats while buttons strained on jackets no doubt made for their younger, slimmer selves.

The church, thankfully, was cool and I sank into the pew, conscious of beads of sweat on my brow caused by the warmth of the day and the strain of making conversation with so many new people in such a short time. I knew only too well that there was more of the same to follow at Molly and Charlie's cottage after the service.

I confess I paid less attention than I should have to the christening ceremony. In my head, I was running through the names of everyone I had met and wondering whether I could recall them correctly. I experienced a pang when Joseph's godparents stepped forward – if I had met the family earlier, might I have been considered for such a role? Then I dismissed the notion. I'd already decided that I didn't wish to become too embroiled in the Dawson family, their son and daughters, grandchildren, nieces and nephews. I wanted to stay a little apart from them, to observe them. I was beginning to formulate a plan but, as yet, I was unsure of how to put it into action. I was prepared to bide my time.

Chapter Nine

With the ceremony over, and baby Joseph having acquitted himself well by not crying during the baptism, we all walked back to the cottage. Once again, I found myself partnered by Charlie, Molly having been drawn into conversation by her sisters.

I heard her ask Lizzie why Aunt Jane wasn't at the service, getting the reply that Uncle William wasn't well and she had stayed at home to tend him. I'd been spared yet another family encounter, although I remembered Aunt Jane quite well. John and I had been regularly invited round to their house, which was next door to Molly's family cottage in Margate. We went to play with Constance, Aunt Jane's grandchild. I remember Aunt Jane as rather stern, although we saw little of her, and the house as being on a grander scale than Molly's. One of the maids, or the cook – Hannah, I think she was called – generally took care of our needs.

I was able to retreat into my memories for, although I walked at Charlie's side, he was much taken up with jolly remarks that passed up and down the group. The short distance between church and cottage was covered before I'd been able to share more than a couple of words with him, and once we were at the gate, I was swept away from his side and ushered into the parlour, while the children were all sent into the garden to play.

I found myself seated next to Molly's youngest sister, Mary, and her husband while Molly busied herself in the kitchen alongside her daughters. Mary wasted no time in asking what had happened to me and where I'd been since they'd last seen me, over twenty years earlier, when my mother (her step-mother) had taken me to Eastlands Farm. I was sure Molly must already have told her all but I dutifully filled her in.

She was pleasingly shocked by my mother having defected shortly after we'd moved away and expressed regret that they hadn't known.

'If only we'd had word!' she exclaimed. 'I know Aunt Jane would never have allowed you to stay there under those circumstances.'

I shrugged. 'It's a shame no one thought to enquire.'

She blushed scarlet and I regretted my words. It wasn't my intention to show my hand in this way.

'No matter,' I said, to smooth things over. 'I haven't come to any harm. I have a good job now, at the Royal Sea Bathing Hospital.'

Again, I was sure Molly must have told her but Mary listened intently and asked questions about the treatment there, expressing surprise that the patients were expected to sleep outside in spring and summer.

'As for the sea bathing . . .' She shook her head. Then a look of horror crossed her face. 'You aren't expected to take patients into the water yourself, are you?'

'No, no,' I hastened to reassure her. 'The dippers do that. They help the patient down the steps of the bathing machine, support them in the water and see them safely back into the machine before it is pulled from the sea.'

Mary shuddered. 'It makes me cold even to think about it. I can't imagine what it must be like to experience it.'

I couldn't, either. We had been encouraged to try it for ourselves but I had declined with barely a moment's consideration.

Margaret had shrieked when the idea was suggested to her. 'If the good Lord had intended us to go into the water He'd have given us fins,' she declared.

I smiled at the memory and caught Mary looking at me with curiosity.

'I was thinking of what another member of staff said to me,' and I repeated Margaret's words. 'She's from the West Indies,' I added. 'I do believe the climate is a great deal warmer there.'

'The West Indies, you say?' Mary said. 'Our cousin Nicholas spent the last years of his life there. I'm not sure whether you ever met him?'

A few minutes' conversation established that Nicholas was mainly at sea when I was young, sailing away on his trip to the West Indies when I was barely three years old.

The discussion with Mary reminded me to ask Margaret more about the islands she came from as soon as I had the chance, but my thoughts were interrupted by a summons to help ourselves from the spread Molly had prepared.

I took my plate out to the garden, for I'd seen Charlie going in that direction. I found him sitting under an apple tree wreathed in blossom, watching the children at play.

'It's always lovely to see the family together,' Charlie remarked, as I sat on the grass next to him, 'but sometimes I just have to make my escape. I spend a lot of time working alone in the gardens and I must have become too used to my own company.'

I half rose at his words, murmuring something about leaving him in peace.

'Oh, heavens, no.' He reached out and grasped my arm, pulling me gently down. 'That truly wasn't intended to be as rude as it sounded. Another example of how unfit I am for polite company.' He gave me a rueful smile. 'Please excuse me. I didn't mean you, of course. I think you are also used to keeping your own counsel. I find your company restful.'

He patted my hand in what was meant as a paternal gesture, I'm sure, but it sent fire through my blood and I felt the colour rise to my cheeks.

'Goodness,' I said, setting my full plate to one side and fanning my face with my cloth napkin. 'It really is warm today.'

'It is,' Charlie agreed. 'It will be very good for the garden. It will bring the flowers along nicely in Mr Powell's borders.' He peered up at the sky through the branches of the tree. 'Provided the sky isn't too clear tonight, that is. It isn't too late in the year for a touch of frost.'

I noticed that he had a glass of ale but no food. I picked up my plate and offered it to him. 'Would you like this? I can fetch another.'

'Bless you, no,' he said. 'You're our guest. I can get my own.' His words made me secretly curse myself for the offer. I wanted to keep him at my side, not drive him indoors.

'Eat,' he said, gesturing at the plate. 'I do believe the pork pie will be particularly good. It was always Catherine's favourite when she was a child, and Molly has had many years to perfect the recipe.'

I contrived in any case to share my plate of food with him, protesting that I'd been handed the plate fully laden and it was far too much for me. We sat on in our blossom bower, talking inconsequentially about this and that – the children at play, the weather, his favourite part of the Woodchurch Manor garden – until we were summoned inside to toast baby Joseph's health and to eat a piece of cake in his honour.

I thought Lizzie, who had been sent to call us in, gave me an odd look so I took care to separate myself from Charlie once we were inside. I stood close to Catherine and Francis, raising my glass in a toast and exclaiming over the impressive christening cake, which Francis said had been sent over from the Woodchurch Manor kitchens.

Shortly afterwards, I sought out Molly and said I must make my return journey for I would have evening duties at the hospital. I took care to express fulsome thanks for my invitation.

'I've had such a delightful day,' I said. 'My head is quite spinning from meeting all the family. I must congratulate you on providing such a lovely celebration for Joseph, who is a charming baby.' I began to wonder whether I was overdoing it, but Molly looked pleased at my words, although her brow was damp from her exertions in the kitchen.

I looked around the crowded room. 'I'm going to slip away without making my farewells to everyone as I don't want to disturb the party but please say goodbye on my behalf.'

Molly smiled. 'Of course. I understand you must get away. It was very good of you to come.' She looked around, a little distracted. 'I wonder whether any of the family from Margate might be able to offer you a ride home in their carriage.'

'Oh, please, no – I wouldn't dream of disturbing anyone. I'll enjoy the walk. It's still a pleasant afternoon and I will be glad of the air.'

'It's a great shame Aunt Jane wasn't able to be here,' Molly said. 'I know she will want to meet you again. Perhaps we can arrange something in Margate before too long.'

Then she was drawn away by George, so I took my chance and slipped out. I made a point of not saying goodbye to Charlie, but as I hurried down the path and onto the lane I turned back towards the house as I fastened the gate. I thought I glimpsed him at the kitchen window but I studiously avoided casting more than a cursory glance in that direction.

I turned my face into the wind, back towards Westbrook. Anyone who encountered me on that journey would have wondered what had happened to wreathe my face in smiles. I couldn't help but feel satisfied. I was tired from the whirl of introductions, but I felt it had gone very well. I was re-establishing myself in the family, building relationships. I just needed an opportunity to present itself.

CHAPTER TEN

My excuse for leaving the christening party – that I had evening duties – was an untruth and I slipped back into the hospital and up to my room in the attic without encountering another member of staff. Margaret lived away, in a rented room in Margate, so I couldn't question her over whether Mrs Murray had reacted to my absence that morning. I had no story prepared for the next day – I simply couldn't think of anything plausible. I could hardly plead illness when it would have been easy to check whether I had lain sick in my bed. Yet I didn't dwell on my predicament – my thoughts were too much occupied with the events of the day – and I fell asleep easily enough that night.

In the morning, I rose and went about my duties as normal, snatching a moment to quiz Margaret as we passed each other, preparing to take our patients back out on the seaward terrace after their breakfast.

'Was my absence noticed? Was anything said?'

'Nothing was said. It doesn't mean it wasn't noticed.' Margaret's matter-of-fact reply awakened in me a sense of unease for the first time.

When we passed again, in the corridor, she said, 'I hope your reunion with your family went well?' I could see she was genuine in her enquiry. I could only nod, for I could see Mrs Murray waiting at the end of the corridor. As I reached her, she spoke.

'When all your patients are outside, Miss Dixon, please see me in my room.'

I could glean nothing from her words or her demeanour, so I could only do as she requested, making sure that all my charges were settled with blankets around their legs and taking my time in positioning them so that the sun wasn't in their eyes. My heart was thumping uncomfortably by the time I knocked on Mrs Murray's door and was bade enter.

I stood before her desk while she finished writing in the ledger that was open before her. I have no doubt it was a strategy to make me uncomfortable and it worked. I now had definite misgivings about my failure to have a ready excuse.

'Now, Miss Dixon,' Mrs Murray said at last, blotting her script and pushing the ledger aside. 'Please explain your absence yesterday morning. I understand that you arranged to exchange free afternoons with Miss Roberts, so you clearly had something that you felt required your attention for a full day.'

I took a deep breath, then told the truth. I explained that I had been invited to attend a christening, that of my great-nephew, at which I would meet family members from whom I had been separated for over twenty years.

'It was the sort of occasion that wouldn't arise again – it seemed like an opportunity I couldn't afford to miss.' I paused. Mrs Murray's expression was inscrutable. 'I'm very sorry to have been absent without permission.'

'And did you think to ask for permission?' Mrs Murray's tone gave nothing away.

'No, I didn't. I feared the request would be denied.'

If I had been in the overseer's position, I would have refused my request. Allow one person to break the rules and others will follow, I thought.

'I see. Well, the fact is, I would have granted your request under the circumstances you describe,' Mrs Murray said. 'But you have placed me in a difficult position. You have been devious, choosing to take leave without my authorisation, and that cannot go unpunished.'

My expression must have given away my confusion. I found it hard to comprehend Mrs Murray's words, that she would have given me leave to go. Life hadn't offered me any leeway in the past. Anything I had, I had got for myself, whether by fighting for it, or through my own resourcefulness. No one had suggested a kindness of this nature before.

'I will need to think about this,' Mrs Murray said. 'You may return to your duties, Miss Dixon. I will let you know my decision in due course.'

I was filled with apprehension. Had my conviction that I knew the overseer's mind put me at risk of dismissal? Now I was forced to wait for her to decide what to do – and this time, I had no idea what that would be. I could only make sure that my conduct that day, and in the days that followed, was blameless.

Margaret was watching for my return and, at the first opportunity, quick to ask me what had happened. For the second time that day, I was surprised that someone had even the slightest interest in my life. I told her that Mrs Murray was considering the matter, but we weren't able to have any further conversation until we were free to eat, the patients always being encouraged to rest after their own midday meal had been served.

We sat on the hard benches in the gloomy room that served as our dining area and I explained what had happened that morning, that I might have been excused Sunday church attendance if I had only told the overseer the circumstances.

'Well, you must hope Mrs Murray decides to be lenient,' Margaret said. 'You enjoyed the day, I take it?'

I described the christening celebration, saying how confusing it had been to meet so many relatives. 'Almost the whole extended family at once – my half-sisters, their husbands and children, some of the children's children . . .' I tailed off as I mentally assembled the whole group. 'There's still a set of relatives to meet – they were kept away by ill-health – so it may all have to be repeated.'

Margaret laughed – a rare occurrence for she was normally a serious woman. I soon realised it was a laugh tinged with bitterness.

'I envy you the chance to reconnect with your family. Mine are unknown. I have no idea where they might live and they have no idea about me, as far as I am aware. My mother is the only person I have in the world and she is so far away.'

I was pleased by the turn that the conversation had taken, for it saved me having to probe her about her family. 'You must know something of your father's history, surely?'

'Very little beyond that he served in the Navy and had spent many years in Jamaica and the Windward Islands.'

I was puzzled. 'You took care of him when he was sick, I believe. You didn't think to ask him then?'

Margaret shrugged. 'Why would I? I didn't imagine then that I would be coming to the country where he was born. In any case, he was too ill, rambling with the fever. Even before

49

that, throughout my childhood, he was unwell. Like many of the British sailors, he struggled with the heat and the climate. He was sick with fever more often than not, and when he wasn't he was drinking rum.'

The picture Margaret painted of her childhood was not a happy one. And yet her father had stayed on – I wondered why. Before I could help myself, I'd blurted it out.

'Then why did he stay there?'

Margaret gave me a look and I wished I could take back the words. It was the first time she had shared confidences with me and my question was both clumsy and rude. To my surprise, though, she answered me.

'I often wondered the same. Partly money, I suppose. I don't think he could buy himself a passage home. But I thought there might be something more, something here that he was trying to avoid.'

I noticed that she didn't mention her existence as a reason for him staying overseas and I felt for her. I knew what it was like to find yourself of no consequence to a parent. In my case, though, with my father dead, it was my sole parent, my mother, who had so little regard for me. Margaret at least had a bond with her mother, from what little she had told me.

She stood up, ready to clear away her plate, and I knew our conversation was all but over. I tried one last question.

'Have you made any attempt to search for your father's family since you've been here? Although I suppose the name Roberts is a common one.' As I spoke, I was thinking that I wouldn't have the first idea where to begin such a search. Naval records, perhaps, but how to find them? I almost didn't hear Margaret's reply.

'Not Roberts.' She looked away from me as she spoke.

'My name is actually Marguerite Robert. It's French, and I soon discovered that, away from home, it's seen as hard to pronounce.' She gave a faint smile. 'I have my mother's name. She and my father weren't married. His name was Goodchild, Nicholas Goodchild.'

CHAPTER ELEVEN

M argaret's words threw me into a state of astonishment. Goodchild – my own name! And yet she couldn't know that for I had never used it at the hospital, being Harriet Dixon to everyone. Nicholas Goodchild, then – I certainly knew of one with that very name: a man who had gone to sea, too. He was the son of my aunt Jane, which I suppose made him some sort of half-cousin to me. I racked my brains to dredge up some memory of him but nothing came to mind. We had left Margate when I was seven. If my mother had had news of the family after that, she certainly didn't pass it on.

I should have said something at once to Margaret about her father's surname matching my own – but I had let the moment pass and now I was in a quandary. She would find it very odd that I hadn't spoken. I roused myself and looked up, thinking to catch her, only to see her leaving the room having already washed her plate and cup. I wanted to stay where I was, trying to impose order on my scrambled thoughts, but I had to go back to my patients. I couldn't afford to let Mrs Murray catch me out in any dereliction of duty.

I decided I would get Margaret's attention at the first possible opportunity and tell her of our connection. I couldn't help marvelling at the turn of Fate that had brought her to the very place of her father's birth – for I was already clear in my mind that all the evidence pointed to my half-cousin being the very same Nicholas Goodchild.

Molly would be able to fill in more details for me, I thought, as I climbed the stairs back up to the seaward terrace. But I would have no chance to pay her a visit for at least two weeks, and I still had to repay Margaret in kind for covering for me on Sunday. I could write to Molly, but I quickly discounted this thought. I felt that my discovery needed to be examined in a face-to-face conversation, for her answers would surely provide me only with more questions.

I was thinking how pleased Margaret would be to have the answer to her parentage before she had even set out to solve the puzzle, and I suppose a smile must have crossed my lips. As Mrs Murray stepped out in front of me, drawing me to a halt, she remarked, 'You are looking rather pleased with yourself, Miss Dixon.'

I cast my gaze to the floor and didn't respond, for I knew that to appear pleased when I was already under a cloud was not a good thing.

'I have decided what's to be done about your misdemeanour,' Mrs Murray continued. 'You will be suspended from duty for three days. You will stay in your room and I will provide you with work to be done. The hospital's sheets and other linen need repairs and, if that work should run out, I feel sure that there is useful sewing to be done for the poor of Margate.'

I made to speak but Mrs Murray held up her hand. 'You are to go to your room now and I will arrange for the work to be delivered to you. The care of your patients will be shared between your fellows and you will have no contact with them. I think that should be sufficient to deter anyone else from trying to follow your example.'

My great wish to speak to Margaret could not be fulfilled for three more days. I would have to curb my impatience as best I could. With Mrs Murray watching me, I made my way back along the corridor and up the staircase at the end that led to the attic rooms. I was seething by the time I got there. My room had just two beds with space enough to stand between them, and a chest of drawers serving as a stand for the bowl and ewer. We were under-staffed so I had the room to myself but, even so, it was tiny. It was already stuffy and my first instinct was to open the window and stand for a minute, looking out, trying to calm myself. I was on the side of the building away from the sea and my window had a view of the fields. The sound of the sea was distant – at least, on a calm day like today. The pleasant aspect was at odds with my mood – I was in a rage and had no outlet. Was I really to be confined here for the next three days?

Mrs Murray was true to her word. I received, with ill humour, a great pile of mending, along with a basket of needles, threads and scissors. My meals were brought up by one of the kitchen staff, who made clear her displeasure at the extra work. That was equalled by the servant girl whose duty it was to deliver water for washing and to remove and empty my chamber pot. I was ashamed that she had to perform this service for me but, although my door was not locked, it was as though Mrs Murray's presence patrolled the attic corridors. My feeling of being watched was so strong that I dared not leave.

I had plenty of time to wonder how my absence had been received on the wards. Mrs Murray was shrewd. I would have to work hard to regain the goodwill of my fellows. They would not have taken kindly to performing my duties as well as their own.

My confinement to my room made me all the more impatient to share my news about Nicholas Goodchild. I had had time to consider how the news would be received by the Goodchild family – Aunt Jane and Uncle William in particular. It would not sit well with them, I was sure.

When I worked in London, I'd been made aware of wealthy households employing African footmen and young boys. According to my employer at the time, they would be dressed in the finest silks and paraded as status symbols. 'The lady of the house keeps the young ones about her – like pets, spoilt pets.' His tone was full of scorn.

But that was in London. A family in Margate who liked to see themselves as pillars of the community (or so my mother had described them): how would they react to Margaret's claim of kinship?

CHAPTER TWELVE

When my punishment was over, I returned to the wards full of anticipation at making my discovery known to Margaret. Imagine my dismay on finding her absent! At the first opportunity, I asked another of the women whether Margaret was ill.

She gave me a strange look. 'No,' she said. 'I think Mrs Murray let her go. On account of her helping you to break the rules.'

I was so shocked that I came to an abrupt halt as I wheeled one of the beds out onto the terrace, causing the woman behind me to cannon into my legs with the iron bedstead she was pushing. In my distress at the news about Margaret, I was barely aware of the pain.

'But when? Where has she gone?'

My informant shrugged. 'She left yesterday. I don't know where.'

The unfairness of the situation hit me hard. Mrs Murray had done everything possible to make sure that no one would risk crossing her in the future.

I tried to go about the business of the day, my mind whirring. The overseer had allowed Margaret to work on, oblivious, then sent her packing when she knew I would be back to work. It still left us under-staffed, and although I wanted to leave the hospital without delay and seek Margaret out, I couldn't leave my post. I would have to wait until the evening, and then I had only the vaguest idea where to look, never having thought to enquire fully about her lodgings. Mrs Murray would know, but I had no doubt that she wouldn't divulge the information. Whenever she came among us on the wards or on the terrace, I set my face to the most neutral expression I could manage, although inwardly I was raging. How could she have behaved in such a way, in particular towards Margaret?

And yet I knew she had done only what I would have done in her position: meted out punishment to discourage others from following suit. I had to swallow the medicine or seek employment elsewhere. Still, no matter how I tried to calm myself, rage rose up again at the thought of Margaret. With Dr Lettsom gone, Mrs Murray no doubt considered it easy to be rid of Margaret. But now I knew that Margaret was my kin, I felt the injustice as keenly as if I'd suffered it myself.

Once we were released from our duties at the end of the day, I hurried to my room to fetch a shawl and a bonnet, without pausing to change out of my work clothes. It was a miserable, damp evening and I didn't relish the prospect of combing the streets in search of Margaret, but I was determined to try to find her. She had mentioned the shops at one end of the high street as being the closest to where she was staying, so I decided to concentrate my search on that side of town. I'd thought little about how I might seek her out, other than by calling at houses and asking whether Margaret Roberts lodged there, but I found myself frustrated early in my quest.

Few wanted to be bothered to answer the door on an evening such as this, growing darker by the minute with squally showers blowing in on the wind. From the suspicious reactions of the few who did answer, I guessed the inhabitants feared that the only people likely to be knocking at this time of the evening were debt collectors or worse. Conscious of my increasingly bedraggled state, and that it wouldn't be wise to be out alone on these streets as darkness fell, I tried one last door. It belonged to a tall, narrow house on the corner of Lovell's Row and the high street and, to my surprise, it opened promptly. A woman a good deal older than myself, neatly dressed and seemingly not at all put out, peered at me.

'I wonder, does Margaret Roberts live here?' I asked, ready to turn away as soon as I'd asked the question, so sure was I that the answer would be the usual dismissal.

'She did live here,' came the reply. 'Will you come inside out of the rain a moment, my dear? You look very miserable standing out there in this weather.'

I stepped into her hallway, apologising for my dampness, but she brushed the apology aside and beckoned me to follow her into the sitting room.

'I've had to light the fire, the weather being more like November than May,' she said, and pointed to a chair beside the fireplace. 'Why don't you sit down and tell me why you're looking for Margaret?'

I wondered at her kindness towards a stranger until she said, 'I can tell by your clothing that you both worked at the same place – the Royal Sea Bathing Hospital over in Westbrook.'

'Did Margaret live here with you?' I asked, conscious that the heat from the fire was causing wisps of steam to rise from my damp skirt.

'She did. I run a lodging house – Widow Palmer's Board and Lodging. In fact, I was expecting a new gentleman to arrive tonight and that was why I answered the door to you.'

'You said Margaret had gone?' I asked.

Mrs Palmer's face, cheerful until then, clouded.

'Such a shame. She was one of the nicest, most well-mannered of my guests and I was sorry to see her leave. I made her promise to come back if she should return to Margate.'

'Do you happen to know where she went? Only ...' I racked my brains to see what I could offer by way of excuse, while preserving discretion. I hadn't been prepared to discover that Margaret had left the area already. 'Only I have something important of hers that she needs. I want to pass it back to her.'

Mrs Palmer shook her head. 'She didn't give me a forwarding address.'

'Do you know where she was going?'

'London, I believe,' Mrs Palmer said.

We stared into the fire for some moments, each of us deep in our thoughts. I could never hope to track down Margaret in London. I only hoped that she had somewhere to go for, from what I had heard, it was a dangerous city for the unwary and especially for a woman on her own.

At last I roused myself, reluctant to tear myself away from the warmth of the room to go back out into the rain.

'I've taken up enough of your evening, Mrs Palmer,' I said, rising. 'But in case you do hear from Margaret, perhaps I could leave my name and address with you and you could let me know.'

'Of course,' Mrs Palmer said, and she got to her feet and opened her bureau, pulling out a sheet of paper and a quill pen.

I dictated my address, care of the hospital, and she read it back to me before blotting the page. A brisk knock at the door prevented her from putting the paper somewhere safe and as I left, thanking her, a gentleman made his entrance, carrying a bag. I presumed he would be taking up Margaret's room, so newly vacated. I hoped Mrs Palmer would remember to stow the address safely away. It was surely my only hope of getting in touch with Margaret again.

I pulled my shawl around my shoulders, grateful that the rain had slowed to a fine drizzle, and turned my steps briskly in the direction of Westbrook and the hospital. I could hardly believe that my eagerly anticipated opportunity to tell Margaret what I knew of her history, and how we were related, had been snatched so cruelly from me.

CHAPTER THIRTEEN

Over the next few days I thought of little else, constantly returning to Margaret's revelation. I could see now that we were not only kin, but we had both been wronged by the Goodchild family. I had suffered from their neglect and Margaret had been denied legitimacy by her father.

My brooding on the matter, and what might be done about it, was interrupted by the arrival of a letter. I thought at first, with a great leap of my heart, that it must be from Margaret. Had she been in touch with Mrs Palmer and learnt that I was enquiring after her? But when I looked to the signature, before reading the letter, it said 'Molly'. I was disappointed, but only for a short time. As I read it, its content suggested an idea to me.

It was to let me know that Aunt Jane, disappointed at being prevented from attending Joseph's christening party, had decided to have a gathering of her own, which she hoped I would attend, with as many other family members as possible. Molly assured me that she would be there, with George, Judith and Joseph, and quite possibly I would find many of the relatives whom I'd already met.

It was to take place on a Sunday afternoon at the end of May. My heart sank. After my recent troubles with Mrs Murray I wasn't sure I would be able to have the time off, but

I was determined to try. The gathering was to be in Margate, next door to the house where I had lived until I was seven years old. I was curious as to how much I would remember.

I wrote back to Molly and said I very much hoped I would be able to come, but it was by no means certain as I had experienced difficulties over taking time off for the christening. Since I had been confined to my room, and Margaret dismissed, my fellow workers had become wary of me. They were even less prepared than before to swap half-day holidays with me.

There had been no word from Margaret as the days passed. Yet, for some reason, when I was summoned to Mrs Murray's room on a Friday more than two weeks after Margaret's departure, I was convinced I was about to receive word of her whereabouts. Despite my anger at the overseer's treatment of me and of Margaret, I knew I had behaved impeccably since and she would have no reason to find fault with me. So I stood before her in expectation of some welcome news. What came was indeed welcome, but unexpected.

'I've been informed that you have been invited to a family gathering this Sunday afternoon, at the home of Mr and Mrs Goodchild, in Princes Crescent,' Mrs Murray said stiffly.

I nodded warily, expecting to be warned off trying to attend.

'Mr Goodchild, who is a patron of this hospital, has spoken to Dr Harwood to inform him that his wife will be most disappointed if you do not attend. Therefore, I am to tell you that you have a free afternoon on Sunday.'

I could tell that she was very put out at having to deliver this news so I was careful to hide my glee, restricting myself to 'Thank you, Mrs Murray,' before nodding to her and withdrawing from the room. I was already planning what I would wear as I walked away from her office and down the corridor. This was not difficult for, apart from the outfit I had worn to the christening, I had only one other good dress. The fabric was lightweight, in a shade of blue that I always felt was very becoming.

Two days later, when I set out to walk to Margate my spirits were high, and the sunshine raised them even further, for we had suffered some unseasonably cool and dull weather since I had last seen the family. It was a short walk, no more than a couple of miles, and it was only as I reached Princes Crescent that I felt a twinge of apprehension. Nearly twenty years had passed since I had set foot in the street and at first it looked very different. I realised eventually that two trees along the road had grown considerably in that time, and an additional house had been built on what was previously an empty plot of land.

Jane and William Goodchild's house was much the same, however – one of the grandest in the road in a terrace of five, a flight of steps rising up to its front door and a kitchen down in the basement. The cottage next door to it was the one I had lived in. I gave it a cursory glance, finding it little changed, before I climbed the steps and rapped on the door, noting the high polish on the knocker.

A maid opened the door and I gave her my bonnet, glancing at myself in the glass before she ushered me into the drawing room. I was relieved to see Charles and Molly already in attendance, with George and Judith, who was proudly displaying baby Joseph to Aunt Jane. My aunt looked much older than she had when I had last seen her, which was hardly surprising as she must now have been in her late sixties. Her hair had turned white and her face was lined. Uncle William, whose illness had prevented their attendance at the christening party, seemed to have shrunk in stature. He was a little stooped and his hair was thinning but he clearly still enjoyed commanding a room. He was holding forth to Charlie and George, who appeared to be nodding in polite agreement at everything he said.

Molly, at Aunt Jane's side, spotted me and called me over. 'Aunt Jane, you remember Harriet, Ann's daughter? She used to come and play here when she was young.'

'Goodness me, Harriet, I'm not sure I would ever have recognised you! How well you look. Pull up a chair and sit beside me – I want to hear all about what you've been doing since I last saw you. I know you are working at the hospital – Molly told me of your troubles there. I'm very pleased that William was able to intervene so that you could join us today. Your overseer is a difficult woman, by all accounts.'

I sat down and managed to make polite responses to Aunt Jane's enquiries about my mother, taking satisfaction in her shock at the news that she had remarried such a short time after leaving Margate.

'Well …' Aunt Jane clearly wanted to say something further but was holding back. 'Did you hear that, Molly? Ann married again, shortly after she left here. I always did think …' Molly put her hand on her aunt's arm and she stopped mid-sentence. She turned to me. 'So, tell me more about your work at the hospital.'

I launched into a description of the routine there and how patients were treated for scrofula and other ailments by plentiful fresh air and regular immersions in the sea. Aunt Jane shuddered at the description of sea bathing and murmured, 'How could anyone think that a good idea?'

I could see that I was losing her attention for her gaze had started to wander around the room.

'I met a relative of yours at the hospital, Aunt. A close relative.'

I had her attention now, but not fully as yet.

'Oh? A patient being treated there?'

'No,' I said. 'The daughter of your son, Nicholas.'

Aunt Jane's head snapped away from her perusal of the room. Her faded blue eyes regarded me intently and her brows were drawn together in a frown.

'Constance? What is she doing there? Has she fallen ill? I thought she was in London with her mother.'

Aunt Jane's voice must have risen for I saw Uncle William looking in our direction. The maid was bringing in a heavily laden tray and there was a slight lull as other family members moved aside to make way for her.

'No, Aunt Jane. She's called Margaret – well, Marguerite, really. She was born in Jamaica but lived in Martinique. When her father, Nicholas Goodchild, died she came here in the hope of finding her relatives.'

Aunt Jane, who had just been handed a glass of wine by the maid, let it slip from her fingers. It smashed on the floor, scattering liquid and glass fragments. I stood up quickly, hoping my dress had been spared.

Molly exclaimed and the maid turned white with fright and hurried from the room – in search of something to clear up the mess, no doubt.

The other guests moved a little closer, as if aware that the mishap wasn't entirely due to clumsiness.

'What are you saying, girl?' Aunt Jane was pale, but with fury I sensed. I was a little taken aback and hesitated, so that she said, 'Nicholas does have a child, a daughter, Constance, by his wife, Sarah.' She glared at me and I noticed that Molly had gone pale, too, and put a protective arm around her aunt's shoulders.

The maid reappeared with a cloth, a dustpan and brush. The poor girl was now quite scarlet as she set about clearing up, for the whole room had gone quiet. Aunt Jane clearly did not want to speak further in front of a servant and the rest of the guests did not want to miss any of the developing drama.

'That will do,' Aunt Jane said sharply, after a minute or so had elapsed. There was still more work to be done to clear up but the maid obediently gathered everything together and left the room, almost in tears.

'Well, that's as may be,' I said, taking up the conversation again. 'But I believe he lived for many years in the West Indies. Margaret is twenty-two now and I would have brought her to meet you today if Mrs Murray hadn't dismissed her, without cause. She's left Margate but I am hoping to persuade her to return, once she knows I have found her family.'

I had expected my news to be a surprise and the complete silence in the room told me that indeed it was.

Uncle William moved forward to stand at his wife's side. 'Twenty-two, you say?' He turned to his wife. 'And how old is Constance?'

'Twenty-six,' she whispered.

Uncle William frowned. He addressed me, 'And this . . . person of your acquaintance, what does she want from us?'

'Want?' I was puzzled. 'Why, to get to know you. She has only her mother, who is now living in Jamaica. She came here in an effort to learn more of her father. She has been living in Margate for a few weeks now – that is, until she left for London.'

It was my turn to frown. It would all have been so much easier if Margaret was here with me to explain matters.

There was another silence and I could tell that both Aunt Jane and Uncle William wanted to ask further questions, or one further question in particular. I suspected it would be about the colour of Margaret's skin.

At that moment there was diversion: the door opened and someone else made an entrance, the young maid hovering anxiously in the background. I recognised the latest visitor but couldn't put a name to the face, until her apron gave me the clue I sought. It was Hannah, the cook, still working there. She also looked much older: her cheeks were faded and her hair, caught back under her cap, was now as white as Aunt Jane's. I remembered it had been greying when I visited the house as a child and she fed me in the kitchen.

She seemed oblivious to the atmosphere in the room and went over to the table, straightening bottles and glasses, before saying, 'I heard there had been a little accident. I trust all is well now?' She didn't wait for an answer but turned to the maid and said, 'Bring up the food to the dining room. These good people must be hungry by now. And I heard that Harriet was here. Where is she?'

She looked around the room before her eyes alighted on me. 'There you are! Let me take a good look at you.' She shook her head. 'I would never have known you. You've turned into quite a beauty, like your mother.'

I tried to digest her words, marvelling at how my aunt and uncle allowed Hannah such freedom among their guests. I presumed it was because, having been with them such a long time, she was almost one of the family. Then, as she refilled glasses, she came to a halt in front of George.

'I don't believe we have ever met, although you must have been in the area for a year or two now. But I'd have known you anywhere. You have your father's eyes.'

Hannah turned to look at Molly, who had gasped audibly. Her hand trembled as she placed her glass on a side table. The ensuing silence was broken only by the ticking of the grandfather clock.

Hannah looked from Molly to George, then at Charlie. Her faded cheeks reddened and she put her hand to her mouth. 'Have I said . . .?' She couldn't finish her sentence.

'You knew my father?' George demanded. He turned from Hannah to Molly, his face full of accusation. She looked down at the floor.

I didn't know what to make of it. Charlie was George's father, wasn't he? But I could see that all was not well. The expression on Charlie's face as he stared at Molly sent a chill right through me before he, too, put down his glass and left the room.

CHAPTER FOURTEEN

The gathering broke up in disarray. Uncle William helped Aunt Jane from the room, throwing me a look of fury that discouraged me from saying anything further to my aunt. George left the room shortly after his father – at least, he followed Charlie out, the man I had assumed to be his father. I think Molly must have been taken away by her sisters for, shortly afterwards, I found myself standing alone in the drawing room, a scattering of half-empty glasses the only sign that a party had been in progress.

My stomach rumbled. I wasn't ready to go back to the hospital yet, so I thought I would make myself useful. I took up several glasses and went towards the basement stairs, pausing at the top when I heard muffled sobbing. I supposed that, rather than the young maid, it must be Hannah, over-come by the scene that had followed her apparently incautious words. I trod firmly on the stairs, to make sure my descent was audible, and arrived in the kitchen to find Hannah at the table, face averted, and the young maid beside her, wringing her hands.

I set the glasses on the table, then addressed the girl.

'The guests have departed so we may as well clear the drawing room and the dining room. Will you help me?'

Without waiting for an answer, I turned on my heel and went back up the stairs. The maid followed and between us we had the room set to rights within twenty minutes, the glasses neatly stacked ready to be washed.

The young maid, whom I learnt was called Elsie, set to work in the scullery without being prompted, while I surveyed the full serving dishes of food. I could hear only the odd sniff from Hannah now, so I ventured a question. 'What would you like done with this food? Shall we cover it and put it in the larder?'

She waved a hand dismissively and fell to sobbing again. I sighed, fetched myself a plate from the dresser, pulled up a chair and settled down to choose a selection from the array before me.

After a further twenty minutes, my hunger had eased and Hannah finally appeared to have composed herself. I thought it might be a good moment to ask her to explain what had happened earlier, and what she had meant by her words to George.

I asked Elsie to pour us some wine, from the bottles that had been opened ready for the guests, and then, relieved when the jangling of a bell from upstairs called her away, I turned to Hannah.

'What happened just now, Hannah? Why did everyone react as they did?'

When I had last sat in a kitchen with Hannah, I had been a young child and would never have dared to address her as I just had. Now I felt as though I had the upper hand, even if in truth I had also caused upset upstairs, although Hannah hadn't been there to witness it.

Her voice was trembling as she spoke. 'When I saw George standing there in the drawing room, it was almost as though

I was seeing the young master, Nicholas, just as he was all those years ago. But then I realised he wasn't so much like his father – only in the eyes – and I just blurted it out. I couldn't help myself.' Hannah dabbed at her swollen eyes with the corner of her apron.

'My tongue got the better of me, I suppose. Molly told me years ago that she was having a baby by her cousin, Nicholas. Then she ran away. When she came back, after three years, she told me she'd lost the baby. I believed her at the time, but when a year or so ago I heard that she'd been reunited with a child – a son, now grown – that she'd had to leave behind in London, I did wonder. She let everyone believe that this son was the result of a short-lived infatuation in the city.'

Hannah paused and took some sips of her wine. I poured a little more into her glass. 'You've had a shock,' I said soothingly. 'This will help.'

She needed little encouragement and finished the glass quickly, so I topped it up again, while taking small sips of my own drink.

I was glad of the break in her tale for my brain was whirring. If George was Nicholas's son, it seemed Charlie hadn't known and neither had George. And, since Margaret was also Nicholas's child, Aunt Jane had two new grandchildren whose existence she had been ignorant of all these years. It would be a shock to Constance, too, of course.

I began to wonder how the ages of these three compared, and it was hard to stop a smile spreading across my face. My half-cousin Nicholas must have been quite a character. I was sad not to have made his acquaintance.

I was startled out of my thoughts when Hannah let out a wail, the memory of what had just happened having, I suppose, visited her afresh.

'What have I done? I've brought shame on Molly. What will her aunt think of her now? And Charlie? And George? I don't think it was welcome news.'

I thought this was an understatement but I made soothing noises and patted Hannah's hand. 'Perhaps I can help,' I said. 'I have only recently been reacquainted with the family. I didn't know any of this history so it's much less of a shock to me.'

This wasn't strictly true. I was as surprised as anyone else, but I could see how to turn this to my advantage. 'I can talk to Charlie, and to George. And to Molly, of course. I'm sure I can help smooth things over.'

My news about Margaret had rather faded into the background in this afternoon of revelations, I thought, but perhaps it was no bad thing. Margaret wasn't on hand to prove her existence so pressing her case could wait.

Meanwhile, if I could make myself indispensable to Molly's family, perhaps I could act as a go-between. There were a lot of people in the extended Goodchild family who would be struggling to digest the news they had received that very afternoon. I would make it my mission to help.

I stood up. 'Don't upset yourself, Hannah. If you had spotted George's resemblance to Nicholas, surely it was only a matter of time before someone else did.'

Even as I spoke it occurred to me that Hannah had realised the connection because of the knowledge she'd had when Molly fled – knowledge of the relationship between Molly and her cousin. Without that knowledge, it was unlikely that anyone else would have reached the same conclusion. But my words seemed to comfort Hannah.

Elsie had now returned to the kitchen, saying that Aunt Jane had taken to her bed. She wanted brandy and water sent up. She had requested that Hannah be the one to deliver it.

I felt sorry for Hannah as I took my leave. I suspected Aunt Jane would be merciless in her questioning, and demand to know what she had said to George to cause such a reaction. She would be very unhappy to learn that her son had yet another secret offspring, and that Hannah and Molly had kept it from her all these years.

I was grateful to her, though. She had given me what I needed. Charlie's puzzling reference to George during Joseph's christening party as 'her son' rather than 'our son' made sense now. I walked back to the hospital with a spring in my step and my head held high.

It was a complete surprise to me when the two men who had so recently occupied my thoughts stepped from the White Hart inn as I passed along the harbour. They had their backs to me and were talking closely together; I suppose I could have passed them by without a word but I hesitated, unsure whether to speak to them or not. At that moment, Charlie turned and saw me.

'Harriet.' He sounded neither pleased nor displeased to see me – just a little weary, perhaps.

'Charlie, George.' I nodded at George who had now turned towards me, too. 'I'm on my way back to Westbrook.' I felt as though I needed to make it plain I had come across them by chance, in case they thought otherwise. After that, I could hardly think of what to say to them.

'I was sorry to witness your distress this afternoon.' This was a clumsy beginning, I felt, for Charlie began to frown. 'If there is anything I can do to help – I know it must have been a great shock to you both, hearing about Nicholas in this way . . .'

I trailed off, as an expression of shock spread across their faces.

'Nicholas?' George said.

'Yes, your father,' I said, and left it a moment or two before saying, 'Oh, I'm so sorry – I didn't realise you hadn't known his identity.' I knew full well that Hannah hadn't shared that piece of information in the drawing room, but I put my hand to my mouth and cast my eyes to the ground.

'Please forgive me,' I said, looking up at them beseechingly. 'I spoke out of turn. I fear I am the bearer of unwelcome news.'

Both George and Charlie looked grim, but Charlie spoke up.

'It is as well to know. You must excuse our manners – today has been full of surprises.'

I reiterated that if I could help, I would be only too glad to do so, then went on my way to Westbrook. I glanced back as I crossed the road – there was no sign of either man. Perhaps they had continued on their journey home, but I thought it more likely they had returned to the inn to contemplate my revelation.

PART TWO

MOLLY

Chapter Fifteen

When Molly set out for her aunt Jane's house on a sunny Sunday at the end of May, she had the happy assurance of a woman content with her life. She was forty-four years old, had been married for twenty-four of those years, and of her four children, three were happily married with children of their own. Her remaining daughter, Agnes, had chosen a different path, that of an artist, and she was as proud of her as she was of the others.

That morning, she had attended church on the Woodchurch estate on the arm of her husband, Charlie, accompanied by her son George, his wife Judith and her newest grandchild, Joseph, who happily slept throughout the service. Her youngest daughter, Catherine, was there too, with her husband Francis, the son of the owner of Woodchurch Manor, and their daughter Eleanor. Molly could be forgiven for looking around her family with a sense of pride. On that sunny morning, none of them knew of the darkness on the horizon.

After church, Molly spoke awhile with Catherine, who was apologetic for being unable to join the family gathering in Margate that afternoon, due to a prior engagement with the Powells. Although Molly was sorry not to have Catherine's company, it meant that they were able to borrow the Powells' carriage for the journey since the family wouldn't require it. She knew how lucky they were that Mr Powell allowed Charlie this privilege: he had held him in great esteem as his head gardener of the past twenty-six years.

In the past, when she was younger, Molly would have covered the distance to Margate – some four or five miles – on foot. Now she feared she had become stout and lazy. As she sat in the carriage, she looked across at Charlie, who was passing the journey deep in thought while gazing out of the window. He was still handsome, his brown hair threaded with silver, his face tanned and lined from being outdoors in all weathers. Molly rather suspected he was pondering a new planting scheme for the garden – he'd mentioned something to her about it the previous night and she'd nodded as though she was listening. If truth be told, she'd heard his plans for the garden so many times over the years that she'd ceased to pay too much attention. He didn't seem to mind – expressing his thoughts aloud seemed to help get them in order.

Joseph, cradled in his mother's arms as she sat beside Molly, snuffled and sighed, and George, sitting beside Charlie, leant over to gently touch his son's face. He smiled at Judith, and Molly's heart contracted with pride as she looked at him. How lucky she was to have him back in her life! It had been two years now – two years since chance had brought him to Woodchurch Manor after he'd left the Navy. Two years since she had discovered that he was the son she'd had to leave behind in the Foundling Hospital twenty-four years earlier. He'd been a little younger than baby Joseph, a realisation that made Molly bite her lip and stare out of the window. Such melancholy thoughts hit her only rarely, these days. Even so, she knew she would never get over what she had done. She could only hope that with each year that passed the memory of her action would fade and the pain would ease.

In the end it was Charlie who had helped bring George back to Molly, and it was Judith's presence that had helped him make up his mind to stay. Molly knew that she had many good things to be thankful for in her life. Her family had brought her great happiness; she expected to see Sally, her eldest, at Aunt Jane's party, with her children, Grace and Simon. Molly had spent a great deal of time with her grand-children when they were babies, but she had seen less of them once Eleanor, Catherine's daughter, and now Joseph had come along. It was always the babies Molly loved the most, although she felt guilty for even allowing the thought. Could it be because she had given up George as a baby, leaving her ever greedy to make up for the time she had lost?

The carriage was drawing to a halt – they had arrived in Princes Crescent already. She felt a sense of anticipation. Harriet would be there, her half-sister who had been living away from them for so long but was now back, working in the area. Molly had already seen her two or three times, but it would be Aunt Jane and Uncle William's first encounter. They were both getting on in years now and Molly wondered whether Aunt Jane would remember Harriet, whom she'd known only as a small girl.

Uncharitable feelings arose, unbidden, in Molly's breast and threatened to disturb her equilibrium. Would it have been better if they had all remained in ignorance of Harriet's whereabouts? She had felt sorry for her as a child, but there was something brittle and hard-edged about her now. Molly pushed away the memory of Lizzie, following Joseph's chris-tening party, telling her to be careful, that Harriet seemed to be paying Charlie a good deal of attention. She would take care to be welcoming to Harriet today, she resolved, and keep her at her side. It was clear that she had suffered a good deal. Perhaps she just needed to make up for lost time and get to know her half-sister properly.

Charlie had started to grumble about missing their usual Sunday dinner, which they generally had soon after their return from church.

'I'm sure Hannah will have been busy cooking,' Molly said soothingly. 'She likes to have the chance to show off her skills. But we won't linger once it is served – Aunt Jane and Uncle William tire quickly, these days, and they may well send everyone on their way after an hour or two.'

They got down from the carriage to be greeted at once by Sally and her family, quickly followed by Lizzie and Mary, Molly's sisters, who still shared the cottage next door to Aunt Jane, with their husbands and children. They were all swept into the house on a tide of laughter and shared greetings.

After twenty minutes or so, the visitors had dispersed around the room in little knots, some sitting, others standing. Charlie had taken up his favourite position, one elbow propped on the mantelpiece as he talked to Uncle William. As a trustee of Prospect House, the poorhouse that was just a few streets away, William liked to hold forth about his good works there. But there was no need for that today – only family was present and they had heard his tales more than once.

George and Judith were taking Joseph around the room so that everyone might exclaim about how much he had changed since they'd last seen him, even though that had been just a few weeks previously. Molly settled down at Aunt Jane's side and called to them to bring Joseph to meet his great-great-aunt. After a few minutes' conversation, during which the usual pleasantries were exchanged, George excused himself and went to stand with Charlie by the fireplace.

The door opened and Harriet, wearing a dress in a very becoming shade of blue, was ushered into the room by the maid. Harriet hesitated on the threshold, looking around, and Molly, thinking she might feel daunted to discover the room already so full of people, raised her hand to attract her attention. She smiled at her to encourage her to come over.

Intent on making sure Aunt Jane would realise who Harriet was, Molly introduced her as Ann's daughter, earning a frown from Harriet. While her half-sister, at Aunt Jane's request, described what had happened to her since she left Margate as a child, Molly's attention started to wander. She realised, just in time, that Aunt Jane was about to make an acerbic comment about Ann, to whom she'd never warmed. Molly put a restraining hand on her aunt's arm and was greatly relieved when she swallowed her words.

Molly was just thinking it was time to take Harriet away to talk to some of the other guests, when her aunt took a sharp breath. Harriet had been talking about someone called Margaret, who worked at the hospital alongside her. As Molly focused on the conversation once more, she was in time to hear Harriet say that this woman was the daughter of Nicholas Goodchild, Aunt Jane's son. Aunt Jane's wine glass, only recently delivered to her by Elsie, the young maid, slipped through her fingers and crashed to the floor.

Molly got to her feet, slow to comprehend the meaning of Harriet's words, but aware of the expression on her half-sister's face. It began as triumph, quickly replaced by worry at the effect of her words. The other guests had turned towards them when the glass smashed; from the obvious tension between Aunt Jane and Harriet they could tell that this wasn't a simple accident and began to edge closer.

Molly heard the anger in her aunt's tone as she told Harriet that she must be mistaken, that Nicholas indeed had a child, a daughter – but a daughter called Constance – as well as a wife. All the time, Molly was thinking of Nicholas's other child, the one no one knew about; the one who was standing in the room just a few paces from her: his son George. She prayed that her face was inscrutable although she could be forgiven for appearing as shocked as anyone by Harriet's words. Even as she struggled with the turmoil of her thoughts, with the suggestion that Nicholas had yet another secret child, she could never have anticipated what was to come next.

CHAPTER SIXTEEN

When the door opened again and Hannah entered the room, Molly was relieved by the diversion. Hannah had been Aunt Jane and Uncle William's cook for many years, and she was almost like family to them. Elsie, the maid, was hovering in the hallway behind her – she had probably told Hannah that all was not well in the drawing room. Hannah, quick to sense the atmosphere, despatched Elsie to the kitchen to bring up the food to the dining room – feeding people was both a comfort and a solution to a problem in Hannah's view. Then she busied herself going around the room, refilling glasses, the job that Elsie had been doing before Aunt Jane's accident had sent her scurrying away. Molly turned her attention to her aunt once more, worried about the shock she had received.

As she straightened Aunt Jane's cushions and checked that her dress had escaped the spilt wine, she heard Hannah greet Harriet. Molly remembered that Harriet and little John had been invited to the house when they were young to play with Constance. In that unguarded moment, when Molly was thinking back to Harriet as a child – a trusting little thing – and smiling at the memory, she failed to anticipate that her world was about to be turned on its head.

It never occurred to her that Hannah hadn't seen George before, even though he had now been home for two years. There hadn't been any get-togethers at the Princes Crescent house for a while; when the family had met up it had been at Woodchurch Manor, gatherings that hadn't included Hannah.

Molly had always been careful to let everyone think that George had been the result of a brief liaison in London, with a man she had never seen since. She thought it was better to let her friends, family and the good people of Margate judge her as they chose, rather than let the truth come out. The truth being Molly's infatuation with Nicholas, her cousin, his seduction of her (in which she was a not entirely unwilling participant) and her naive belief that they would marry.

Only her father, now dead, and Hannah had known that Molly was with child when she fled from Margate all those years previously. And only those same two people had known the identity of the father.

It seemed that Hannah just couldn't help herself. Faced for the first time with George, as she moved around the room with jugs of ale and wine, she said what no one else had ever suspected. With her words, 'You have your father's eyes,' Molly's world fell apart.

She couldn't move, out of fear. She'd let Charlie and George believe the half-truth, that George was the result of an unfortunate infatuation; if they had conceived the idea that this was something that had happened in London, she hadn't disabused them of the notion. It had been hard enough to recover from the fact that she hadn't been honest with Charlie about George's existence, and for George to forgive what he saw as a betrayal: how she had gone on to have a

84

family but failed to reclaim him. It had been so much easier at the time to let the half-truth remain.

Now Molly could only watch Charlie's face as it dawned on him that she had been less than open with him, that at least one other person knew the truth of George's parentage, while she had kept it from him. He left the room and George wasn't slow to follow.

Molly could remember very little of the immediate after-math. She sank to her knees and Lizzie hastened to her side. Hannah could be heard saying, 'I'm sorry,' over and over again, then Lizzie and Mary helped Molly from the room and took her to their house next door.

They sat her down in the kitchen and there followed a discussion in low tones with Paul and Michael, after which the men and children were gone, shut away in another room perhaps. Or maybe they had been sent in search of Charlie and George. Molly's heart contracted painfully: she wanted to see them both, but she dreaded it, too.

She sat at the kitchen table, rolling stray breadcrumbs into a pellet, her head empty of thoughts. She didn't realise she was shivering until Lizzie put a shawl around her shoulders. Then Mary gave her a glass of something – brandy, most likely – and told her to drink it. It burnt her throat as it went down and made her cough and splutter, and that helped to clear the fog from her brain, if only briefly.

'They don't know,' Molly said suddenly. She looked up and caught Lizzie and Mary watching her. Their faces were full of concern, but the frown on Lizzie's brow told of her puzzlement.

'Don't know?' she asked.

Molly looked down at the table again. Hannah's words, less than an hour ago, had made her thoughts leap straight to Nicholas. It was so obvious to Hannah, and so obvious to

Molly that she had thought surely everyone would make the deduction. But no name had been uttered. Charlie and George had left Aunt Jane's drawing room in disgust at her deception. They were yet to learn the name of George's father. Molly could hardly bear to think of their reaction – and everyone else's – when she had to reveal the truth, the one final piece she had withheld.

'They don't know the name of George's father,' she whispered. She bit her lip and stared fiercely at the table, looking at the scarred surface and the rough grain of the wood, tracing the knots in it with her finger.

The silence in the room was complete and Molly knew without looking that Lizzie and Mary would be watching, waiting to hear what she had to say.

'It was Nicholas,' she said, looking up from the table to face them.

'Nicholas?' Mary was puzzled but Molly could see from Lizzie's face that she had understood immediately.

'Cousin Nicholas,' Lizzie said, turning to Mary. 'Aunt Jane's son. The black sheep of the family. Oh, Molly.'

Her last words, addressed to her sister, were sorrowful. Molly began to cry again, reliving what Harriet had said to Aunt Jane. Nicholas's children: George, Constance, and now an unknown daughter from the West Indies.

'Did you love him?' This from Mary.

Molly stared at her, tears running down her cheeks. It felt like an odd question. She hadn't thought of Nicholas in years, but when she was young and foolish she had fancied herself in love with him. She knew better now.

'I've only ever loved one man,' Molly replied. 'Charlie.'

The sickening realisation of what her deception had done struck her afresh and Molly wept even harder. If only

86

she could turn back the clock and undo it all, not George's birth, of course, but her behaviour afterwards, decisions she had made that had seemed so sensible at the time but now – now it seemed she must pay the price over and over again.

CHAPTER SEVENTEEN

Paul and Michael came back into the house through the kitchen door, the children in tow. Molly did her best to hide her distress from them, looking down at the table and shielding her face with her hand. She heard Paul say to Lizzie in low tones, 'No sign,' and she knew then that they had been despatched to find Charlie and George, as she had suspected.

She experienced a wave of panic. What was she to do? Should she return home? Had the carriage already left without her, bearing everyone else back to the Woodchurch estate?

There was more quiet conversation, this time between Lizzie and Mary. Then Molly heard the kitchen door open and close once more. Lizzie sat at the table and took her hand.

'I want to go home.' Molly was suddenly fretful. 'I need to talk to Charlie. And to George. I must explain. I have to make it right.' She whispered the last few words, unsure whether, in fact, she would be able to make anything right. But George should hear from her who his father was, and she had to explain to Charlie what had happened all those years ago.

Molly stood up, all at once impatient to be on her way. 'I must go, Lizzie. I must find them, and go home.'

Lizzie made more soothing noises. 'Mary has gone next door to see if there is any news. Perhaps Charlie and George returned to the house, looking for you.' She didn't sound convinced.

Molly got up and began to pace the floor. She would have gone to Aunt Jane's herself except that she wasn't sure what kind of welcome she might receive. Her face burnt with shame. What would her aunt think of her? Nicholas, her only son. And Molly, her niece and employed in her house at the time. Their shameful encounters, all taking place under her aunt's roof, without her suspecting. Could she get away with changing the story to spare her aunt? For Molly was the only one left alive who knew the whole truth of it. Then she was filled with despair. Hadn't she just proved that the consequences of lies and half-truths caught up with you in the end? If Aunt Jane asked her, she would have to tell her what she wanted to know.

The kitchen door opened and Mary came in. She looked at Lizzie and shook her head.

'I'm sorry, Molly,' Mary said. 'No one knows where Charlie and George are. Judith took Joseph home in the carriage because he was grizzling and neither Charlie nor George had returned to Aunt Jane's house by then. Michael and Paul walked around Margate looking for them but didn't find them. Perhaps they set off to walk home.'

Molly sat down again abruptly. She didn't know what to do. The carriage had gone and no one knew her husband and son's whereabouts. Should she try to get home? Or should she stay the night in Margate with her sisters?

Her head ached and she felt exhausted. She had no idea what time it was, but it was still light outside so it was not yet evening. She supposed she felt tired because she hadn't eaten – none of them had. Molly thought of all Hannah's hard work in preparing the food, all gone to waste, and felt a pang of anguish. Hannah would be so upset at what had happened but it wasn't her fault. She should have told her Charlie and George didn't know the whole truth.

A knock at the door made everyone start. Molly's heart filled with hope and terror at the same time. Had Charlie and George come to fetch her? Would they forgive her?

The same thoughts must have been running through her sisters' heads for Lizzie's voice was trembling as she called, 'Come in.'

The door opened and it took a moment or two for Molly to comprehend that Elsie, the maid from next door, stood there, not her husband and son.

'Please, madam.' She addressed the room in general and avoided looking at any of them. 'The mistress has ordered her carriage and she says you are to take it and go home. She will send it for you again tomorrow, when she would like to talk to you.'

She bobbed a curtsey and left the kitchen before anyone could speak.

'Go home,' Molly repeated. She wasn't at all sure now whether that was what she wanted to do. Particularly to return the next day for an interview with Aunt Jane. But it was too late – it had already been decided. In the quiet of the kitchen, they could all hear the rumble of the carriage wheels and the jangle of the horse's harness as it drew to a halt outside.

Molly turned to her sisters. 'I suppose I must go,' she said. She was their big sister, the one who had always taken care of them, but now she looked to them for help.

'It will be all right,' Lizzie said, after a moment or two. 'They'll understand. It's just a shock. For everyone. It makes no difference.'

But Molly knew it did. Once George had a name for his father, he would want to know everything. And Charlie would surely despise her for what she had done. Aunt Jane's belief in her son must already have been rocked by Harriet's revelations; she must be wondering whether there were still more secrets to be revealed. Constance's mother, Sophie, would discover that George was barely older than her own daughter. And Molly was no longer the wife and mother that everyone thought they knew. She had behaved badly and covered it up and now her past had caught up with her. And she was shamed by it.

CHAPTER EIGHTEEN

It felt strange to Molly to step outside her sisters' house and discover that the day was still bright and warm, far removed from her despondent mood. She passed the journey home in gazing out of the carriage window but couldn't have told anyone what she saw. She appeared to be looking out, but her thoughts were all turned inwards.

When the carriage stopped in the lane and she realised they had arrived, she didn't want to get down. She wasn't ready to face yet more trouble, but she could hardly sit in the carriage any longer. The coachman, clearly following instructions, asked what time he should collect her the next day. Molly, not having considered the question, tentatively suggested two o'clock. He nodded, shook the reins and the carriage started back.

Molly stopped for a moment on the path and looked at their cottage, sensing that no one was at home. She let herself into the kitchen and called hesitantly, 'Charlie?' There was no reply and she hadn't expected one. Now she was back, she didn't know what to do with herself.

She needed to keep busy, to distract herself from fretting over where Charlie had got to. She supposed she should force herself to eat something, although she had no appetite. She looked in the larder and discovered the remains of a beef and ale pie. It was only after she'd forced down a slice that it occurred to her to go and find Judith.

Molly hurried out of the door at once, without even clearing away her plate, intent on discovering whether Judith had news of George. Their cottage lay just a few doors along the small terrace. Here, all was calm and peaceful: Joseph was asleep in his cradle and Judith was attending to household duties as though nothing unusual had happened. She invited Molly in and gave her a hug, then offered her refreshment, which she declined.

'Do you know where George is?' Molly asked.

'On his way home from Margate, I expect,' was the reply. 'Not best pleased that I took the carriage and he had to walk.' Judith smiled as she spoke.

'He's going to be angry with me,' Molly said. She could see no point in pretending otherwise.

Judith frowned. 'A little upset, perhaps. But I see no reason for him to be angry.'

Of course, Molly thought, she wasn't aware of who George's father was. Or that George had once met him, when he was in the Royal Navy and his captain had asked him to take some money to a man living in Martinique, someone who had once also been in the Navy. This man, called Nicholas Goodchild, was ill and living in straitened circumstances. That was all George had been able to tell Aunt Jane the previous year, when the coincidence of this man being her son had been discovered. Molly had kept it from George that this was his father, for what good would it do to tell him? Nicholas Goodchild was surely dead by then.

Joseph began to stir and ordinarily Molly would have been pleased, for it would have given her the chance to keep him company while his mother busied herself around the house.

Today, though, she was agitated and couldn't find it in her to settle to anything. She stood up, keen to return home now that she knew George was not to be found there.

At that moment, the gate creaked and footsteps sounded on the path. Molly froze and looked at Judith, knowing she had heard them too. It could surely only be George?

The door opened and in he stepped. He looked surprised to find his mother there and Molly could tell in an instant that he had been drinking. His cheeks were flushed, his eyes bright and he had a curious air about him.

'Molly,' he said. He'd never called her 'Mother', or any variation of it, having known her as Molly Dawson before either of them had realised she was his mother. It had never bothered her: she had just been happy to have him in her life after so many long years spent apart. Now, though, she was reading things into his intonation and his expression even though she should have known better than to make judgements when a man had been to the inn. She didn't dare to ask whether he was angry with her, in case he wasn't. It wouldn't do to put the idea into his head. She felt as though she must wait until he spoke again.

Judith stepped in to fill the awkward silence. 'Did you walk back?' she asked. Then, without waiting for an answer, 'Would you pick up your son?'

Joseph had started to cry, a wail that was rising in volume with each second that passed. George stepped forward to scoop him out of his cradle then, his son in his arms, he turned to Molly.

'You should have told me, Molly. Told me I'd met my father. I know it makes no odds – I wouldn't have realised at the time. But I would have liked to know whose son I was – I am. And now I not only discover the name of my father, but that I have two half-sisters whom I never knew existed. And all the while I'd been thinking myself the product of a chance encounter in London. That's what you wanted me to think, isn't it?' The look he gave her was full of accusation.

Judith was looking puzzled for, of course, she was missing a vital piece of information: that Nicholas Goodchild was George's father. Molly had cause to be puzzled, too, but for another reason. How had George come by this knowledge? Hannah's words had only made it plain that she knew who his father was. She hadn't divulged his name.

Molly wanted to ask the question but before she could speak, George said, 'Molly, would you mind leaving us now? I have a lot to think about and to discuss with Judith.'

Judith frowned at his words but didn't try to prevent her going.

'Charlie will be home too, I expect,' she said to Molly, coming to the door to see her out. She meant it to be reassuring. She wasn't to know that the words filled Molly with dread.

CHAPTER NINETEEN

On her return, Molly's cottage looked just as it had when the carriage had dropped her off earlier: blank-faced and strangely unwelcoming. The flowers she'd tended in the garden over the years, nurturing them as lovingly as the ones Charlie looked after at Woodchurch Manor, held no pleasure for her that day. Normally she would have stopped on the path to nip off a spent bloom or take notice of a new blossom. Today she passed her flowers without a glance.

During all the years of her marriage, the only other time she had felt anxiety over seeing Charlie was also because of George. Or, more correctly Molly supposed, it had been over her veiling of the truth surrounding the son she had loved so dearly and had had to give up. It was this last thought that struck home and filled her with a kind of fierce pride as she entered the house. She'd done wrong, it was true, but she liked to think it was for the right reasons: out of love and a wish to do her best for George.

Charlie was sitting at the kitchen table, apparently deep in thought. When he looked up at Molly's entrance, his cheeks were flushed, too, and she supposed he had joined George in visiting an inn or two on the way home. This was unlike Charlie: he would have a drink of ale when a social occasion demanded it, but he wouldn't seek it out.

He stared at her for a moment or two, then turned away again.

'Judith took the carriage. You must have had to walk home,' she ventured.

She thought he might ask how she had made the journey, although perhaps Aunt Jane's carriage had passed them by without Molly noticing. It was more than likely, though, that they had taken the more direct route across the fields. Absorbed in pondering this, she wasn't ready for his words when they came.

'So, Nicholas Goodchild, eh? Your own cousin. No wonder you turned me down all those years ago. You had your sights set on better things. Your uncle's money, for one.'

Charlie's tone was one she'd never heard from him before – cold, hard. Shaken, Molly began to reply but he held up his hand. He continued, 'And look what a prospect he turned out to be. Three children by three different women and only married to one of them. A shame it wasn't you, I suppose.'

He turned away from Molly again, hunching his shoulders. She ventured towards him, reaching out a hand. She wanted only to make amends but he flinched and spat out, 'Don't touch me!'

She recoiled. Then her anger flared. 'Charlie, I know I was foolish and misguided. I've had to live with the knowledge for many years now. And I realise it was wrong to keep the name of George's father a secret, but I honestly didn't see what good it would do to tell George or you. By the time George became known to me, Nicholas Goodchild had been gone for many years, most likely dead. And by then I was only too well aware of the sort of man he was.'

She paused, not sure how to phrase what she wanted to ask.

'Hannah saw a resemblance to Nicholas in George, but only because she was one of just two people who knew of what had happened, before I ran away to London. But she didn't say a word about Nicholas at Aunt Jane's party – just that George looked like his father. And the only other person who knew was my own father and he's dead. So how did you . . .?'

She halted, unable to ask the question.

'How did I find you out, do you mean?' Charlie's voice was icy. 'Well, Harriet felt George and I should know. She told us.'

'Harriet?' Molly was astonished. She couldn't think of any way that Harriet, who had been just a child at the time, could have acquired such knowledge.

Charlie was speaking again. 'George and I came across her as we left the White Hart. We'd gone there to try to make some sense of what we'd heard. I have to say, though, that if we hadn't met Harriet we'd still be wondering.' He glared at his wife.

Would it have been better if they *had* still been wondering? Molly asked herself. Wouldn't it have been better if the truth had come from her, in her own way? She could at least have tried to explain to George – to them both – why she'd kept that one last secret.

As if Charlie had read her mind, he said, 'What else have you lied about, Molly? What else have you hidden from us all?'

As he said 'us all', she remembered that she still had to face Aunt Jane the following day. She quailed inwardly at the thought, but pushed it aside. It was more important now to try to make amends to Charlie.

She protested that there was nothing else, and reiterated that she'd kept the truth about Nicholas Goodchild a secret to protect George, Aunt Jane, Sarah and Constance, not just herself.

Seeking to return their relationship to a more normal footing, she set out the meat pie and a plate on the table, but as she went to the dresser drawer to fetch knives and forks, Charlie stood up and left the room. Molly heard his tread on the stairs and the bedroom door slam, while she stood like a statue, the cutlery in her hand.

That night, Molly slept in Agnes's old room, since her bedroom door, closed against her, felt too forbidding to broach. She passed a fitful night, tossing and turning, although she must have fallen asleep before dawn, for when she awoke it was daylight, the birds were singing and Charlie had left for work.

Chapter Twenty

Molly passed the hours until her aunt's carriage was due to return in needless cleaning and tidying of the house. She couldn't bear to be alone with her thoughts so threw herself into clearing out the cupboards of the kitchen dresser. Unable to reach a decision as to whether to keep things or throw them away, she simply returned them to their original home. She was glad when the clock showed that, with just half an hour until the carriage was due, it was time to get ready. The morning's pointless endeavours had persuaded her of the wisdom in having the interview with Aunt Jane, even though she didn't anticipate it would be easy.

The carriage arrived promptly and Molly took her seat without a backward glance at her home. She half wondered whether Charlie might be watching her leave from somewhere in the Woodchurch estate grounds. Then it dawned on her that he had no knowledge of her planned return to her aunt's. There had been no chance to share news of it with him the previous evening and she hadn't thought to leave him a note. Molly was taken aback. She hadn't known where Charlie was after he'd left her aunt's house and now he wouldn't know where she was. Such things simply didn't happen in their marriage. It felt as though the life she'd built was crumbling around her.

Her mood, when she descended from the carriage in Princes Crescent, was very different from that of the day before. She found it hard to believe that just twenty-four hours had passed. Yesterday she had felt the warmth and security of her family around her. Now she couldn't have felt more alone.

Elsie opened the door promptly to her knock and she was shown into the drawing room, which bore no trace of the party. Molly could smell beeswax polish and wondered whether Elsie had been given the job of erasing all evidence of the gathering, mopping the floors and polishing the furniture so that nothing might remind Aunt Jane of what had passed.

Her aunt wasn't in the room and Molly was too unsettled to sit and wait. She wandered around, picking up ornaments and putting them down again without even noticing what they were. A vase of pale pink roses stood on a side table and a waft of their perfume raised a memory of when she had lived with her aunt and brought back roses for her from the Prospect House gardens. The head gardener there, Mr Fleming, knew of her liking for them. Charlie had been there, too – Molly was reminded of how awkward he had been with her at first, eager, shy and embarrassed all at once. She would have smiled at the memory if it hadn't been too painful in light of everything that had just happened.

She was alert for sounds of her aunt's footsteps and so, when she came into the room, leaning on the stick that she had recently taken to using, Molly was as composed and ready as she was ever likely to be.

'Sit down, sit down.' Aunt Jane waved her stick irritably at Molly as she took up her customary chair. 'You may leave us, Elsie.'

The maid had been hovering, no doubt expecting to be asked to bring refreshments, and looked surprised to be sent away. Molly wished that she could follow her down to the kitchen, to Hannah's domain, and take a seat there instead of in the uncomfortable ladderback chair assigned to her.

'I've spoken to Hannah and she's told me what she said to your son yesterday, and why she said it. What do you have to say for yourself?' Aunt Jane demanded.

Molly, although expecting the question, was taken aback by its bluntness. 'I – oh – I'm sorry, Aunt.' She paused. 'I know it must have come as a shock. It was all so long ago. I was young. Foolish, I suppose.' She halted once more.

It felt ludicrous. So much trouble over one man, over something that had happened so many years earlier. Was Molly never to cease being held to account for it? Nicholas had escaped all censure, at the time and now, in death.

'Foolish and headstrong,' Aunt Jane snapped. 'I took you in as a favour to your father. I blamed that wife of his, Ann, for the unhappiness in his household. Now I'm not so sure.' She glared at Molly.

There was a silence, while Molly contemplated the events all those years ago: Nicholas creeping up to her room in the attic of the house, while his parents and sisters slept, unsuspecting, on the floor below. How it had all felt so strange and exciting, how she had been sure he planned to marry her. Now, looking at it through her aunt's eyes, she saw it differently. Did she suspect Molly had set out to trap her precious son with a cheap and sordid affair? Although surely, if that was the case, she must see that Molly wouldn't have run away without a word.

She was about to put this point to her when Aunt Jane spoke again.

'That boy has brought nothing but trouble to this household.' She seemed deflated: all the anger had left her. 'Asking Sarah to marry him when he was carrying on with you.' Aunt Jane's mouth set in a thin line. 'And then deciding to leave all his responsibilities behind and start a new life in the West Indies. Whatever was in his head? Heaven knows, we still have to face the consequences of that decision.'

Molly could scarcely believe her ears. Her aunt had always believed that Nicholas could do no wrong. She'd been distraught when he was sent home from his naval academy under a cloud, then despatched to sea by his father. Now Aunt Jane seemed prepared to believe that Nicholas might not have been the wonderful son she had believed him to be.

'Did he know?' Aunt Jane had reverted to her earlier, accusatory tone. 'Was he supporting his son?'

'No!' Molly protested. Then she hesitated. 'Well, I did tell him. But by then he was betrothed to Sarah. And he did give me some money. But it was to make me go away.' The cruel memory of that moment came back to her. She'd realised then that she would have to make her own way in the world.

'You didn't think to come to us for help?' her aunt demanded.

Molly could only stare at her aunt, who looked away.

'No, I suppose not,' her aunt said. 'I can see why you didn't.' With a visible effort, she forced herself to say, 'I hope that we might become better acquainted with George, now that we know he is our grandson.'

Molly didn't know how to answer. It would be a decision for George to make, once he had come to terms with what he had just learnt about his father. If he ever did.

Aunt Jane shook her head. 'It has been a lot to take in. You will have to excuse me, Molly, if I've seemed a little harsh in my words to you today. It would seem that so many things I have believed over the last few years were wrong – based on a lie.'

Molly, seeing how frail her aunt looked, was concerned for her. 'Where is Uncle William?' she asked. 'Shall I call him?'

'He's gone to Greenwich,' Aunt Jane said. 'To fetch Sarah and Constance. And to see whether he can get news of this Margaret Roberts. Another of yesterday's surprising discoveries.'

Molly gave a start when her aunt banged on the floor with her cane, but the intention became clear when Elsie appeared in the room within a minute of the summons.

'Show Molly out,' Aunt Jane said. 'And ask Hannah to help me up to my room.'

And so Molly found herself dismissed, without the customary farewell kiss on the cheek, and with no chance to speak to Hannah. At a loss as to what to do next, she could only think to go next door, in the hope of finding her sisters at home.

CHAPTER TWENTY-ONE

L izzie and Mary listened to Molly's account of her interview with Aunt Jane, their indignation plain to see.

'They always thought they were superior to us,' Lizzie said crossly. 'As if having money somehow makes you a better person. Well, at least Aunt Jane knows the truth about Nicholas now.'

'Did she ask you anything about what you did in London? About how you managed on your own there, with a baby?' Mary demanded.

Molly was glad her aunt hadn't asked her. It wasn't information that she wanted to share with anyone. Not even her sisters, who had clearly been wondering about it.

Lizzie, cross and quite pink in the face, had her own questions.

'Was Charlie there when you got home yesterday?' she asked. 'And what about George? Did you tell them about Nicholas?'

'No,' Molly said. 'Harriet had already done that for me.'

'Harriet?' Lizzie and Mary spoke in unison.

'Yes,' Molly said. 'She walked by as they were leaving the White Hart down on the harbour. I don't know how she knew or why she told them. It would have been better coming from me.'

There was silence in the room as Lizzie and Mary digested the news. They were all sitting around the kitchen table in the sisters' cottage once more. Lizzie had been quick to offer Molly tea when she heard Aunt Jane hadn't seen fit to do so. Now Molly turned her empty cup between her fingers and frowned into it.

'What did they say?' Mary asked her at last.

'They weren't happy.' Molly sighed. 'George asked me to leave his house and Charlie picked a fight with me, then went to bed. I slept in Agnes's room.'

Her stark depiction of the events of the previous evening further roused her sisters.

'Oh, for goodness' sake!' Lizzie exclaimed, impatient. 'It's not as if you committed a crime. If anything, you were the victim. You've never tried to do anything but the best for George, for your family and for Charlie. Can't they see that?'

Molly shrugged. 'Well, they'd both had a few drinks. Maybe it will be easier to talk to them today.'

'Stay here with us,' Mary said. 'I don't think you should go back. At least, not yet,' she added, seeing Molly's expression. 'Let them miss you, so that they realise how much you matter to them. A few days away will help them get used to the news.'

'Do you think so?' Molly was doubtful. She was keen to get home as soon as possible and have another attempt at making them understand.

'Mary's right,' Lizzie declared. 'Stay here for a day or two. We hardly ever get the chance to spend time together.'

Molly hesitated. Charlie didn't even know that she had come to Margate. Wouldn't he be worried if she wasn't there when he got home? She looked around her sisters' kitchen, familiar from when she had lived in the cottage as a young girl but now so much more homely. All at once, the thought of going back to spend another night like the previous one was too much to contemplate. If she stayed here, she would be distracted from her woes for a little while. And there was a pie in the larder at home. Charlie wouldn't starve.

'All right, I'll stay,' she said. 'But do you have room for me?' She was suddenly doubtful.

'Of course,' Mary said. 'You can have Lewis's room. He can sleep in the parlour. He works such long hours in the bakery that he's hardly here anyway.'

And so it was decided. Mary settled down to help the sisters prepare that night's dinner and for a few hours she was able to forget her troubles. Every now and then, though, she remembered what had happened, and what must still be faced at home. Two days passed in this way, and the third had begun, Molly wrestling with the decision over when to return. Her conscience told her it was time, but her heart failed her. She half thought Charlie would send a message to her sisters, asking whether she was there, but nothing had been heard from him.

And now, after a walk to the harbour and back, under-taken in the hope that the fresh air might bring clarity, she saw an unfamiliar figure loitering at the roadside beside her sisters' house in Princes Crescent. She was tall and slender, standing with a very straight back and wearing a cotton gown printed in a shade of green that was rather brighter than anything Molly had seen before.

'Can I help you?' Molly asked, thinking that perhaps the woman was lost.

The woman turned and Molly registered at once that her features and skin tone marked her out as not of these parts. Even as the thought crossed her mind, she made the deduction.

'Margaret?' she ventured. 'Miss Roberts,' she added hastily, remembering that they had never been introduced.

The woman looked at her sharply. 'And whom do I have the pleasure of addressing?' she asked.

'I'm Molly – Molly Dawson.' Molly paused. '*Are* you Margaret Roberts? And are you looking for someone?'

Margaret looked her up and down. 'How do you know who I am?' she asked.

'Through Harriet,' Molly replied. 'Harriet told us about you.'

'Harriet?' Margaret looked surprised, then recovered herself. 'Harriet, indeed. Well, I'm looking for William Goodchild,' she went on. 'He's been asking questions around London, looking for me, so I thought I'd better come to his house and find out what he wants.'

Molly scrutinised Margaret's face and thought she could see a resemblance to George's features there. All at once, she needed to sit down.

'William Goodchild is my uncle but I'm not sure whether he's at home. Will you come into my sisters' house, next door?' Molly said. 'I was just about to go in. You could wait there.'

'Thank you,' Margaret said. She looked weary, all of a sudden. Molly thought she must have taken a very early coach from London to have arrived by this hour in Margate.

She led the way into her sisters' kitchen and surprised them both, Mary kneading dough for a loaf for dinner and Lizzie sweeping the floor.

'Do you have to scatter flour everywhere while I'm trying to sweep up?' Lizzie complained, then straightened to see what had caused her sister to stop and stare.

'This is Margaret Roberts,' Molly said. Her voice sounded loud in the sudden silence that had fallen. Seeing the look on

108

Lizzie and Mary's faces, Molly felt a rush of sympathy for Margaret. She wondered whether she had become used to this reaction, which she must face every day.

'I found her out in the street, looking for Uncle William. I thought she might need some refreshment after her long journey from London. And perhaps we can answer some questions for her, about her family.'

Even as she spoke, Molly thought that here was yet another person to whom she would need to explain her son's parentage. Margaret was about to discover a few things about her father, Nicholas, that would come as a shock. Although it was quite possible, Molly supposed, that she was better acquainted with her father's true character than any of his family in Margate.

CHAPTER TWENTY-TWO

Molly registered Margaret's straight-backed posture once more when they were all seated around the kitchen table. She had a dignity and composure about her, Molly decided, that she certainly didn't recognise in her own daughters. Her heart lurched as she thought of them: Sally in Westgate with Grace and Simon; Catherine at Woodchurch Manor with Eleanor. What would Catherine be thinking of her mother – for news of the revelations about George's father must surely have reached her? And Agnes, too, somewhere in London or Ramsgate, or between the two. How Molly wished she was at her side now!

Lizzie served everyone with lemonade, remarking on the heat of the day as she did so, and then silence fell. Molly saw that her sisters were looking at her, in expectation of her starting the conversation.

But it was Margaret who spoke first. 'Thank you for inviting me in. I confess, I was eager to meet the man whom I assume to be my relative, but a little anxious, too. The message that I received from him in London felt more of an order than a friendly greeting. I knew I needed to come to Margate in order to discover more.'

'That sounds like Uncle William,' Molly said, with a wry smile. 'How did he trace you, though? Harriet said that you ...' She hesitated, choosing her words with care. She remembered that Harriet had implied Margaret's dismissal from the hospital. 'She said that you'd moved on, to London,' she managed finally, 'but she didn't know where.'

'It was easy enough to find out,' Margaret said, frowning. 'The hospital had a forwarding address for me. After all, they had arranged my temporary transfer to look after a private patient in London.'

'And Uncle William visited you there?' Molly was puzzled, for it didn't sound as though Margaret and her uncle had yet met.

'No, he was in London on Monday and called at the house, but I was tending my patient. He told the maid he had other business to see to and couldn't stay, but he left a message, with the coach fare, asking me to come to Margate as soon as possible. He said he had something important to tell me.' Margaret sipped her drink. 'Then when I got here, I realised I couldn't read the house number on his note – the ink had smudged.'

Molly remembered her aunt had mentioned Uncle William's trip to Greenwich. She looked at her sisters. 'Is Uncle William back? Did he bring Sarah and Constance with him?'

Mary seemed uncomfortable. 'Uncle William has returned, but without Sarah. I think she was upset. She asked for some time to come to terms with the news.'

Molly looked down at the table, stricken. Here was yet another consequence that must be faced because of her secrets. It was true that she hadn't gone out of her way to see Nicholas's wife, Sarah, over the years, but meeting her at social gatherings had been unavoidable. She had always been civil to her, if only to avoid arousing suspicion.

Her aunt and uncle had taken good care of Sarah, and Constance, Nicholas's daughter. Over the years they had maintained the pretence that Nicholas would return, only quietly giving up when George had unwittingly shared news of having seen him. Since the sighting had been some years earlier, when Nicholas had appeared very ill, Aunt Jane had quite naturally assumed the worst.

Molly had been glad when Sarah went to live in Greenwich, taking Constance with her. George and Constance were just a few months apart in age and Molly had been worried that someone might remark on a resemblance between them. But their paths had never crossed, and once the move to Greenwich was complete, Molly had relaxed, thinking her secret was safe.

Now a lull in the conversation round the table pulled her back from her musings. Once more, she was aware that her sisters were gazing at her but this time Margaret, too, had an expectant expression on her face. Molly realised that she had been asked a question.

'I'm sorry,' Molly apologised. 'What did you ask me?'

Margaret answered her: 'I asked about Sarah and Constance. Who are they and why are they relevant?'

Molly looked to her sisters for help but they avoided her eyes. She took a deep breath.

'Sarah is – was – married to Nicholas Goodchild, Uncle William's son. And Constance is their daughter.'

Margaret's demeanour changed only slightly, in that she looked down at her hands in her lap. After a moment she looked up again and said, 'Will you tell me more?'

Molly sighed, then plunged into the tale that had to be told.

'Nicholas married Sarah in Chatham in 1789, just before his ship sailed. Constance was born while he was at sea. He never returned, and the last the family heard of him, he had left the Navy and was living in the West Indies.'

'He had met my mother,' Margaret said softly.

'None of us have seen him since he went away. Uncle William managed to trace him once or twice during that time and sent money, but the only news we had was that he was ill.'

'Yellow fever,' Margaret said. 'A lot of sailors suffered from it. Only a few survived, and in those who did it had a habit of recurring. He drank to take his mind off it.'

She turned once more to Molly. 'So I have a half-sister?' she asked.

'Constance.' Molly nodded. 'I think she must be older than you. She is twenty-six. And you, you must be in your early twenties?'

It was a guess on Molly's part, for Margaret had a mature air about her.

'I'm twenty-two,' Margaret said. 'All those years and I never knew I had a sister.' She shook her head; it was clear that the idea was strange to her.

'Not just a sister,' Lizzie said.

Molly glared at her but Lizzie went on, 'There's no point in keeping it from her,' she said. 'The whole town probably knows by now. It's as well Margaret hears it from us.'

Margaret's gaze was now focused on Molly's face. Molly found herself distracted all at once by the flashes of resemblance she could see between her and George.

'What else should I know?' Margaret asked.

'You have a half-brother, George, too,' Molly said.

'A brother?' Margaret frowned. 'But you said Sarah and my father only married just before he set sail. And he didn't see her again. So how—?'

'George is my son,' Molly said.

In the silence that followed, she heard the clip-clop of hoofs and a rumble of wheels as a horse and cart proceeded along Princes Crescent. The driver's voice rang out in greeting on the still air, and Molly could hear a less distinct reply from the street. Dust motes floated in the sunlight that poured through the window and the kitchen cat, which was curled up in the patch of warmth created on the stone-flagged floor, stretched and yawned.

Molly knew she had to go on. 'George is almost exactly the same age as Constance. I was living next door with my aunt and uncle at the time and Nicholas was at home on leave. I was young and foolish and I thought Nicholas would marry me. But he didn't. He married Sarah.' Molly paused. She had been about to add that Nicholas wanted nothing to do with her baby, but thought better of it. Better not to completely blacken his character in the eyes of his daughter.

'So I ran off to London. I had to give George up to the Foundling Hospital shortly after he was born. I thought I would never see him again. He only came back into my life, quite by chance, two years ago.'

Molly was close to tears as she thought about the painful history she had left out in the telling of her tale to Margaret.

'I see,' Margaret said. There was a long silence. 'So I have quite a family,' she said finally.

'Yes,' Molly said. 'But Harriet's news of your existence came as a shock and I'm afraid no one took it well. Particularly George. I hadn't . . .' the words almost choked her '. . . I hadn't told him who his father was, you see. He thought it was someone in London, someone lost to me, not my cousin Nicholas.'

'A surprise for everyone,' Margaret said drily. Perhaps she had some inkling of her father's nature, Molly thought.

Margaret drained her glass and stood up. 'Well, I suppose I should meet this uncle and aunt of yours – my grandparents – before the day is over. Would anyone care to come with me and make the introductions?'

CHAPTER TWENTY-THREE

Lizzie and Mary readily volunteered to take Margaret next door. Molly quailed at the thought but she had a feeling her sisters rather relished witnessing their aunt and uncle's reaction.

Left alone, she was faced with the task of keeping busy to fill the time until they returned. She had finished sweeping the kitchen, brought in the washing from the yard and folded it and was wondering whether to set about cooking dinner when the kitchen door opened and Lizzie and Mary stepped inside.

'Margaret isn't with you?' Molly was surprised.

'No, she's gone to see her old landlady,' Lizzie said.

Mary burst out, 'I just can't imagine what Uncle William was thinking!'

Lizzie shook her head, lips pursed. 'I'm surprised that Margaret remained as calm as she did.'

'What happened?' Molly looked from Lizzie to Mary. 'What did Uncle William do?'

'He thought he could offer her money to go away.' Mary looked ready to explode with indignation. 'His own flesh and blood. I suppose she is an unexpected addition to the family but I don't imagine he'd think to offer money to George in the same way.'

Molly, who had been standing up until this point, sat down suddenly. 'What do you mean?'

'Nothing was said about George,' Lizzie said hastily. 'Don't worry. Mary was just making a comparison. Uncle William obviously chose to believe that Margaret came to Margate to get her hands on the family money.'

'So he offered her what he described as a "generous sum" to make herself scarce.' Mary was so cross she could barely speak. 'What I meant was, he hasn't sought to ask George to make himself scarce. I daresay it's the colour of Margaret's skin that offends him.'

'Now, Mary,' Lizzie protested, 'we can't know that for sure. Perhaps it's because Margaret was born when Nicholas was already married to Sarah.'

'As was George,' Mary pointed out.

Molly was keen to steer the conversation away from the repeated references to George. 'How did Margaret react?' she asked.

'She was very calm and self-possessed. She said she had no need of his money as she was capable of making her own way in the world,' Lizzie said.

'And then she said she planned to return to her work in Margate and she hoped that in time we might all be better acquainted,' Mary said. 'Uncle William went bright red and I quite feared for his health.'

She began to laugh and Molly couldn't suppress a smile at the image she created.

'How was Aunt Jane?' she asked, suddenly serious again.

'She didn't say a word and looked rather as though she might cry,' Lizzie said.

The sisters fell silent, contemplating the upset created in the lives of their relatives.

'Don't forget about Hannah,' Mary reminded Lizzie.

'Oh, yes – Uncle William and Aunt Jane are going to Greenwich for a few days to stay with Sarah and Constance. Hannah's mother is sick and she's worried about her, given how old she is. They've told Hannah to take the time off to visit her. She asked to speak to you before she goes.'

Molly still hadn't managed to have a word with Hannah so the cook's distress at letting slip the truth about George's ancestry hadn't been addressed.

'I'd prefer to avoid Aunt Jane and Uncle William at the moment,' Molly said. She didn't want to go next door to see Hannah and run the risk of meeting them.

'Hannah's going to come here on the pretext of borrowing some flour,' Mary said. 'So you don't need to worry.'

'I was planning to go home today,' Molly said. All at once, she felt she had been away too long. It was time to go back and speak to Charlie and George once more.

'Talk to Hannah first,' Lizzie said, before adding mysteriously, 'She's got something to say that might interest you.'

Molly didn't have long to wait to satisfy the curiosity that Lizzie's words had aroused. Hannah appeared in the kitchen within the hour, still in her work apron and clutching an earthenware jar.

'I've come to borrow flour, in case anyone thinks to ask,' she said, 'but really I need to speak to you, Molly.'

Lizzie and Mary tactfully withdrew from the kitchen, leaving Hannah and Molly face to face.

Hannah barely waited for the door to close behind them before she began. 'I can't tell you how sorry I am for what I did. I couldn't help myself. When I saw George, I knew it was him straight away. He has such a resemblance to Nicholas around the eyes. I remember thinking, *And Molly told me she'd lost Nicholas's baby when she was in London and yet here he is, without a doubt.* And the words were out of my mouth before I could stop them.' Hannah shook her head sorrowfully. 'It's a bad business, what with George and the other one, the young lady. Your aunt and uncle don't know what to do with themselves over it. You know how your uncle likes to appear above reproach in the town.

'That's why they're going to Greenwich. I think he's hoping that the gossip in Margate will die away if he's not here. And at last I've got the chance to go and visit my mother in Faversham. I gather things aren't too easy for you at home and I thought you might like to come along. It might allow things to blow over for you, too.' Hannah gave Molly a shrewd glance as she spoke.

'Oh, I don't know.' Molly was taken aback. 'I've been away too long already. I think I should go home – it's time we all had a proper talk.'

'I'll be leaving on Friday,' Hannah said, getting to her feet. 'Go back and see how things are. The offer is there if you change your mind. I'd like it if you could come with me.'

As soon as Hannah had gone, Lizzie and Mary came back into the kitchen, wanting to know what had been said. Molly was inclined to be dismissive. 'I'm set on going back tomorrow. It was kind of Hannah to make the offer, but I think enough time has passed. I'm better off at home now.'

'Barely any time has passed,' Lizzie protested. 'Don't you think it would be better to let them start to worry about your absence?'

Molly shook her head. 'I've made up my mind. I've been away long enough. I've enjoyed my stay and I'm sure it has been good for me,' she added hastily, fearful of seeming ungrateful, 'but I really do feel it's time to go home. And I'm sure Lewis would be glad to have his bed back.'

Early the following morning, Molly said her goodbyes and made her way to the inn on the western edge of town, where she found a ride as far as Woodchurch Manor with a carter heading for Canterbury. She looked out across the fields as the wagon rolled along. She tried to tell herself that what she felt was nervous excitement but she knew it was apprehension. She wasn't sure what sort of welcome she could expect to receive.

Chapter Twenty-Four

When Molly walked back through the door of her cottage, it felt different. Unloved and empty, she thought. Charlie was tidy by nature so he had cleared up after his meals, but she had a feeling he had spent barely any time there. This wasn't unusual: in the summer the gardens kept him occupied from dawn until dusk and she rather thought he had come home only to eat and sleep.

There would be long hours to occupy until he came in from work, Molly thought, regretting having set out so early. She looked in the larder and saw the pie had been finished, but a freshly killed rabbit – no doubt caught in one of the kitchen-garden traps – lay on the cold slab. Molly set about skinning it and making a stew, which passed a couple of hours. Leaving the pot to simmer, she went to pay a visit to Judith, thinking she might be able to glean how things stood with George and Charlie.

Judith answered the door to Molly's knock and looked surprised and uncomfortable to see her there. 'I didn't know you were home,' she said. She stood in the doorway and didn't invite Molly in.

Molly was puzzled by her behaviour. 'How is Joseph?' she asked.

'He's napping,' Judith said. She still didn't move from the doorway.

'Judith, what is it?' Molly asked. 'Have I done something wrong?'

She knew that the answer was yes, in George's eyes, but she didn't understand why Judith was behaving in this way.

'George has asked me not to let you in,' Judith said. She was clearly embarrassed and couldn't meet Molly's gaze.

'His own mother?' Molly was astonished.

'I'm sorry. He's angry that you kept the truth about his father from him.' Judith turned her head as the sound of a wail reached the doorstep. 'Joseph has woken up. I must go.'

Before Molly could reply, she found herself faced with the closed door. She stood there for a moment, then turned on her heel and went home, her cheeks burning with humiliation. Unable to settle to any of the household tasks she conjured up to occupy herself, she decided to go to the one place she could be sure of finding Charlie and George: the gardens. Ordinarily, she would have left them in peace in their workplace but her increasing agitation meant she couldn't wait until the evening to have a discussion with Charlie. It would be too easy for him to plead tiredness as an excuse to avoid her.

Molly mentally rehearsed what she wanted to say as she followed her usual route to the gardens, entering adjacent to the gate into the walled garden. Head down, she didn't notice Mr Powell in her path and would have cannoned straight into him if he hadn't reached out to grasp her arm.

'Mrs Dawson! Where are you going at such a pace?'

'Oh, Mr Powell, I'm so sorry.' Molly was flustered. 'My mind was elsewhere. I'm looking for Charlie. Or George.'

Molly saw that Mr Powell was regarding her quizzically. 'Have you been away? I don't believe I've seen you for a few days,' he said.

'I've been spending some time with my sisters, in Margate.' Molly knew her cheeks had reddened as she spoke. Had Charlie mentioned they had fallen out? Otherwise why would Mr Powell remark on her absence?

'Charlie will be pleased to have you back. You'll find him with George in the glasshouse.' Mr Powell nodded to her and moved on.

As Molly opened the gate into the walled garden, it occurred to her that Charlie hadn't known where she had gone. He was unable to dissemble – if Mr Powell had asked about his wife, he would undoubtedly have said that he didn't know where she was.

Molly could see her husband and son – one sandy head, the other brown – as they bent over a tray of plants in the glasshouse. They looked up as she pushed open the door and she couldn't miss their expressions. Neither was pleased to see her. Charlie's lips were set in a thin line and he gave her a cold look, while George drew his brows together in a frown, threw down his trowel and made to turn away.

'Don't go,' Molly said, addressing George. 'I'm glad to find you both together. I just wanted to say—' She stopped, all the words she had rehearsed on her way over driven from her mind by her encounter with Mr Powell.

She started again. 'I saw Mr Powell. He said I'd find you here.' And be pleased to see me, she thought wryly. 'And I saw Judith.'

She thought she saw a flicker of discomfort cross George's face.

'Charlie, I'm sorry I left without saying where I was going. Aunt Jane had asked me to return to speak to her and I intended to come straight back, but I stayed with my sisters instead, and for longer than I intended. I'm sorry,' she repeated, for Charlie's countenance was as grim as when she had started.

'And, George, Judith told me I wasn't welcome. I know I've upset you – upset you both. My intentions were good. I didn't see what purpose it would serve to tell you about Nicholas,' Molly stumbled over his name, 'when I hadn't seen him in over twenty years. I knew he was living abroad and disgraced.' She closed her eyes briefly as she came to a halt.

Neither Charlie nor George had spoken, and their demeanour had not changed. They appeared unimpressed by her attempts to explain and Molly was at a loss. A minute passed while they faced each other in silence – a minute that felt like an eternity to Molly – before George spoke.

'It seems that others knew well enough. Did you think to make us both a laughing stock?'

Molly stared, shocked. What did he mean?

'Hannah knew,' George went on. 'And Harriet. So why didn't you think to share the truth with us?'

'Hannah had no knowledge of it,' Molly protested. 'She guessed when she saw you, last Sunday. As for Harriet ...' Molly frowned, trying to unravel how she could have known about Nicholas. 'I don't know,' she had to confess. 'But I really don't believe it was common knowledge.' Although it might be now, she thought ruefully. 'I realise you think I did wrong. I wish I could make you understand that I believed keeping this last secret was the right thing to do.'

'Last secret?' George now looked even angrier than he had done when she walked in. 'You kept me a secret for nearly twenty-five years. And when I asked you about my father, you said he was someone you barely knew. How can I trust a word you say?'

Molly wanted to protest that it hadn't seemed like an untruth. She had felt she hardly knew Nicholas. He'd been away at school and then at sea, and when he returned and she became entangled with him, she had created her own version of him, a figment of her imagination. The true Nicholas was someone else entirely. But she didn't think George would be prepared to hear such an explanation.

She looked at Charlie. Did he understand? They had never had a serious quarrel in all their years together and she didn't think she could bear his disapproval. Her hopes were dashed when he said, 'There was no need to come back, Molly. We were managing very well without you.'

Molly gasped. She felt winded, as though his words were physical punches. She turned and left the glasshouse, blinded by tears. She half expected to hear Charlie calling after her, 'Molly, come back,' but there was nothing – no kindly hand on her shoulder and no sound other than the creak and clang of the gate as it shut behind her.

CHAPTER TWENTY-FIVE

Back at the cottage, Molly went straight upstairs to her bedroom and pulled Charlie's battered leather travel bag from beneath the bed. She took two dresses and a skirt from their peg on the wall and folded them into the bag with trembling hands. Then she went to the chest of drawers and picked out a blouse and chemise and pushed them into the bag. In her haste to be gone, she didn't stop to consider whether she had what she needed, although she did remember to take all the coins from a drawstring bag tucked into the bottom drawer.

She took her shawl and bonnet from behind the door and walked down the path without looking back. She struck out across the fields, staying away from the road and taking the path she had used years ago, when she had first come to visit Charlie at Woodchurch Manor. The memory brought a fresh rush of tears and she had to stop and put down the bag while she fumbled for a handkerchief. The sight of this, embroidered with her initial in one corner, only served to remind her of the token she had left with George at the Foundling Hospital. Instead of staunching her tears, the handkerchief was soaked within moments.

Finally, fear of someone who knew her coming across her in her distressed state drove Molly onwards. She would return to Margate, to her sisters, and she would take up Hannah's offer. Molly was oblivious to her surroundings as she walked: the fresh scent of the countryside warmed by the late-afternoon sun, the birdsong, the glint of blue sea in the far distance. Her thoughts were all turned inwards as she forced herself to consider the future. If her marriage was over, she must find a means to support herself. Could she be a cook, like Hannah? Or a companion to an older lady such as Aunt Jane? Or work at the Royal Sea Bathing Hospital, like Margaret and Harriet? None of these ideas brought her solace and she arrived at her sisters' in a sorry state.

The two families were sitting around the kitchen table when Molly knocked, then pushed open the door. All faces turned towards her. Lizzie stepped away from the stove and hurried to Molly's side.

'Come into the parlour. You look as though you need to sit down. No, leave your bag there,' for Molly had stooped wearily to pick it up again.

'Mary, serve the soup,' she said over her shoulder, then opened the door into the parlour and shut it firmly behind them.

When Molly was seated, thankful for the coolness of the room after her walk, Lizzie said, 'Whatever has happened, Molly? I didn't imagine we would see you back here so soon.'

Molly half rose. 'I'm sorry – I didn't think. Lewis will be expecting to have his room back. I only left this morning. It feels so long ago.'

'Stay where you are,' Lizzie said firmly. 'And tell me what's wrong. But, first, let me get you a drink. You look very hot.'

Lizzie left the room, returning swiftly with a glass of lemonade, which Molly gulped gratefully. Then, revived, she recounted her woes to Lizzie, explaining how Charlie and George had behaved when she sought them out.

'And Charlie said he didn't know why I'd bothered coming back. That they were doing very well without me.' Molly's voice broke as she reached the end of her tale.

'Oh, nonsense,' Lizzie said, taking her sister's hand and squeezing it. 'I'm sure he doesn't mean it. It sounds like hurt pride to me. He's bound to come around.'

Molly began to weep again, but she was exhausted by it and her head ached. 'Lizzie, we've hardly ever quarrelled. He meant it, I'm sure. My marriage is over.'

'Hush, Molly.' Lizzie spoke robustly. 'He'll come to his senses and see that none of this is as bad as either of you think. What difference does it make to you both? Charlie accepted George and understood how he came to be given up as a foundling – he would have realised that he had a father. Now he knows that the father was Nicholas. It must have come as a surprise, but surely it's hardly a disaster.' Lizzie's voice tailed off as they both contemplated Charlie's likely feelings on the matter. 'Look, come and eat. You'll feel better with some food inside you.'

Molly raised a faint smile. 'You sound like Hannah. She sees food as the solution to all ills.'

Lizzie stood up. 'I'll send one of the girls next door to tell Hannah you will be travelling with her to Faversham tomorrow.' She stopped. 'At least, I suppose that's why you've brought the bag?' She looked enquiringly at Molly, who nodded her assent. 'Now, let's eat.'

'I'm not hungry,' Molly said. In reality, she couldn't face sitting at the table and listening to the conversation as everyone talked about their day and what they had been doing. It would be too much of a contrast to her own sad family, torn apart by her actions.

'I'll ask Mary to bring you something in here,' Lizzie said. 'And she can keep you company while I send someone next door with a message.'

Mary arrived with a bowl of soup and some bread for Molly, shortly after Lizzie had left the room. She didn't ask her sister what was wrong – Molly supposed Lizzie must have quickly filled her in. The delicious aroma of the soup made Molly realise she was hungry, but she only managed to eat a few spoonfuls before a wave of despair overtook her and she pushed the bowl aside. Seeing Mary's anxious expression, she dipped her bread into the bowl and took a few token bites before leaving that, too.

'I'm sorry, Mary.'

Mary suppressed a sigh and cleared the bowl away. 'It will do you good to take a trip to Faversham with Hannah,' she said, when she returned. 'It will be a change of scene for you, with nothing to remind you of your worries. And when you come back, why, I'm sure everything will be as right as rain and we'll all go on as we did before.'

CHAPTER TWENTY-SIX

Molly was glad to take a seat beside Hannah, both of them squashed onto the narrow bench beside the carter as the horse pulled its load of barrels out of the yard of the inn. It hadn't been too difficult to find a cart taking a direct route to Faversham: with two breweries based there, usually one had ale to deliver and empty barrels to return.

Molly was on edge for the first part of the journey because they must pass the turning to the Woodchurch Manor estate. She had an unreasoning fear of being spotted by someone who would tell Charlie he had seen her. Then she wondered at herself: since Charlie had been so dismissive of her the day before, surely he would not care.

Once they had passed the turning, she relaxed and listened to the conversation between Hannah and the carter until the memory returned to her of the first time she had journeyed beyond this point, twenty-six years ago. Then she had been in desperate straits, having fled her aunt's house to go to Chatham in search of Nicholas who was soon to board his ship, intent on telling him she was carrying his baby. She had never travelled beyond five miles out of Margate until then and she marvelled now at how brave she had been. She had gone on to live in London and given birth to George. If only that part of her life had played out in a different way. She remembered that Hannah, when she had learnt that she was with child, had told her not to worry, that they would 'find a way'. She wondered now what she had meant by that. How different would her life have been if she had let herself be guided by Hannah?

Molly noticed that Hannah kept glancing at her until, finally, she laid her hand over Molly's and said, 'I'm looking forward to showing you Faversham and, I confess, to seeing it myself after being away for so long.'

Then she pointed out the hop fields bordering the road they travelled on – the hop bines, not yet in flower, trailing over their wooden supports. She described to Molly how teams of pickers would journey down from London to set up camp and join the locals in picking the hops in September.

Molly was intrigued and wondered aloud why she'd never seen hop fields around Woodchurch Manor.

'It's a mix of things.' The carter had been listening and now joined in. 'The hops don't do so well in the wind, especially if there's salt in the air. Go a few miles inland and you'll find them, though. The land's sheltered here, see,' and he gestured to the fields either side of the road. 'Plenty of sunshine, not too much wind and a good soil. It's a difficult crop, though. The farmers around here are only happy to give over their land to them because the breweries in Faversham mean there's a ready market for hops.'

He lapsed back into silence as Hannah pointed out the oast houses set among the fields, and explained how the harvested hops were set to dry, spread out over a kiln on the floor of the conical towers, the cowled vents at the top releasing the moisture.

'You'll know when we're close to Faversham if it's a brewing day – you can't miss it,' Hannah said. 'The smell hangs

131

over the town until the wind carries it away. They say you don't have to step into an inn to get drunk in the town – you just have to sniff the air.'

Molly was charmed by the landscape as the cart rumbled on and found herself looking forward to reaching Faversham. It had been a very long time since she had done anything other than bring up her family and keep house, with the occasional visit to Margate, or even rarer trip to Canterbury forming the highlights of her year. She had slept badly and that morning had been dreading the thought of their journey: now, it felt like a delightful adventure and her spirits rose at the prospect of what might be to come.

The carter let them down close to the marketplace in Faversham. It was apparent to Molly that the town was smaller than Margate, but there was a bustle about it: because it was market day, Hannah said. They had passed several small shops – a draper's, a milliner's and a dressmaker's – that Molly was already looking forward to visiting.

Hannah wished to make some purchases in the market and Molly drifted along after her, happy to enjoy the novelty of browsing. It all seemed delightfully new: the fruit and vegetables, meat, fish and cheese were no different from anything available in Margate, but somehow the way everything was displayed made it all appear so much more appealing. Even the banter of the stallholders seemed cheerier. The aroma of the last strawberries of the season, warmed by the sun on the stall, made her mouth water.

Hannah tucked her final purchase, a loaf of bread, into the basket she had brought with her from Margate, with just such a shopping trip in mind.

'There, I think we have everything we need,' she said, turning to Molly. 'We'll go to my mother's now and have something to

eat. We can come out again later for a walk around the town.'
She checked herself. 'I do declare you're looking better already,
Molly. The Faversham air must agree with you.'

Molly smiled. 'I was just thinking that I can't remember
the last time I visited a market without the responsibility of
dinner to create. It's a rare treat.'

'Good,' Hannah said, smiling back. 'Exactly as I hoped it
would be. Now, it's not far to my home.' She turned into a
narrow passageway behind one of the market stalls and led
Molly between the high walls of the buildings on either side
into a little grassy area, which she cut across, to enter an
alleyway on the other side. They followed this, taking a
dog-leg turn at the end to come out in a short lane of terraced
houses, facing a high brick wall.

'Here we are,' Hannah said over her shoulder. 'Fountain
Road.'

Molly's heart sank a little. The feeling of being enclosed
within a town was impossible to escape, and although it was
a sunny day, little brightness penetrated as far as the front
doors. It could hardly have been more unlike the airy, open
aspect of her cottage at Woodchurch Manor.

Hannah was already knocking at the door of a house in
the centre of the terrace. She opened it without waiting for a
response and Molly, suddenly nervous at the prospect of
meeting Hannah's mother, could only step inside after her.

The room was even gloomier than the street outside and it
took Molly's eyes a moment to adjust. A small fire burnt in
the grate and the curtains were partly closed. Hannah was
bending over what appeared to be a makeshift bed, on a
couch against the far wall.

'Ma, I'm here to look after you. And I've brought Molly
with me, as I told you in my letter. How are you today?'

Hannah spoke loudly and clearly and Molly supposed her elderly mother must be deaf. She moved towards the foot of the couch to get a better view and to introduce herself. Even so, she could see very little of Hannah's mother: between the frilled cap on her head and the blankets pulled up beneath her chin, only a small part of her face was visible. Her body barely raised the blankets: there was no evidence of Hannah's full cheeks and rounded figure. But her voice was surprisingly strong.

'I'm better than I was, I thank 'ee. An' happy to see the both of you.' Her eyes, bright and brown, fixed themselves on Molly before focusing on her daughter. 'Although what you will think of me once you see how ill-kept the place is, I can't imagine.'

'Don't fret, Ma,' Hannah said, patting her mother's hand, which rested tiny and frail-boned on the blankets. 'We'll soon have it put to rights. And I'm going to see about feeding you up a bit, starting right now.' She took up the basket and went through to the back of the house, where Molly could see a small kitchen and scullery.

Molly stood awkwardly by the couch. Should she stay and make conversation? Then she saw that the old lady had shut her eyes – either tired out by her brief exchange of words or, perhaps, to prevent any further conversation.

She moved to the kitchen doorway. 'What can I do to help?'

Hannah had laid out her purchases and was already heating a pan on the tiny stove. 'I'm going to cook these sprats for us and make a pan of soup for Ma. Why don't you take your things upstairs? You'll be on the top floor but I dare say you'll need to make up the bed. And perhaps give the room a clean.' She gave Molly an apologetic look. 'Ma's been ill for weeks now, and although I've been sending money for a neighbour to feed her and do some housekeeping, it doesn't look as though she's put herself out. We might need to spend the rest of the day setting the place to rights.'

Molly reassured her – after all, they were there to look after her mother – then took her bag and climbed the narrow wooden staircase hidden behind a door in the corner of the room. At first sight, the bedroom suggested by Hannah was depressingly dirty and smelt fusty, as though it had been shut up for some time. She put her bag on the bed and beat a hasty retreat to the ground floor. Later, restored by a meal of sprats fresh from the market, fried with onions and herbs, bread to mop the plate, and washed down by a glass of small beer, Molly set to work.

She flung open the window, shook out the bedcovers and swept the floor. With the windows washed and the bedding hung out to air, the room began to feel much fresher and Molly descended to the floor below to do the same for Hannah's mother's room. Molly wondered whether the old lady would ever be able to climb the stairs again to use it, but it needed to be made ready for Hannah. As she worked, she noticed that the upstairs rooms weren't so affected by the high wall: judging by the position of the sun, they would both be woken by its rays first thing in the morning.

Downstairs, Hannah had finished making soup and was now baking and preparing a fowl for their dinner. While everything was cooking, she'd swept the sitting room and opened the curtains to make it feel brighter, more homely and less like a sick room. Yet when Molly came down to ask where to find the linen for the beds, she saw Hannah sitting by her mother, looking anxious: perhaps her mother's health was rather worse than she had been led to believe.

CHAPTER TWENTY-SEVEN

Molly's guess that she would be woken by the sun was correct – the following morning, light was streaming through the thin curtains when she opened her eyes. At first, she struggled to place where she was: the bed and window were in entirely the wrong position. Then the mists of sleep departed and she remembered that she was in Faversham, with a day of exploring ahead of her.

Her feeling that Hannah was worried about her mother had been confirmed the previous evening. While the old lady dozed, after managing a little soup for dinner but spurning her daughter's delicious chicken as 'too rich', Hannah had suggested a short stroll to Molly so that she could point out places of interest.

'I fear I will be a great deal taken up with Ma,' she said, as soon as they were outside. 'I won't be able to accompany you as much as I had hoped. But the town is small and I can show you the direction you might take to walk and get some air.'

They retraced their steps to the marketplace, much quieter now that the stalls had packed up. 'Use this to guide you,' Hannah said, indicating the building that took up one edge of the marketplace. Most of the ground floor was open, the building above it, with its domed clock tower, supported by great wooden arches. 'It's the Guildhall and the original covered market – everyone here knows it and if you get lost, just ask to be directed back to it.'

With the Guildhall at their backs, she led Molly away along a street of houses older than Hannah's own. 'The abbey was out along this road,' she said, 'but it's long gone now. And there are breweries set behind these houses.'

Molly sniffed the air. The aroma of brewing was another useful guide to where she was in the town, she thought, as she followed Hannah down a side turning.

'This leads to the Creek and the quays,' she said. 'You'd do well to avoid going there on your own, although they are busy by day. There are always ships coming and going with the tide, bringing in what's needed to make the gunpowder, then taking barrels of the finished stuff away. Some ply a trade with London, while other ships come from far overseas. You'll see sailors from all over on the quays and in the town.'

They loitered for a moment on the bridge, looking out along the Creek as the sun sank behind them. Ships were moored all along the water's edge and the quayside was busy, male voices raised and laughing on the warm air.

'There's no shortage of inns here,' Molly said. She could see three within a few yards of where they stood, on either side of the water.

'They're mainly for the sailors,' Hannah said. 'There's even more in town. It's said you can't go more than a few paces without being able to quench your thirst.'

They walked on, crossing the Creek to walk for a short way before crossing back at the next bridge. Hannah stopped and turned, pointing to where the road ran out of town. 'That's Dark Hill up there – the road runs alongside Stonebridge

Pond, a nice enough walk on a summer's day. Beyond there's Davington and Oare: the gunpowder works are out there. We'll go this way home. I don't want to leave Ma alone for too long.'

She turned and led Molly back into town, along a row of half-timbered cottages that Molly thought must be at least two hundred years old. The upper floors hung over the lower storeys, and the walls and windows sloped where the ground must have moved over time. The cottages were interspersed at regular intervals with inns: they passed at least five on the short walk that took them back to the Guildhall.

'Now, show me that you can remember the way to Fountain Road,' Hannah said, smiling. Molly's sense of direction was good: they were standing outside the house a couple of minutes later, as dusk started to fall.

'Time to light the lamp,' Hannah said, opening the door into a sitting room lit only by the glow of the fire.

Now Molly was in bed, luxuriating for a moment longer in the thought that a whole day lay before her, with no need for her to be anywhere or do anything for anyone. Noises from below alerted her to the fact that Hannah was already up and about, so she threw a shawl around her shoulders and went down the stairs to see whether she could help.

'Bless you, no,' Hannah said. 'Ma had a good night and I plan to stay here so that I can keep her company. It looks like a lovely day – are you happy to make the most of it and take a proper look at the town?'

Molly made a polite offer to remain there with her but Hannah wouldn't hear of it so, within the hour, she stepped through the front door and paused a moment on the step, sniffing the air. The brewery was at work, for the breeze carried an aroma of hops, as well as a tang of brackish water. It wasn't the salty smell of the sea as they were too far inland so it had to be the Creek, Molly decided. She would have liked to turn in that direction first but she had written a note to her sisters over breakfast, to tell them of her safe arrival, and it needed posting. She had every expectation of enjoying her stay, she had written, before wondering whether to ask if they had heard from Charlie or George.

It felt odd not to be writing to her husband, to tell him that she was well and to give him notice of when to expect her home. But he had made it clear that she was no longer welcome there.

Molly closed her eyes briefly at the memory, then set her shoulders and stepped into Fountain Road, ready to follow the directions to the post office Hannah had given to her. She handed over the folded letter, hoping her sisters would be happy enough to pay the postage when they received it. Then she stepped back out onto the street and hesitated, irresolute. Should she make for Stonebridge Pond or walk out of the town along the Creek? Hannah's mention of the gunpowder works the previous evening came back to her, making the decision for her. George had taken a job at a place he referred to as the Works when he was barely sixteen years old, and she remembered him saying he had lived in Davington, which Hannah had said was on the other side of the pond.

Molly turned in the direction of West Street, now busier than it had been when they had walked that way the previous evening. Women of her age, baskets on their arm, set out to make their purchases for the day, greeting one another as they passed. Molly exchanged smiles with one or two and her spirits rose even further as she walked along. The roadway was busy, carts laden with goods, and solo horsemen looked purposeful as they rode through the town.

It wasn't long before Molly reached Stonebridge Pond and she turned off the road onto a path alongside the water. The pond was larger than she had expected from the glimpse she'd caught on the previous evening, and the centre was filled with a series of small islands, covered with trees and shrubs. Water fowl were busy, upending themselves as they searched for food below the surface. Molly stopped to watch, smiling at their antics. Then her attention was caught by a boat being propelled swiftly along. The boatman was standing and driving a long pole into the water to move and guide the craft. He nodded to her as he came past and she turned to see him manoeuvre with skill into a narrow waterway leading off the pond, before he vanished from view.

She turned back to the path, wondering over this unusual sight, and came almost at once upon a man seated on the bank, fishing. On impulse, she said, 'The boat that just came by – can you tell me why the man was standing?'

'The punt, you mean?' The fisherman smiled at Molly. 'I take it you're not from these parts?' He didn't wait for a reply but continued, 'They use them at the gunpowder works. To move the powder and other things around the site.'

'Is the Works around here, then?' Molly looked at the grand building on the other side of the pond as she spoke.

The man followed her gaze. 'Bless you, no. That's the priory over there. There's more than one gunpowder works in the area but the nearest one is that way,' he pointed back to where the road passed over the pond, 'on the other side of the bridge, a little way upstream.'

Molly turned, as if to set off in that direction but the man added, 'You'll find there's no admittance. Not unless you work there. A dangerous business, making gunpowder.'

He turned back to his fishing and Molly thanked him, then moved on. She'd have to ask Hannah more about the gunpowder industry in the area, she decided, regretting not having quizzed George. She wondered whether he had ever passed this way, alongside the pond.

The path had brought her into a lane that she remembered from the previous evening. She caught a whiff of the brackish smell she had noticed in Fountain Road that morning, making her wrinkle her nose. The route was less pleasant by day – the buildings that last night had been shuttered and quiet were now revealed as warehouses and workshops associated with the wharves that lay alongside. The ringing sound of hammering came from a forge, where horses shifted in their traces as they waited to be released from their carts and led in for shoeing.

Molly felt uncomfortable: she was sure that curious eyes were following her. As another whiff of the unpleasant smell reached her, recognition dawned. The tide was out in the Creek, the boats moored alongside listing as they settled into the exposed banks of mud. The reek came from the mud and the pools of dirty water collecting there. Molly's intention to walk alongside the Creek evaporated and she turned her steps back towards town, formulating a new plan as she did so.

CHAPTER TWENTY-EIGHT

Molly indulged herself during the afternoon by visiting the milliners and the drapers she had noticed the previous day. At the back of her mind was the thought that she couldn't make any purchases, for she had no idea what her future held. If she was to be forced to seek work and somewhere to live, she couldn't risk spending any of her money. But it was nice to pretend. She introduced herself in both shops as a visitor to Faversham, there for a few days and keen to see what they could offer that was different from Margate. Seeing her as a potential customer, they were affable and eager to please.

The draper had just received a new delivery of printed cottons and Molly was sorely tempted, especially when he said the dressmaker next door would undoubtedly be able to complete an order for her before she left the town. She promised to go away and think about it.

The milliner a few doors along was more than happy to let Molly try on several different styles of bonnet while she chatted about the weather, the town and its visitors. She didn't seem unduly disappointed when Molly said that she couldn't decide, but might return with a friend in the next day or so. By the time she was making her way back to Fountain Road at the end of the afternoon, she had decided that Faversham was a delightful place.

Her exploration the following day took her out in the direction of the ruined abbey that Hannah had mentioned. She quickly found herself among fields and orchards but never discovered the abbey, for a succession of heavy rain showers sent her back into town and to Fountain Road.

After that, she began to feel a little guilty about spending so much time away from Hannah, while she cared for her ailing mother, so she helped her each day with the household chores that were gradually restoring the little house to the comfortable home it had once been. Now that her daughter was on hand to care for her, Hannah's mother was making great strides towards recovery and had progressed from sitting up in her bed to getting up for short periods. The regular meals of nourishing broths seemed to bear out Hannah's theory that there was little that couldn't be cured by good food.

As the days passed and she fell into a new kind of routine in Faversham, Molly began to think she could live there very happily, if it wasn't for the fact that her children weren't close by. It didn't stop her daydreaming about finding work in the town, and perhaps renting the top bedroom in Fountain Road. The letter that arrived one morning from her sisters put paid to such dreams. She read it at the breakfast table, where Hannah's mother had joined them for the first time. The letter, in Lizzie's hand, began apologetically. It referred to some 'goings-on' since Molly left, which Lizzie and Mary had debated over, but finally decided must be shared with their sister.

Molly stopped reading and frowned, puzzled. What 'goings-on' could Lizzie be referring to? And why did they think to protect her from news of them? She read on.

I'm sorry to have to tell you that Charlie appears to have taken leave of his senses. He attended a ball in the Assembly Rooms on the first Saturday in June, with George and Judith. We had been persuaded to go by the children – Susan and Helena were particularly excited, as you can imagine. Harriet was there, with Margaret, and we couldn't help but notice that Charlie danced several dances with Harriet, including the waltz, and was seen leaving with her. I'm afraid to say that since then they have also been seen out walking together on the coastal path near Westgate, by Sally's in-laws.

I think that you must cut short your stay in Faversham and return before Charlie's reputation is destroyed. The ball has given the matrons of Margate much to discuss and we can't bear to see you wronged in this way.

Your loving sisters,
Lizzie and Mary

Molly read the letter at least twice more before the full meaning sank in. At first, she was distracted by Lizzie's listing of the family members at the ball, and Margaret, too, whom she'd thought back in London. As for the news about Charlie, it was so far removed from everything she knew about her husband that she didn't know what to make of it. Charlie avoided social occasions whenever possible and he didn't dance. Could Lizzie have made a mistake? But rereading the letter confirmed that Charlie was the subject, and her sisters were linking his name with Harriet's.

Molly let the letter fall from her hands to the table. She felt as though she must have been away from home for a year, so much had changed in her absence. It was bewildering.

She looked up to see Hannah watching her.

'What is it Molly? You've turned quite pale. Not bad news, I hope?'

Molly pushed the letter across the table to Hannah. 'Read it. It's from my sisters. I confess, I'm struggling to understand it.'

Hannah was embarrassed. 'Molly, I don't read very well. I'm slow – would you read it to me?'

'Of course.' It was Molly's turn to feel shamed, but the flush on her cheeks only increased as she read the letter aloud. This time, it was caused by rage as Lizzie's words hit home. Harriet! Molly's half-sister, whom she'd welcomed into her home. And now it seemed as though she thought to take advantage of Molly's troubles, and her absence, to make a fool of Charlie.

'Oh, Molly, this is my fault.'

Molly saw that tears were rolling down Hannah's cheeks. 'Of course it isn't.' She was quick to reassure her. 'I wanted to come and stay here with you. It's not your fault that I'm away from home.'

'I spoke to Harriet after your aunt's party, when everyone had left.' Hannah looked distraught. 'I told her why I'd thought George was Nicholas's son. And she said that she knew all of you and she would try to smooth things over between you, but she's used the rift between you all as her chance to get closer to Charlie.'

'But why?' Molly couldn't follow Hannah's reasoning. 'Charlie must be at least fifteen years older than Harriet.' Even as the words came out of her mouth she couldn't believe what she was saying.

'I don't know,' Hannah said. 'She lost her father at a young age – could that have anything to do with it? I suppose Charlie seems strong and wise. Perhaps Harriet is like her mother, Ann – an opportunist.'

Molly barely heard her last words. 'Wise! I'd hardly call Charlie wise if he's been behaving like this.'

She stood up from the table in agitation. 'I'll have to go back, Hannah. I must leave at once. I'm sorry.'

Molly's hands shook as she packed her bag, her mind in turmoil. Her thoughts ranged wildly. How would she get home? What would Charlie say to her when she got back? What would she say to him? She had fancied her marriage all but over. Now, faced with such a reality, she was ready to fight for it.

She descended the stairs to find Hannah waiting anxiously.

'I've put some food together for your journey,' she said, thrusting a paper package into Molly's hand. 'You must go and enquire about the stage coach to Canterbury. There's one about noon, I think. But you may do better to ask around the inns on the edge of town. Perhaps there will be a wagon or cart setting out in your direction.'

Hannah was putting a brave face on it, but Molly knew she would be lucky to find a means to get to Woodchurch Manor before the day was over. She bent and kissed Hannah's mother, who was still sitting, bemused, at the breakfast table, and embraced Hannah. Then she stepped out into Fountain Road, her mood at odds with the beautiful sunshine, and her heart full of anxiety.

PART THREE

HARRIET

Chapter Twenty-Nine

I hadn't expected matters to move on so swiftly after I'd encountered Charlie and George outside the White Hart. I'd taken up my duties at the hospital as usual on the Monday morning, my head still full of the previous day's events. Aunt Jane's son the father of Molly's son – and neither Charlie nor George knowing it! It was a delicious scandal. And I was in the thick of it. I was hard put to concentrate throughout the day. My thoughts kept returning to Charlie and George's expressions when I'd given them the news. How fortunate that Hannah's tongue had been loosened by her distress. Now I just needed to find a way to make this work to my advantage.

It was to take less time than I had imagined. In the middle of the week, I was instructed by Mrs Murray, the overseer, to take one of the newly arrived patients into the garden.

'I know you like spending time out there,' she said, giving me a look as she said it that made me wonder whether she knew more about my motives than I cared to reveal.

I didn't mind, though. I liked this particular patient – he was more cheerful than the others and respectful towards those who tended him. He was asking me questions about how I came to be working at the hospital as I wheeled him around the garden, and I was spinning him an elaborate tale of being abandoned by my mother and forced to make my own way in the world. It wasn't far from the truth, after all, and it might earn me a good tip when he left.

I could scarcely believe it when I saw a familiar figure walking along the path towards me.

'Charlie!' I exclaimed, when he was almost upon us. 'It's a while since we've seen you in the garden.' I hoped my cheeks weren't as pink as they felt.

'I was rather hoping to find you here,' Charlie said, completely ignoring my patient, who was now looking between us with a puzzled frown. 'I need to have a word.'

'I'm afraid that isn't possible at the moment,' I said, hoping that my voice was under control even though my heart beat wildly. I indicated my patient and Charlie gave him a curt nod as if he'd just noticed him.

'I'll wait out here for you, then,' he said, turning on his heel and walking away before I'd had a chance to reply.

'He's the husband of my half-sister,' I said, by way of explanation to my charge.

The man gave me a knowing look. 'Really? I could tell you were – acquainted.'

'We are,' I said firmly. 'There's a bit of trouble in the family at the moment. I hope you will excuse his lack of manners.' I wheeled the patient away, taking care to ensure he felt that he had spent a good amount of time in the garden. I didn't want to run the risk of him making a complaint to Mrs Murray.

Once he was safely back on the seaward terrace, I announced to anyone who cared to listen that I would be making an inventory of the linen cupboard if I was needed. I spoke with authority, certain no one would think to challenge me. I knew Mrs Murray was in the habit of shutting

150

herself into her office at about this time every day to do paperwork (or so she said). In reality, she would be dozing in her chair, the door firmly locked. I thought I had a clear twenty minutes to find Charlie and discover what he wanted from me.

I was wary of being seen out in the garden by anyone watching from the hospital windows so I stayed in the shadows as much as possible. To my relief, I found Charlie almost at once. He was sitting in the shade outside the gardener's hut, head bent as he stared at the ground.

He looked up at my approach and I saw the frown etched on his forehead.

'Charlie,' I said, at a bit of a loss now we were together. I didn't know why he had come and I wasn't sure how to start the conversation. I sat beside him, making sure I was hidden from the house. I also made sure that I brushed against him as I sat down, but he was oblivious.

'How did you know?' There was no preamble and I thought it was pointless playing games.

'Hannah told me.' If he could be abrupt so could I.

'Hannah? So she's known for years.' He spoke flatly and his expression was so grim I took pity on him.

'No, Charlie. She only realised when she saw George at Aunt Jane's house. She had no idea until then. She saw a resemblance to ...' I hesitated, unsure whether to say 'Nicholas' or 'his father'.

'Then everyone must have seen it. The resemblance.'

'I don't think so. It seems Hannah knew before Molly ran away, but she believed she'd lost the baby. Seeing George unexpectedly, it all came back to her.'

I was disappointed that this was all he wanted of me. 'You haven't asked Molly about it?' I asked.

'She's not at home.' He stood up suddenly. I stayed seated for a moment or two longer, looking up at him. Then I rose.

'I'm sorry to hear that, Charlie. I hope you haven't quarrelled?' I reached out to clasp his hands in mine. 'It's of no consequence, you know. It was so long ago. I'm sure Molly didn't deliberately set out to deceive.' I pressed his hands then released them, but kept my gaze fixed on his face.

'I hope to see you – all of you – very soon. And in happier circumstances. But I must return to work now.' I walked briskly away, pausing to look back before I left the garden. He was still standing, looking after me, an odd expression on his face. Bemused, I thought, or perhaps there was dawning recognition. I smiled as I returned to work. I felt the encounter had gone well.

That week rapidly turned into one of the more interesting ones in my life. The day after Charlie's appearance in the hospital garden there was another unexpected arrival; unexpected by me, at any rate. I was doing my usual morning rounds of the patients, checking to see how they had fared overnight and setting their rooms to rights, when I stood up from making a bed to find myself face to face with Margaret. I was unable to speak, such was my surprise.

'Hello, Harriet,' she said. She greeted me as though she had never been away. I was reminded all at once that I had shared the details of her existence with all those present at Aunt Jane's house without her permission.

'Margaret,' I managed finally. 'But I thought you'd been sent away? I didn't expect to see you again.'

'Sent away?' Margaret frowned. 'Whatever gave you that idea? No – at least, I was sent to London to care for a patient in the last stages of her illness. Dr Harwood thought my experience with my father made me best suited of anyone here. Apart from you, of course, but Mrs Murray had you shut away.'

She spoke cheerfully and I had to remind myself that she knew nothing of what had gone on in her absence.

'Margaret, I have news for you.' I spoke low, so that the patients couldn't hear, and urgently. Should I tell her now? It was best to do so, I thought. She might get to hear of it in a way that showed me in a bad light.

I drew her slightly apart and whispered in her ear, 'I have found your family.' I expected a shocked reaction but she continued to gaze straight ahead. 'And . . .' I hesitated '. . . they are my family, too. We're related – half related.' I frowned as I tried to work out our precise relationship.

There was no time to give Margaret any further details – we were under the beady eye of Mrs Murray, who had arrived to give the orders for the day. Therein lay another surprise: apart from the usual instructions about patient care, which followed a sentence of welcome to Margaret on her return, the overseer had an announcement to make.

'As I am sure you all know, there is to be a ball at the Assembly Rooms a week on Saturday, in honour of the Royal Sea Bathing Hospital.'

We did know. It had been much discussed as it was to be a grand affair, with guests invited down from London. They were patrons of the charity and no doubt the intention was to raise yet more money from them.

Mrs Murray went on, 'It has been decided that those staff who wish to attend, and can be released from their duties, will be able to do so.'

A murmur ran around the room and I glanced at Margaret. It struck me at once that this would be a good moment for her to meet her half-siblings and cousins.

Mrs Murray was still speaking. 'The ball is to take place in both of the Assembly Rooms. The main room will be reserved for invited guests, with a limited number of tickets available in the other room for townspeople and those linked to the hospital. If you would like to attend, let me know by the end of the day.'

'We're going,' I hissed at Margaret, as we began to wheel those patients due their immersions away from the seaward terrace. I didn't have a gown suitable for a ball and I doubted that she did. But it was clear that we weren't expected to join the gentry and I imagined our best frocks would do among the townsfolk. I'd never been to a ball before, but I thought it was the perfect way for Margaret to meet her relatives.

I went about the rest of my work that morning in a fever of impatience. I wished the ball was to take place that weekend, until it dawned on me that I would need more than two days to ensure that I could get the family members together. Helena, Susan and Lewis – Lizzie and Mary's children – should all be there, I decided. And surely George could be prevailed upon too – wouldn't his curiosity about Margaret get the better of him? And the mysterious Constance, of course.

It wasn't until the midday meal that I had another chance to speak to Margaret. I'd had time to get used to the idea that our family lives were intertwined, but it would be a shock for her. In the end, I was the one to be surprised, yet again. It seemed that Uncle William hadn't wasted a minute in tracking her down after I'd shared the news of her existence. By the Tuesday following Aunt Jane's gathering, he'd been in London seeking her out at the address he'd obtained from the hospital. And by Wednesday, when I'd been talking to Charlie in the gardens, Margaret was already back in Margate and discovering more about her family background.

By my reckoning, I could still be the first to introduce her to George. I was keen that no one should overlook my role in uniting the family. Things hadn't gone so well for Molly, of course. Margaret told me that Molly had been at her sisters' and might have gone home now, or perhaps she had gone away with Hannah. Either way, she wasn't in her husband's favour and that suited me very well.

CHAPTER THIRTY

I was quick to inform Mrs Murray that Margaret and I would like to attend the ball. I was careful to tell her that my family, with whom I had become so recently reacquainted, would be there. She'd told me previously that such a situation would have made her look favourably on my request, although I didn't remind her of this. Margaret didn't know what I had done, either. I'd made up my mind that we were going and didn't think I needed to consult her.

I had two things to focus on in the days that remained before the ball: our gowns, and making sure the family attended. With only one half-day free before the Saturday of the ball I was worried about how I could manage both.

I needn't have worried about the family. Balls of this nature were rare enough occurrences at the Assembly Rooms and the townsfolk, young and old, were keen to attend: not only for the entertainment but also in hope of catching a glimpse of the London gentry in all their finery. It was while I was taking advantage of my half-day to purchase evening gloves and a ribbon for my dress that my dilemma over inviting the family was solved. I came across Mary in the high street as I embarked on my errand.

'A beautiful day, Harriet, with a delightful breeze,' she greeted me. 'What brings you into town?'

'It's my half-day, and I must make some purchases – gloves and ribbons – for the ball,' I said.

She laughed. 'You and every other woman in Margate. You'll find Mrs Hughes has sold out. But I believe Helena said that the shop at the top of the high street still has stock.'

I thanked her for the information and asked whether she would be attending.

'Of course,' she said, 'along with most of the town. George and Judith are coming, too: Judith said she wouldn't miss it for the world, baby or not. The nursery maid at Woodchurch Manor has agreed to take care of Joseph. It's a long time since we've had a ball quite as splendid as this. We could almost be in London, don't you think?'

Mary was clearly excited at the prospect and I was happy for she had given me the information I needed, that George would be there. We parted, after a few more pleasantries, and I hurried to the shop she had recommended, fearing that the ladies of Margate might already have bought every frippery available. I was lucky enough to arrive just as a new delivery, 'direct from London', as I was proudly informed, was being unpacked.

Within the half-hour I had the ribbons and gloves I desired, investing in a similar set for Margaret. She had been taken aback when she discovered that I was serious about attending the ball, protesting that she had never been to one and would have no idea what was expected of her. I reassured her, telling her that the floor would be so thronged with people that she had no need to think of dancing and could simply watch from the side. And, of course, she could meet her family.

By the time the day of the ball arrived, I could barely contain my excitement. I had hardly slept the night before, torn between excitement at the spectacle ahead of us, and the thrill at the thought of introducing Margaret.

We both had to work on the actual day, although Mrs Murray allowed us to finish earlier so that we could prepare ourselves. I had been surprised to find that none of the other staff at the hospital would attend. Family commitments or the expense were the excuses. The ball began at eight and we had the luxury of two hours to get ready. I intended to curl and dress my hair: if I couldn't afford to spend money on a new gown that would probably never be worn again, I could at least make an effort with my hair.

To my astonishment, Margaret not only had a set of curling irons, but proved adept at using them. I'd used curling papers the night before but my duties in the day had cost me what little curl they produced. The stiff breeze on the shore when I'd taken my patients for their immersion had whipped my hair free of its cap. Margaret heated her irons in the kitchen range and once I had twisted my hair into a chignon she produced some fetching ringlets to frame my face.

'I didn't think you'd have need of such things,' I said, when she had finished, for Margaret's hair was naturally curly.

'You can use them to straighten hair, as well as curl it,' she said. I thought I detected a hint of reproof in her voice and hoped I hadn't offended her. I'd been at pains to suggest she should bring her gown to work with her, so that she could change in my room and we could leave together. I wanted to promote our kinship, even though of all her relatives I suppose I was the least close.

I was wearing the striped muslin gown I had worn to the christening, with the blue ribbon I'd bought tied at the high waistline. There was enough left over to wrap around my brow. Margaret was wearing a lavender-coloured gown; she had told me her plan in advance and the primrose ribbon I had bought for her waist toned beautifully.

I pulled on my gloves – elbow length as the shopkeeper had advised would be expected for an evening ball, and handed a pair to Margaret. She was puzzled at first, but once I explained what was expected on such an occasion, she thanked me. She looked very well: she carried herself with dignity and her stature and colouring would guarantee attention that evening, I thought. I surveyed myself in the glass and felt quite satisfied, too.

We descended the stairs to find Mrs Murray waiting for us. 'Your tickets,' she said, handing us two rectangles of card. 'Would you be so good as to let the patients see you before you leave? They are as excited as if they are invited, too.'

We did as we were asked; it was gratifying to have them exclaim over us. They were used to seeing us in our drab work outfits so they were bound to find us quite changed, I thought. But would we be suitably dressed for a ball? I wasn't so sure.

As it turned out, we were no worse in appearance than the majority of the Margate folk, and a lot better dressed than most. Some of the ladies, it is true, wore gowns that were clearly more suited to a ball than our day dresses. Their frills and decorations plainly showed that these were worn for dancing and not to church on a Sunday. The rest of us had contented ourselves with doing our best with what we had. It was quickly clear to me that we were attracting a good deal of attention, Margaret's height and striking appearance being unusual in these parts. Neither of us was well known about the place and I was sure a good deal of speculation was taking place behind open fans, revealed by the way that the owners' eyes followed our every move.

My first action, on gaining admission to the first-floor Assembly Rooms, was to take up a position as close as possible to the double doors leading to the larger room. Here, under a richly gilded ceiling, the ball had already begun, the dancers reflected in the enormous mirrors adorning the walls. A thick red rope now barred our entrance to the space and kept us away from the distinguished guests.

I noticed that the few brave couples who had taken to the floor were under the intense scrutiny of their fashionable fellow guests. Many ladies, particularly the older ones, were already seated on the chairs set around the room. I thought I caught a glimpse of Aunt Jane and Uncle William on the far side as the dancers passed in front of them.

It was the ladies' attire that interested me – I feasted my eyes on the silks before a feeling of disappointment overtook me. The dresses were, on the whole, very similar: high-waisted, mostly in pale pastel shades or cream. It was the little details that made one stand out from another – a fabric rose at the bosom or a row of them around a tiered flounce near the hem. Sleeves were short, long sleeves being a preserve of the older ladies, and again it was the detail that counted: tiny silk buttons on a narrow cuff, a satin bow, lace sleeves on a silk dress. I had expected bright patterns on Indian silk, not such a subdued palette. Colour was mostly confined to the fabric slippers peeping from beneath the gowns, displayed during the rise and fall of the steps.

I turned to view the room I was in. We were, on the whole, more colourfully attired, which I supposed marked us out as less fashionable. I was glad of my pale striped muslin. It would have been out of place in the main room but here I felt I could hold up my head with the best of them.

Margaret was becoming restive at my side. 'It's warm already,' she said. 'Shall we find something to drink? I feel as though all eyes are on me, standing here.'

I'd seen enough of the private room for now and I was happy enough to join her to await our turn to be served with punch. Glass at last in hand, I turned my attention to seeking out any of our family members. I failed to realise that Margaret was no longer at my side until I spotted her in conversation with Lizzie while Helena and Susan, Lizzie's daughters, looked on. I was angry with myself: I had planned to be responsible for chaperoning Margaret around the ball and making introductions. She was my discovery and I wanted everyone to remember that. But, then, I knew she had already met Lizzie previously. I reassured myself that it was more important, after all, to be the one to introduce her to George.

CHAPTER THIRTY-ONE

I cast my eyes around the room once more and caught sight of George and Judith as they paused at the entrance. As they stepped forward to join the throng, another figure appeared behind them and I failed to stifle a gasp. It was Charlie. It had never occurred to me that he would come to the ball. From my small acquaintance with him I'd assumed his preoccupations were all with his garden and not with the small-talk and social niceties an occasion such as this demanded. I peered to see beyond him but there was no sign of Molly.

I had to take firm control of myself – my priority was to manage a meeting between George and Margaret and I needed to act now or the moment would be lost. I moved swiftly across the floor to where Margaret and Lizzie still conversed, now joined by Mary and her son, Lewis. I greeted them hastily before seizing Margaret's elbow.

'Please excuse us. There's someone I'd like Margaret to meet.' Before she could object, I was steering her towards George, Judith and Charlie. They were gazing around the room as though unsure what to do next.

'George – and Judith. How delightful. And Charlie, too. I'm so pleased to see you all. And to have the chance to introduce you to your relative, Margaret.'

My words were superfluous – their eyes had been fixed on Margaret since we were several paces from them. No one spoke and I had a sudden flash of fear that I had acted foolishly. Was it too much of a shock to make such an important introduction in such a public place? Margaret, though, rose to the occasion.

'I am delighted to meet you, George, although I fear my existence must have come as a great surprise to your family. As yours is to me, of course,' she added gravely. 'My father never gave any indication of what he had left behind and I'm sorry that you had to find out about me as you did.' Here she glanced in my direction and I ducked my head in acknowledgement of guilt, while inwardly seething. If it hadn't been for me, she might never have found her family – my family.

She stopped talking and still there was silence, until Judith stepped in.

'I am very pleased to meet you, Margaret,' she said, giving her a warm smile. 'You will have to excuse these two.' She indicated George and Charlie. 'I do believe Charlie – Mr Dawson – is angry with us for dragging him here this evening. As for George, well, I hope you will pay us a visit at home before too long so we can become better acquainted.'

She put her arm through Margaret's and, with a swift glance at her husband, drew her away. I watched them go, their heads close as they conversed and walked. I was left alone with Charlie and George.

I turned to Charlie. 'Do I take it you don't care for the Assembly Rooms?'

He grunted. 'Too many people. Too much noise. Too damned hot.' He tugged at his neck tie, easing it away from his collar. He was right about the heat – all the windows

163

were open but unless you stood beneath them there was little benefit.

George smiled wryly. 'We are here to please Judith. Neither of us would have chosen to come otherwise.' He turned to Charlie. 'If you can get by for a couple of hours, we can consider we've done our duty and make our escape.' He nodded to me and moved away and I was pleased to see he had joined Judith and Margaret. I hoped his wife would help ease any awkwardness between them.

Charlie and I stood side by side in silence, observing the crowd. Musicians had been employed to mirror the music being played in the room next door, to enable dancers to take to the floor in this one. Without them, the music from the main room would have been muffled by the press of bodies and the chatter of the people, but I couldn't honestly say that they added anything to the proceedings. They were fewer in number – just a couple of fiddles and a pianoforte, and they invariably finished what they were playing just before, or just after, the other musicians. This led to a strange echo effect of music and applause between the rooms. But we had to make the best of what we had and, after watching the dancers for a while, tapping my feet, then tapping my now-empty glass with my fingers, I turned to Charlie.

'You're supposed to ask me to dance, you know.'

The look he gave me in return was filled with horror. 'I can't dance,' he said bluntly. 'Surely there is someone here who will ask you.' His eyes roved around the room and I feared he was about to prevail upon an acquaintance.

'No matter,' I said hastily. 'But the heat is making me thirsty. Perhaps you could fetch me something to drink.'

He looked relieved and set off to fulfil his errand, while I turned my gaze on the crowd once more. I had lost sight of all the family members and I was surrounded by strangers, so I was pleased by Charlie's swift return, bearing two drinks. We stood in silence for a little while longer and I found myself drinking the punch rather fast, in order to set myself at ease.

'Have you never danced at all?' I asked, at length.

'Never.' Charlie was emphatic.

I was about to ask whether Molly danced, then thought better of it, even though I was curious about her absence.

'I could teach you a few steps,' I offered. I had taught myself to dance from pamphlets, without ever believing I would have occasion to do so. I was eager to try, as I watched the couples move through the cotillion, the men quite scarlet from the heat in the room, intensifying now as the candles had been lit. Wearing a waistcoat, cravat and coat on a warm summer evening in such a confined space must be intolerable, I thought.

I expected another outright refusal from Charlie but he hesitated, so I pressed on.

'I imagine half the men here haven't danced before.' It was true that more than one wrong turn had been made in front of us, others correcting the mistake with good-natured laughter and helping hands.

The music drew to a stuttering close and most of the dancers cleared the floor, in search of air or refreshment. Within five minutes, though, the music struck up again, a reel this time. There was no answering echo from the other room and I guessed they were being served supper.

'This one will be easier than the last,' I promised. I looked up at him, hoping he would be moved by my pleading eyes.

He squared his shoulders and then, to my surprise, made me a small bow and took my hand. I thought he looked anxious as we joined the couples already on the dance floor, but it was too late to back out. We took our places at the end of the set so I was able to hiss instructions to him before it was our turn to lead the dance. It was a good-humoured affair and Charlie managed well, making rueful apologies by gesture whenever he mis-stepped. I thought he would retire as soon as the music was over but George and Judith came to join us and I noticed Margaret further down the line on the arm of a stranger.

The next hour passed in the blink of an eye, or so it seemed. I partnered George for one of the dances, while Judith partnered Charlie. We were so exhausted from laughing that we had to sit out the following dance. Charlie fetched me another drink and I was soon on my feet again, suggesting we should return to the floor. I forgot to pay heed to the gentry in the other room and even to Margaret's whereabouts, so caught up was I with delight in dancing – and with Charlie. We even danced a waltz, which must have been at the request of the London guests, for I'm sure it had never been danced in Margate before. It was quite something to spend a whole dance clasped in the arms of the same man, with none of the usual exchange of partners.

When George and Judith announced it was time for them to leave, I realised the crowd was thinning out. It seemed natural to make my way down the stairs at Charlie's side and it wasn't until I was out in the welcome coolness of the night air that I remembered Margaret. We had arrived together and I wanted to make sure she was all right, even though Charlie offered to drop me at the hospital.

'We're travelling in one of the carriages from Woodchurch Manor,' he said. 'It wouldn't be out of our way.'

I longed to say yes, for now that I'd stopped dancing I realised how tired I was, and how sore my feet. Still, I was about to turn back to seek out Margaret when she arrived beside me, along with Susan, Helena, Lewis and another young man. I could see Lizzie and Mary in the background, yawning. As soon as it was clear to me that she was quite safe, I climbed into the carriage that had drawn up beside us and sank gratefully into the seat beside Charlie.

It was a journey of but ten minutes to the hospital, made longer than usual by the crush of people leaving the Assembly Rooms at the same time. I savoured every minute of it: the warmth of Charlie's body beside me, our closeness. We were thrown together when the carriage rounded a bend in the road and I may have feigned sleep a short while after, allowing my head to droop onto his shoulder. I was only too conscious of the tightness of muscle in his arm as he shifted slightly to support my weight.

When I stepped down from the carriage outside the hospital, and offered my grateful thanks to Charlie, I was intoxicated by more than the wine.

Chapter Thirty-Two

I was as convinced as I could be that Charlie would have had a restless night after the ball. I was sure I would be on his mind and hugged the thought to myself as I worked on the Sunday. Several of the patients asked about the evening. Had we seen anyone of consequence from London? Who had asked us to dance? Did we each have a beau now?

I was quick to say that I had spent the evening with family but felt sure Margaret had made a conquest. She shot me an odd look, which I took to be an admonishment: I suppose she wished to keep her affairs private. In any case, the patients didn't press her on it. Instead, one of the older ladies said to me, 'You should have made use of the opportunity. You're not getting any younger, you know.' Those within earshot laughed and she added, 'Chances will be few and far between to find yourself a husband.'

I smiled sweetly at her and made a face behind her back as I pushed her out onto the seaward terrace after breakfast. I paid little heed to her words in any case: I was still bathed in the afterglow from the evening and not a little footsore and weary from the dancing and unaccustomed late night. I longed to discuss it with Margaret and in particular to discover whose company she had kept for most of the evening.

My need to discuss the ball with Margaret grew almost

unbearable but Mrs Murray seemed determined to keep us apart. After enquiring whether we had had a pleasant evening and asking us for any news of 'the important guests at the main ball', as she put it, she lost interest when we were unable to give her few details beyond my initial impressions of the ladies and their gowns. I began to think she took a perverse pleasure in giving us work that took us to different parts of the hospital, and the whole day passed without an opportunity to question Margaret.

The following day a startling event quite drove the wish from my mind. Passing along the upper landing I glanced out into the garden. The weather had turned gloomy and inclined to rain. I noticed a movement in front of the glasshouse: there stood Charlie, looking up at the hospital building. Had he seen me at the window? I pulled back into the corridor, heart pounding. I was sure the gardener wasn't due to be there that day but perhaps I was mistaken. Was he looking for me? I peeped out of the window and saw that Charlie had now moved away and was standing by the gate at the end of the garden, one hand on the latch. I was puzzled – he stood there motionless for quite some time, turned back once more towards the hospital, then visibly shook himself and left in a hurry, banging the gate behind him.

I stood at the window for a minute or two longer, wondering whether he would return, then heard Mrs Murray calling for me. I hurried down the stairs, but Charlie's mysterious action occupied my thoughts for the rest of the day. Was it possible he had been looking for me? Had his courage failed him? I liked the idea that I was in his thoughts and I worried away at the notion that I must engineer a meeting between us again, before his wish to see me faded.

That same day I was at last able to speak to Margaret about the ball. We took our break for the midday meal together and I wasted no time in asking her how she had enjoyed herself. I barely paid heed to her answer for I was more interested in what she would say to my next question.

'And who was the young man who had the pleasure of your company for most of the evening?' I asked.

'Henry Sayer. He's a friend of Lewis, Mary's son.' Margaret was concentrating on finishing her meal, cleaning her plate with a piece of bread, and didn't seem put out by my questions.

'And will you see him again?' I asked.

'We've made an arrangement for this coming Sunday, my half-day,' she replied.

'What does he do?' I asked.

'He works at the bakery, with Lewis,' Margaret said.

I frowned. 'In the bakery? Margaret, I feel sure you could do better for yourself. Why, you've travelled halfway across the world to get here, you have a skill and yet you contemplate wasting yourself on a boy who works in the bakery?'

I'd gone too far. Margaret's expression changed, and when she spoke, it was in chilly tones. 'You seem to be making a lot of assumptions. First of all, I'll be meeting Henry on Sunday for only the second time. That doesn't mean I'm about to make a lifelong commitment to him. And what do you know of his prospects or ambitions? Have you ever spoken to him? As for my life, have you ever considered the ease or otherwise of living in Margate for the likes of me?'

I was quite taken aback by her cold fury. She hesitated, then continued, 'And even if your wild imaginings proved correct, far better to set my sights on someone attainable, than on another woman's husband.'

She stood up abruptly, almost knocking over her chair in her haste to be gone from me. My cheeks flamed at her words. She meant to hurt me and she had, I suppose. Although I had been oblivious to it at the ball, Charlie's behaviour must have been noticed by other members of the family: Molly's sisters, Lizzie and Mary. My half-sisters. It would surely only be a matter of time before word reached Molly, wherever she was.

'I'm not answerable for the consequences of Molly lying to her husband and son.' My parting shot was delayed and I'm not sure whether Margaret was still within hearing.

I was determined not to let her words ruffle me, but I was only partially successful. My duties kept me busy for the rest of that day but, alone in my room that evening, I contemplated what lay ahead. I was sure that I had captured Charlie's interest and now I needed to capitalise on this, while he and Molly were, I suspected, estranged. I could see a dreary future working at the Royal Sea Bathing Hospital stretching before me unless I acted now. And I shouldn't lose sight of my original intentions: making the Goodchild family see that, while they might have spurned me as a child and abandoned me to my fate, I was nevertheless cleverer than they were. I had brought them Margaret, to upset Aunt Jane and Uncle William's comfortable existence, and now I thought I could see a way to wreak revenge on Molly and her family.

Chapter Thirty-Three

Charlie appeared in the garden again before the week was out. I noticed him, deep in conversation with the gardener, as I passed along the landing with an armful of linen. I had spent rather more time than I should looking out over that garden in the expectation of seeing him, yet his presence, although half expected, caused my heart to lurch. I immediately wished to find a way to join him, but it was impossible. I had been given the task of changing the bed linen and, in any case, without the excuse of a patient to wheel around the borders I had no place out there. I found myself pressed up against the window, the pile of linen clutched to my breast with one hand, the palm of the other pressed against the pane.

He looked up, perhaps attracted by the movement, and for a moment it seemed as though our gazes locked, even though we were surely too far apart. He stood motionless and I felt a rush of blood through my veins and a fire in my cheeks. Then he raised his hand, as though in greeting, and turned back to his work with the gardener. I stood on for a moment or so longer and noticed him glance up again before, resolute, I walked away. Let him long for another glimpse. I had begun to feel anxious that time would drift by while I was trapped in my hospital duties, Charlie in his garden, and neither of us would find the opportunity to meet again to follow up on the rapport we had established at the ball. Seeing him twice in the hospital garden in one week gave me hope. Was I wrong in thinking that Charlie was seeking me out? I didn't have long to wait to find out.

That Sunday, just over a week after the ball, I was going about my duties with bad grace, envious of Margaret as she left for her half-day and her meeting with Henry Sayer. She practically skipped from the building – I saw her from the seaward terrace as she left. The shore path was busy with couples and families taking a Sunday stroll after church and I gave them no more than a cursory glance, until my eye was caught by a familiar, solitary figure, gazing out to sea. Surely it was Charlie, but what was he doing here today? He had no reason to visit the garden so I had to assume that something else had drawn him to Westbrook on the day that most people spent in the company of their families.

As I watched, he turned back towards the building and began to walk around the wall, vanishing from sight. I tried to attend to my patients and put the sighting out of my mind, but barely ten minutes later the little girl employed to help in the kitchens sidled up to me. She looked anxious at being in a part of the building unfamiliar to her, and gabbled out her message.

'There's a man as wants to see you in the garden. He says he's known to you an' he'll wait there for you.'

She scuttled away before I could ask her anything, although in truth there was no need. It could only be Charlie looking for me. But how long would he wait? I did my best to appear as though her message was a trivial thing, of no consequence to me. I carried on tucking the blankets around the patients and settling them in sheltered positions, as the cloudy skies held the threat of rain.

It was a good half-hour before I was able to make my escape from the terrace. I slipped down the staircase and out into the garden before caution got the better of me. As I had before, I skirted the edge of the garden, staying close to the shrubbery and hoping my drab clothing would hide me if anyone chanced to look out. Charlie saw me and came forward to meet me by the gardener's hut. I was about to open the conversation with some nonsensical comment about the weather when he blurted out, 'Harriet, I haven't been able to stop thinking about you.'

I gasped: this was just as I had hoped. Then I collected myself. 'Why, Charlie, whatever do you mean?'

He stepped back. 'I beg your pardon. You must excuse me – I spoke out of turn.'

I was not about to let the moment slip away so I held his gaze before dropping my eyes to the ground and saying, 'I have been much troubled, too.'

'You have?' He was eager and hopeful again.

'Yes, you have been much on my mind.' It was true, of course, but perhaps not in the way he imagined. There was no denying my attraction to Charlie, but my reasons for seeking to bind him to me were complicated. At this point, making mischief in his marriage to show Molly and her family how wrong they were to abandon me was part of it, as well as a wish for an adventure, perhaps.

I glanced over my shoulder. 'Charlie, this is wrong. You are a married man. And I will be in the most terrible trouble if I'm spotted out here with you.'

To my surprise, he laughed, but his expression was bitter. 'I've lost all faith in Molly. My marriage might as well be over.' Then he looked stricken. 'I don't wish to get you into trouble.' He surveyed the hospital windows before he raised my hand to his lips, almost crushing my fingers with his fierce pressure, and kissed it.

'I will wait for you to finish work, Harriet. We must talk. You will find me on the shore.'

He strode away, towards the back gate of the garden, and I turned to the house. My legs were trembling and I could feel the impression of his lips on my hand as though he had burnt me with a brand. I slipped back inside, unnoticed, and resumed my duties, although I couldn't say how I got through the hours until the end of the day.

Released at last, I hurried upstairs and changed out of my work clothes. A quick glance out of the window showed that the clouds had cleared and the evening held the promise of some late sunshine. I dressed in my blue gown as quickly as possible, although now my fingers shook as I tried to do up the buttons. Then I seized a shawl, to guard against sea breezes, and snatched up my bonnet, tying the ribbons as I hurried down the stairs.

Would Charlie still be there? Would I be able to find him? What did he want to say to me? My mind whirled with possibilities as I hurried to the shore. I'd made my token protest about his marriage. Charlie's response had been quite clear. Now I cared only for myself and for my future.

Chapter Thirty-Four

Ineedn't have worried about finding Charlie: he was obviously looking out for me, and as I began to walk along the path he rose from a bench and came to meet me. I felt awkward and exposed out in the open, away from the privacy of the garden, but as soon as Charlie arrived in front of me, I could see he had eyes only for me.

'Thank you for joining me, Harriet,' he began, reaching for my hand. 'There's much I want to say.'

I was alarmed and drew back. 'Charlie, it's Sunday and this is a public place. Let's walk on a little.'

I was keen to keep up appearances as best I could. Yet I knew it wouldn't do to be seen out walking together, even though we were, in a way, related. I was unsure whether it would be better to follow the path towards Margate, where a few couples were taking the air, or in the other direction, which would be quieter but give rise to speculation if we were seen by anyone who knew Charlie.

He had already decided, though. He steered me onto the rougher path towards Westgate, where few chose to walk. I wasn't sure I liked the decision. Charlie seemed different, somehow. More impulsive and wilder than the man I thought I knew. I resolved to be on my guard. I didn't doubt, though, that by the end of our walk we would have reached a better understanding.

In an effort to lighten the mood I asked him teasingly whether he had enjoyed his evening at the ball. 'Judith said you were reluctant to come. And you told me that you didn't dance.' I raised an eyebrow. 'Yet anyone would have thought you spent every Friday evening at the Assembly Rooms, dancing the night away.'

'I swear I told you the truth.' Charlie's expression was earnest. 'Judith thought it would do me good – I'd been in low spirits. I had no mind to watch the people of Margate cavorting around and my feet are used to traipsing about the garden rather than performing dance steps. But it seems you bewitched me and my feet – they were only too eager to do your bidding.'

I laughed, relieved that he was no longer quite so intense, but I had noted what he said about being in low spirits. I was determined to discover why, although his earlier words about troubles in his marriage had given me an indication. We walked on in silence for a while and I wondered how long it would take him to get to the point of why he had wanted so urgently to see me. The sight of a ship in full sail, moving at quite a pace a little way out to sea, finally brought me to a halt. We both stood and watched it.

'I wonder where it's bound,' I said. Away on an adventure, I thought, and wished with every fibre of my being that we were going with it. Charlie was standing so close to me that I could sense every breath he took. On impulse, I turned to him.

'Charlie, am I right in thinking you would like to spend more time with me?'

He, too, had been gazing out to sea but at my words he turned to me. He didn't speak – I'm not sure he could – but his expression held both longing and fear.

'You know we can't be seen together like this while you are living with Molly,' I said.

He appeared bewildered. 'But she is away.'

That explained why he had come to the ball alone, I thought. 'Then now would be a good time to leave the cottage. Is there somewhere you can go?'

I saw the shock on his face as he registered my words. He really was quite naive, I thought. Had I turned his head so completely that he had no notion of the scandal that would erupt if my name was linked with his? If his marriage appeared to be over, society would be more forgiving of him in the end, less so of me. I wanted to disrupt things, but not destroy my reputation in the process.

We began to walk on, Charlie gazing at his feet, deep in thought. A couple passed us, arm in arm, and they nodded to Charlie but he failed to notice them. I ignored them, averting my head as if to gaze out to sea, hoping my bonnet hid my face.

'I could stay with George, I suppose,' Charlie said at last. 'He's angry with Molly. He'll understand why I don't want to be at home.'

'Good,' I said briskly. 'Then, once you are no longer under the same roof as your wife, we can consider how to further our ... relationship.'

I glanced around me. The couple had passed on into the distance and no one else was in sight. 'Shall we seal our agreement with a kiss?' I asked, hoping it wasn't too risky a move, too soon. I was taken aback by the eagerness with which Charlie responded, seizing me around the waist and planting his lips so firmly on mine that he knocked my bonnet askew with his ardour.

'Goodness,' I said, disengaging myself to smooth my dress and right my bonnet. I was made quite breathless by his fervour and not a little worried that control of the situation was slipping out of my grasp. I'd intended suggesting it was time to walk back but I needed to compose myself. So we walked on a little further and I steered the conversation to safer ground, asking after his garden.

He recounted his plans for the summer months, his face clouding as he recalled there were only a few weeks before the annual garden party at Woodchurch Manor. 'I hope you will come,' he said, turning to me, all eagerness once more.

'I've never been to one. Tell me what happens,' I replied.

He described the events of the day, the tours of the garden and around the lake, tea on the lawn accompanied by music, speeches by Mr Powell, his employer.

'And the whole family comes – all the grandchildren,' he finished.

I smiled and nodded, all the time thinking sourly of how unwelcome I would be. By now, we had walked quite a way. The wind had got up, forcing me to snatch at my bonnet while my dress billowed around me. The sky was still blue but clouds were gathering.

'I think it's time to return,' I said. I didn't want to be caught out in a summer storm.

Before I could stop him, Charlie took me by the shoulders and turned me to face him. 'I can't return without another kiss. I will need something to think of in all the hours we must spend apart.'

'Not here,' I protested, even though as far as I could see the path was quite empty.

The passage of feet had worn a track away from the main path through the grass to a cove. He guided me down and it was easy to find a spot sheltered from view, behind a cluster of fallen rocks. I felt easier about submitting to his kisses there, even enjoying them. It had been a long time since I'd found myself in a man's arms, delighting in the passion I had aroused. I'm not sure who was the most reluctant when I finally broke free.

'Charlie,' I said, gently pushing him from me. I didn't say it with any great urgency but I was pleased to see that he stepped back at once. I adjusted my gown around my shoulders and replaced my bonnet, hoping I didn't look as dishevelled as I felt. Charlie gave me his hand to help me scramble back onto the path and we turned our faces towards Westbrook, and Margate beyond. I took it for granted that he would see me safely back, before returning to Woodchurch Manor.

We had gone barely a few steps beyond the cove when I saw the couple who had passed us earlier. This time, Charlie recognised them before they were upon us and his steps faltered. They stood aside to let us pass and greetings were exchanged.

'You know them?' I asked, as soon as they were out of earshot.

'Mr and Mrs Joshua Symonds,' he said. 'Sally, my daughter, is married to their son. They live close by, in Westgate.'

He wore a grim expression. I imagine he feared they would tell Sally they had seen her father in the company of a younger woman who most definitely wasn't his wife. I said nothing, but smiled to myself. I rather thought that if Charlie didn't move out, Molly would make the decision for him.

I hadn't counted, though, on word spreading so quickly with regard to Charlie and me. Shut away in the hospital, I had no notion that we were the subject of scurrilous gossip. Lizzie and Mary had already been made uneasy by Charlie's behaviour at the ball, and his attentions to me. Our Sunday walk by the sea had been observed and this was enough to make them write to Molly. They also spoke to Aunt Jane, who in turn discussed matters with Uncle William, which precipitated a visit to the hospital governors.

The Tuesday following my walk with Charlie, I was called into the overseer's office.

'There's a reason we don't like to employ unmarried women,' Mrs Murray began.

I adopted a puzzled expression, although her words put me immediately on guard.

'Allow them a little leeway, make a concession or two, and before you know it, you've been taken advantage of.' Mrs Murray was working herself up as she spoke.

'You've brought your own name, and the Royal Sea Bathing Hospital, into disrepute, Miss Dixon. You're to leave today. Collect your things from your room, bring your work clothes to me when you've changed and I'll have your wages waiting for you.'

I tried to protest and to ask her what I was supposed to have done but I was treated to her withering scorn.

'I wasn't born yesterday. I know all about the likes of you. You'd do well to leave Margate. The hospital is prepared to give you a good reference to help you on your way. I think you will discover that there are those in town who can make life difficult for you should you remain here. I'm sure London would suit you very well.'

It wasn't lost on me that, although some in Margate considered it to be the height of fashion and a fascinating place, others saw London as a den of iniquity, the rightful home of fallen women. I suspect Mrs Murray subscribed to the latter viewpoint. I drew myself to my full height, put my nose in the air and swept from the room.

181

Her words had initially come as a shock, but as I packed my few things I began to see this turn of Fate as an opportunity. It had forced my hand but perhaps this was no bad thing. I would throw myself on Charlie's mercy and ask him to find a home for me – perhaps even for the pair of us. And if he hesitated, I would threaten to leave the area, go to London and never return.

I finished my packing with a glad heart and was back in Mrs Murray's office to collect my wages within the hour. Leaving my box for collection, I stepped out into the sunshine, lifting my face to feel the breeze on my skin. I would find Charlie and put my proposal to him. I was confident of success and, in any case, I had my nest-egg to fall back on. My collection of rings, gold chains and money, misplaced over months by hospital residents, nestled in the pocket tied under my skirts. Never let it be said that Harriet Dixon wasn't well prepared.

PART FOUR

MOLLY

Chapter Thirty-Five

All the way back to Woodchurch Manor, on her slow journey from Faversham, Molly had gone over and over all the things she wanted to say to Charlie. Yet as soon as she saw him, all reasonable thought had fled and she had harangued him like a fishwife, without giving him the chance to tell his side of the story.

She'd concluded, 'She must be half your age. You'll make a spectacle of yourself. What will everyone say? And she's family! She's my half-sister.'

Charlie just looked at her.

Molly wished the words back into her mouth the moment she had spoken. But it was true nevertheless. They would be a laughing stock, whispered about behind people's hands. There would be those who would say it was no more than she deserved. Molly's face burnt with shame and indignation.

'She's schemed for this, Charlie. I don't like to say this of my little sister, but she's like Ann, her mother. She set out to steal you, a married man, and you've let her. How could you?'

Somewhere at the back of Molly's mind was the thought that she should be calm and conciliatory, try to win Charlie round to her point of view. Instead, she wanted to shake him; to shout so loudly her words would penetrate his skull and make him understand how his behaviour looked to everyone else.

He turned away from her. 'Molly, I'm going now. I can't talk to you when you're like this.'

She swallowed hard. She was allowing her humiliation to colour her words. 'Charlie, all our years together – do they count for nothing? I know there have been difficult times but we've brought up three daughters – Sally, Agnes, Catherine. What will they say?'

Molly stopped. She'd wanted to say something about their love for each other, but the words just wouldn't come. When Charlie turned back towards her, it sparked a brief flicker of hope in Molly's heart.

'And what do you suppose they think about you, Molly? Now they know you carried on lying to them, just when they'd got used to the idea they had a brother you had kept a secret. He can't bear to be near you. I know how he feels.'

Charlie turned on his heel and strode towards the door. He hesitated a moment, his hand on the latch, and then he was gone, the door banging behind him.

Afterwards, Molly wondered whether he had paused because he expected her to throw herself at him, fling herself to the floor and beg him not to leave. Or had he, perhaps, had second thoughts about his harsh words? As it was, she did fall to her knees, but only after he had gone. She didn't know how long she knelt on the cold, hard floor or where her thoughts went during that time. When she finally struggled to her feet, using the chair and the table to force her chilled, cramped body into an upright position, it was dark. She didn't want to light a lamp and force herself to go about the routine of making herself something to eat. Instead, she stumbled up the stairs and climbed onto the bed fully clothed, pulling a blanket over herself. She stared into the darkness for a long while, but her eyes must have closed for she woke up to find light creeping into the room through the window, where she had failed to draw the curtains.

Molly turned on her side and thought about getting up. Then she wondered whether there was any point. She could make herself some food, she supposed, but she didn't know whether she felt hungry. She tried to consider this but it took too much effort. She must have fallen into a doze for when she awoke again it was brighter, patches of blue appearing among the clearing clouds outside. She lay on her back and watched birds fly across the sky, and tried to drag her thoughts back to the conversation with Charlie. Why had she allowed hurt pride to get the better of her? Anger had caused a cold, hard nugget in her heart and her thoughts were too full of one person alone, and the damage they had caused: Harriet. Had he gone to see her? Was he with her now? The thought was so painful that she gasped and closed her eyes, only for images of Harriet's face to dance across her eyelids. Why couldn't Charlie see her for what she was? He was such a sensible, practical man, so caring. How could he have been so easily drawn in by her? Had Molly been complacent, believing Charlie must see that all their years together were worth far more than the excitement of a ridiculous flirtation?

Then she was reminded of what had led to this. She had thought she was doing the right thing in withholding the fact that Nicholas was George's father, hardly daring to think about the problems it would cause if the truth became known. Now, that deception was magnified. She had made a terrible mess of everyone's lives, including her own. She had lost the man she loved – and not just to another woman, for it felt as though the Charlie she had known since they were both fourteen years old had changed into someone unrecognisable. Someone who no longer loved or cared for her or his family. Why had he so quickly turned to Harriet? Lizzie had been right to warn her against her half-sister. She would never have made the journey to Faversham if she could have foreseen such a thing might happen. Tears seeped from her eyes and ran down her cheeks, unchecked. She didn't have the energy to wipe them away.

When Molly roused again, the failing light told her it was evening. She was parched, her throat dry and her tongue felt swollen. She must at least get up and drink something, throw some water on her face, change her clothes. It was only the necessity of using the chamber pot that drove her from the bed. Standing up, she felt dizzy. She made herself go downstairs and drink a little water, then took bread and the butter dish from the pantry. She cut a slice from the loaf but it was an effort to force it down. Nothing else held any appeal – not cheese, ham, a slice of pie that someone – Judith perhaps – must have made. Molly stood at the window and gazed out over the garden, barely taking in what she saw. It should have been full of scent and colour at this point in the year, but Charlie hadn't seen fit to water it while she was away and her precious plants had withered and died. It was a sign of the man he had become, she supposed: so possessed by another that his previous life meant nothing to him.

Heavy with despair, she turned and slowly mounted the stairs again. The stale atmosphere in the bedroom struck her and she opened the window, taken aback by the freshness of the air that wafted in. Shivering all at once, she climbed back onto the bed and turned onto her side again. This time, she stared unseeing at the wall until the painted boards danced before her eyes and she had to close them.

CHAPTER THIRTY-SIX

Molly discovered more about Charlie's whereabouts when Lizzie and Mary appeared on her doorstep two days later. She hadn't sent word of her return but no doubt she had been spotted on the coach from Canterbury or at some other point on her troubled and weary journey from Faversham, and that little nugget of gossip had made its way to them.

Molly let in her sisters without a word, but before she could ask them what they would like by way of refreshment, they both flung their arms around her. They remained clasped like this for a minute or two, while tears ran afresh down Molly's cheeks.

'Now, you're to sit down,' Lizzie told her. 'We've brought food with us. We came to see what we could do to help.'

Molly was mainly concerned to hear as much as possible about the ball at the Assembly Rooms. Lizzie and Mary were apologetic – they had little to offer beyond what had been in the letter. Judith and George had apparently persuaded Charlie to go with them to the ball, for Judith feared he was moping in Molly's absence. (Hearing this was enough to raise Molly's spirits a little.)

He had spent the evening in Harriet's company and had danced the night away, to the sisters' astonishment. Outside, afterwards, he had been seen handing Harriet up into a carriage, then getting in himself.

Mary, seeing Molly's stricken expression, hastened to add, 'But it was the carriage for Woodchurch Manor. George and Judith were in it, too. I dare say they dropped Harriet at the hospital. I'm sure you can find out more from them.'

'And the walk by the sea at Westgate?' Molly asked.

Lizzie's expression was hard to read. 'They were seen by Sally's in-laws. They were deep in conversation and didn't notice Mr and Mrs Symonds on the first occasion, but they passed again later and I gather Charlie seemed surprised to see them. Harriet looked—' Lizzie stopped.

'Harriet looked?' Molly prompted.

Lizzie flushed. 'I don't know. I really couldn't say.' She refused to be drawn any further.

'And now he's with her!' Molly exclaimed.

'Is he?' Lizzie and Mary spoke in unison.

'He must be. He hasn't been here for the last two days.' Molly was tearful once more.

Mary frowned. 'Are you sure? I heard he was staying with George and Judith.'

Molly was taken aback. Her son and his wife lived in the same terrace of cottages, just a few doors down. She would surely have seen Charlie if he was there. Then she remembered the long hours he worked in the summer months, leaving at dawn and returning when it was dark, all his attention focused on getting the grounds ready for the garden party.

'Who told you he was there?' she asked.

Mary looked embarrassed. 'I think Margaret told Henry who told Lewis.'

'Margaret? Henry?' Molly was confused. She'd barely been in Faversham above two weeks: how had so much happened in that time?

Lizzie had news she was eager to share. 'Harriet has been dismissed from the hospital. Uncle William spoke to the governors and they let her go at once. She's been told to leave Margate.'

'And has she?' Molly spoke faintly.

'She hasn't been seen since.' Lizzie's voice was firm. Molly supposed she ought to be thankful but she'd have felt safer if Harriet had been cloistered in the hospital, with work to keep her occupied. Now she could be anywhere, with time on her hands. And eager to spend it with Charlie, no doubt.

Lizzie and Mary busied themselves, laying out the food they had brought with them. Molly was secretly impatient to be free of them so that she could go and knock on Judith's door, and discover whether Charlie had moved in there. And she would ask about George, too. Her heart gave a jolt: she'd barely given George a thought amid all the upset of the last few days. Whatever was the matter with her? Her only son, whom she'd missed so very much when he was lost to her. Now that she had him back in her life, she mustn't squander this precious time. He was angry with her, but she must find a way to make it right. She thought back to Charlie's words, spoken in anger two days earlier.

'Your daughters – what do they think of you?' He'd implied they thought less of her for keeping the identity of George's father a secret. She hated the idea. Now that the truth was out in the open, it did feel as though she had made the wrong decision. Yet, at the time, it had seemed the only course of action she could take.

She saw that Lizzie and Mary were looking at her.

'Did you say something? I'm sorry – I was thinking about George. And the girls. I knew George was angry with me but I didn't realise I'd upset my daughters, too.'

'Who said that?' Lizzie asked, then answered her own question. 'I suppose it was Charlie. I don't think the girls are angry. Surprised, perhaps.' She frowned. 'George might take a bit of persuading that you had his best interests at heart, keeping the name of his father a secret. But now, let's eat.'

The three of them sat at the table. Molly surveyed the array of delicacies that her sisters had brought to tempt her – a pork pie, which only served to remind her it was Catherine's favourite food as a child, a roast fowl, some hard white cheese and stewed gooseberries. She could only pick at the food she put on her plate, despite her sisters' anxious glances. Her thoughts had turned to how she might begin to put things right with her family.

As Lizzie and Mary cleared the table after their meal, putting the leftovers into the larder for Molly to have later, Lizzie spoke: 'Molly, why don't you come back with us to Margate?'

She shook her head. 'No, I must stay here. I can't let George be lost to me again. And I need to talk to Sally, Agnes and Catherine – we haven't spoken since it became known that Nicholas was George's father. I shouldn't have gone away to Faversham with Hannah when there were so many things here that needed my attention.'

Mary added her pleas to Lizzie's in an attempt to persuade Molly, but to no avail. Molly stood firm: there was to be no more running away from the consequences of her past actions. She would stay and face whatever needed to be faced.

Chapter Thirty-Seven

Molly, who had been so impatient to see Judith and discover whether Charlie was staying with her and George, found she was nervous as she stood on their doorstep later that afternoon. The last time she had visited – which seemed like half a lifetime ago but was just three weeks previously – Judith had said she couldn't let her in, that George wouldn't allow it. She supposed she still wouldn't be welcome, but she needed to ask the question: was Charlie living there? It would give her some comfort if he was.

Her knock was tentative but Judith answered quickly. Molly wondered whether she'd seen her from the window as she walked up the path. She spoke quickly, in case Judith closed the door on her.

'I'm sorry – I know George has said I'm not welcome and I don't want to put you in a difficult position – but I needed to ask whether Charlie is staying with you. I came back from Faversham two days ago and he left the house. We argued.' Molly's voice faltered. 'I was worried about him.'

Judith stood in silence on the doorstep for a moment. Then she opened the door wider and stood aside. 'You'd better come in,' she said.

Molly was surprised but stepped in at once, thanking her. She went immediately to Joseph, who was lying in his cradle, wide awake. It was the one that had been used by her girls, one after another, then passed around the babies of the family. The wood was now scuffed and scarred, and although it had never been used by George, it made her happy that at least his son had it now. She bent down and buried her nose in Joseph's neck, then kissed his cheek as he beamed and gurgled.

'He's changed since I last saw you,' she said to Judith.

Judith smiled briefly, then responded to the question Molly had asked on the doorstep.

'Charlie's staying here,' she said. 'And neither George nor Charlie will thank me for inviting you in but I can't stand by and watch Charlie make a fool of himself over Harriet. He's behaving as though he's moonstruck. And she's a scheming miss, if I'm not mistaken.' Two spots of colour in Judith's cheeks showed her indignation.

Molly was pleased by her words, while at the same time feeling a lurch of pain. Although she'd told herself that her marriage was over, in her heart of hearts she didn't believe it. She couldn't bear to think of Charlie infatuated with Harriet. Was she in love with him, or was she playing with him? There was such an age difference: Charlie was married with children and grandchildren, for Heaven's sake.

All this ran through Molly's head before she replied. 'Scheming?'

'Yes,' Judith replied firmly. 'Oh, Molly, if you could have seen her at the Assembly Rooms ball. Gazing up into Charlie's eyes and hanging on his every word. She even got him out onto the dance floor – and kept him there.' Judith laughed wryly. 'He's not the most elegant dancer, or particularly light on his feet. You could tell he'd never had a lesson in his life. He was mostly going left when everyone else was going right.'

Molly's lips twitched, in spite of herself. She could picture it only too well.

'All the time, though, he was oblivious,' Judith continued. 'He had eyes only for Harriet. And then he offered her a ride home. In our carriage, with George and me. We had no say – the privilege of using the carriage is Charlie's, because Mr Powell thinks so well of him. I don't think he'd have thought so much of him if he could have seen him then.'

Judith's indignation gave way to contrition. 'Molly, I'm so sorry. It's my fault. I persuaded him to come with us to the ball. He'd been moping around since you left and I thought it would take his mind off things. With so many relatives there, I assumed he would spend the evening talking to them and watching the young people dance. If I'd known . . .' Judith tailed off.

'It's not your fault,' Molly said, laying her hand on Judith's arm. 'Please don't blame yourself. Harriet is the one at fault. And Charlie – he should know better. He was angry with me, but this, it's – it's . . .' Molly struggled to describe her feelings then settled on, 'It's humiliating.'

Joseph began to grizzle, diverting their attention, and Judith took him from his cradle. The two women devoted themselves to entertaining him until, worn out, his eyelids drooped and fluttered and he fell asleep in Molly's arms. She was soothed by the warm weight of him: what did anything else count for in the presence of his innocence?

'Do you want me to say something to Charlie?' Judith asked suddenly. 'I've had a hard job stopping my tongue but he's my father-in-law. And he dotes on Joseph.' She smiled at him as he slept. 'Yet I'd like him to know what I think. And I won't have that woman in my house, of course,' she added.

'Has George said anything?' Molly asked.

'No.' Judith looked troubled. 'I don't think he was comfortable with Charlie's behaviour at the ball but it's difficult for him. The two of them work together. And although George is angry with you, I suspect he doesn't feel that gives Charlie the right to act in this way. At least, I would hope that's what he thinks.' Judith pursed her lips at the idea of George condoning Charlie's actions. 'Do you think his conduct at the ball was just a moment of madness?' she asked Molly.

Molly shook her head. 'Perhaps not,' she said, and related what she had heard about Charlie's Sunday walk along the coast.

Judith looked horrified. 'I wondered where he'd gone. He came to church with us, then barely graced us with his presence while we ate before saying he had something to attend to. Then he took himself off. I assumed it was something to do with the gardens. He came back in a good humour so I thought he'd sorted out the problem.'

They contemplated her words, then Molly said, 'Harriet has been dismissed by the hospital: it was Uncle William's doing, I gather. But I don't know where she is now.' She turned anguished eyes on Judith. 'Will you tell me if Charlie decides to move out?'

'He won't,' Judith said firmly. 'He and George are really busy in the gardens, working dawn till dusk. You know what it's like in the summer, preparing for the garden party. He can't afford to take time off, or to stay somewhere that isn't right on the doorstep of work.'

It was small consolation, Molly thought. Who was to say that Charlie wasn't counting the days until summer – or the garden party – was over when he would be free to spend more time with Harriet?

She stood up and gently deposited the sleeping Joseph in Judith's arms. He stirred briefly, then nuzzled into the warmth of his mother. Molly's body ached and she felt tired: much older than her forty-four years.

'I'll go home now but thank you, Judith, for inviting me in and for talking so freely to me.'

'I'm just sorry I had to turn you away before.' Judith paused. 'I won't say anything to George or Charlie about your visit. And nor will Joseph.' She smiled at her sleeping infant. 'But please come and see us whenever you can. We'll try to work out what to do for the best.'

Molly let herself out and made her way home, her heart lighter than it had been for days. While Charlie remained at George and Judith's, she felt there was a glimmer of hope in her situation.

Chapter Thirty-Eight

O ver the following days, Molly tried to get used to the feeling that her world was out of kilter. She woke each day from an uneasy sleep, momentarily free of the memory of what was wrong, only for the sight of the untouched pillow beside her to remind her anew of how things stood. She struggled to fill her days, now she had only herself to care for. It hardly seemed worth cooking for one, there was little cleaning to be done and the garden, usually a source of pride, held no charm for her. It was sorely neglected. She supposed she should look to the future and began to think back to Faversham: while staying with Hannah she had dreamt about making a new start there.

Could such a thing be possible? Molly knew only too well how blame was apportioned in marital upsets: the husband, after the townsfolk had voiced some initial indignation and outrage, generally escaped lasting censure. The fault lay with the wife for not providing a loving home, or so the reasoning went. Faversham was far enough from Margate for her to be able to establish herself there as a respectable widow, under an assumed name, of course. But what work could she do? And what about her children and grandchildren?

Molly knew that if she was to make such a move she must consult her daughters. She hadn't paid any of them a visit since the news about George's father had come out. There was no excuse for not seeing Catherine, who, after all, lived at Woodchurch Manor. She hadn't been present at the fateful gathering at Aunt Jane's, and Molly was unsure how much she had heard about it. It made sense to visit her first, then take a trip to Westgate on another day to see Sally. Agnes had written to say that she would be in Ramsgate for the rest of the summer: perhaps she would make the journey home before too long.

Molly went to see Judith regularly, apart from on Sunday when George was at home. She had fallen into the habit of calling in at the same time in the afternoon, when she was most likely to find Joseph awake. It was the highlight of an otherwise very empty day. That afternoon when she knocked on the door and Judith opened it, Molly heard voices within. She at once stepped back and said, 'You have visitors. I'll come back another time, if I may?'

'No, no, come in. It's Catherine and Eleanor, come to see Joseph.'

Molly was perturbed. She'd planned to see Catherine, but alone. Now it was too late – she could hardly refuse to see her own daughter. Judith was waiting, so she raised a smile and said, 'How lovely,' before stepping inside.

Catherine was kneeling on the floor, her chestnut curls hiding her face as she held Eleanor and bent over Joseph, waving a rattle for him.

'You forget so quickly,' Catherine said, looking up at her mother. 'It was only a year ago that Eleanor was like this, and now she's walking and starting to talk.' She smiled and kissed the top of her daughter's head. 'How are you, Ma? I've been meaning to come and see you but every day something cropped up to prevent me. I feel like I haven't seen you for weeks.'

Catherine's expression was guileless – Molly had the impression her enquiry was genuine enough. Had she really not heard how Molly had earned Charlie and George's displeasure? Or of Harriet's association with Charlie?

Molly settled herself in a chair and Eleanor vacated her mother's lap and rushed over to clamber onto her grand-mother's knee. The first few minutes were spent in cuddles, kisses and tickles before Eleanor slipped off and went in search of Judith in the kitchen, no doubt hoping to find a treat.

Molly took a deep breath: she should broach her worries with Catherine now, before Judith returned.

'Have you heard . . .' she hesitated, then pressed on '. . . have you heard what happened at Aunt Jane's Sunday gathering a few weeks ago?'

Catherine turned away from Joseph to her mother, caus-ing him to wail at the loss of his entertainer. She scooped him up onto her lap before turning her attention back to Molly.

'Do you mean about George's father being Aunt Jane's son?'

Molly was relieved. At least she didn't have to explain herself. 'Yes, I do. And I realised that you ought to have heard it from me, not from someone else.'

'Judith told me,' Catherine replied. 'Don't worry, Ma. It was a surprise but, after all, we knew that George must have a father.' She shrugged. 'We never knew Nicholas so really it doesn't matter to me. I gather George is upset with you, though.'

'Yes,' Molly replied. 'And he isn't the only one. Your father, too.'

Catherine sighed. 'Judith told me something of that as well. He's staying here at the moment?'

Molly nodded.

'I haven't seen him,' Catherine said, 'but I hope he comes to his senses soon.'

Joseph began to wriggle and distracted her. Molly wondered whether she should say anything about Harriet. Did Catherine know? Had she seen anything of her sister, Sally, who must know since her husband's parents had seen Charlie and Harriet together?

Before she'd decided whether or not to enquire further, Judith came back into the room, closely followed by Eleanor, her mouth surrounded by crumbs.

'Someone couldn't wait,' Judith said. 'Shall we sit in the garden? The sun is out for a change but there's plenty of shade and we can have the lemonade I made this morning.'

Catherine and Molly got to their feet and followed Judith out through the kitchen into the garden, where she'd spread a blanket beneath a tree and brought out chairs from the kitchen. The three women sat and drank lemonade and talked of inconsequential things, while Molly tried to drive her worry from her mind. Should she mention Harriet? If Catherine didn't know, was there any point in making her view her father in a different light? Molly had the impression her daughter thought she and Charlie had had an argument that would sort itself out in time. Perhaps it was better to leave it like that for now.

CHAPTER THIRTY-NINE

Two days later, on Sunday, Molly found herself at a loss as to what to do with her time. It was grey with a chill wind, and heavy rain earlier in the day had discouraged her from attending church. In any case, she was unsure whether Charlie and George would be there and was fearful of their reaction if they were. She stood in the bedroom and gazed out across the field. It looked as though more rain was in the offing; she supposed it would be good for the gardens. Charlie was always fretting at this time of year about watering the plants so that they were in perfect condition for the garden party.

The garden party – Molly had been there every year since Mr Powell had begun the tradition, ten years earlier. Each year, he called Charlie up onto the bandstand that served as his stage to thank his head gardener for bringing the grounds to their full glory in time for the party. And he invited Molly to come up too, to thank her for supporting her husband while he worked so hard. But what would happen this year? If she was still estranged from Charlie, should she even go? She couldn't bear the idea of people whispering behind their hands about him and Harriet. They'd be gossiping about the goings-on at the ball. Or, worse still, would Charlie's behaviour in the weeks remaining before the garden party have given them even more to wag their tongues about?

Molly buried her head in her hands. She tried to bring a picture of Charlie to mind, to remember the exact timbre of his voice, the colour of his eyes, the flecks of gold among the brown. In panic, she felt as though the memory of him was slipping away. How could that happen so quickly? He'd been gone less than ten days. Although she supposed it was nearly a month since the Sunday party at Aunt Jane's. She'd seen little of him since then.

Through her misery, Molly became aware of a noise. Was it a rapping at the door? She thought at once of Charlie and her heart leapt. But of course he wouldn't come knocking – he'd just walk in. She stood up from the bed and hurried down the stairs, hoping it wouldn't appear obvious that she had been crying.

When she opened the door, it took her a moment or two to realise who was standing there. 'Margaret!' she exclaimed. 'Come in. I couldn't think what you were doing here at first, then remembered that Judith said you were visiting.'

She wondered whether to show her into the parlour, but Margaret looked as though she would be perfectly content in the kitchen. She'd already taken off her bonnet and laid it on the table and now stood looking out of the window.

'You have a beautiful view,' she said, turning to Molly. 'The countryside around here is lovely. Up until now, I'd only seen Margate and London since I arrived in this country. I'm so happy I came out here today to visit George and Judith. And you, of course.'

Molly pulled out a chair for her to sit down, then took the seat opposite. 'And how was your afternoon? Did you get to know George a little better?'

'I did.' Margaret was enthusiastic. 'They made me so welcome. I've spent time with them before, of course, at the ball but today was so much better: we could have a proper conversation. And I met Joseph, too. He's delightful.' She smiled at the memory, then became serious. 'But, Molly, I gather all is not well between you and George. I feel partly responsible. If I hadn't come here in search of my family, and if Harriet hadn't taken it on herself to share my history at your aunt's party, then George would have been none the wiser.'

'Nonsense.' Molly spoke briskly. 'It wasn't anything to do with Harriet or you. It was Hannah, Aunt Jane's cook, who recognised George as Nicholas's son. She did have a reason to think it, though no one else in the room would have suspected, I'm sure.'

Margaret looked puzzled so Molly briefly explained how she had told Hannah she was expecting Nicholas's baby over twenty-five years earlier, when she'd lived in Aunt Jane's house. 'But then I told her I'd lost the child. It seemed easier and, in a way, it was true. He was lost to me. I'm glad that you and George are getting to know each other now. I'm sure he's got a lot of questions about his father and you are the only person who can answer them. Even Constance knows next to nothing about Nicholas.' She paused. 'Have you met Constance yet?'

Margaret shook her head. 'She hasn't been back to Margate since the news came out. I'm not sure she ever will. I'd like to meet her, but I might feel awkward. As though I stole her father. George and I seem to have more in common, somehow.'

'The first time you met was at the ball?' Molly asked.

'Yes. I think he would have avoided me if it hadn't been for Judith. She made sure that we spoke and I'm so pleased she did.' Margaret smiled.

'And I hear that you met someone else, too?' Molly asked.

'Ah, you mean Henry. Henry Sayer. He works with your nephew, Lewis. It was a lovely evening.' Margaret's smile grew broader.

'I wish I'd been there,' Molly said.

'You should have been.' Margaret was suddenly serious. 'To be honest, I felt uncomfortable about going. I only went because Harriet insisted. I didn't think it was fitting for the likes of us, workers at the Sea Bathing Hospital, but she was very persuasive. It was only later I realised what she had been up to. I spent most of my time in the company of George and Judith, your nieces and Lewis. If I'd realised what was going on, I'd have taken Harriet away at once.' Margaret looked mortified at the memory.

Molly shook her head. 'Please – you mustn't blame yourself in any way. The fault lies with Harriet, and with Charlie. And, I suppose, with me. If I had been there, none of this would have happened.'

'I understand your husband is staying with George and Judith?' Margaret asked, after a pause.

'Yes, he is. I'm afraid both George and Charlie are angry with me at the moment.' Molly wouldn't ordinarily have admitted as much to someone she didn't know well, but she'd been drawn to Margaret on first meeting her. She seemed to have an understanding beyond her years.

'Well, I think that's unfair.' Margaret was indignant, then remembered her manners. 'I do beg your pardon. But it's Mr Dawson who isn't behaving well from what I've seen.'

'Yes.' Molly spoke with sadness. 'Was he with you this afternoon?'

'No, he wasn't. I think Judith thought he might be in Woodchurch Manor gardens.'

'George didn't go out there with him?'

Margaret looked troubled. 'No, he was with us.'

Molly abruptly changed her line of questioning. 'I hear Harriet has been dismissed from the hospital. Do you know where she's gone? Has she left the area?'

'She has, but she hasn't gone far. I believe she's taken a room in Ramsgate.'

'Ramsgate?' Molly's thoughts flew to her daughter, Agnes, who had written to say she was staying in the town.

Margaret looked at Molly. 'You don't think she's still in touch with your husband?'

'I don't know,' Molly said. 'But I plan to find out.'

CHAPTER FORTY

Margaret couldn't stay very much longer, for she needed to walk back to Margate and the skies held the threat of rain, but she promised to return another day and stay longer. Molly had questions she wanted to ask, about Margaret's father and their life in the West Indies, but her thoughts were too full of her own predicament. She would have to pursue that topic another day.

After Margaret had left, she felt uplifted and ready to make plans. She would visit Sally as soon as possible, she decided, for she had yet to discuss with her the revelations about George's father. And Sally must be wondering about her own father, Molly reflected, for she would be only too well aware that he had been seen in the company of Harriet, walking on the coastal path near Westgate. She would also visit Agnes in Ramsgate, sending word to her the very next day.

Huddled by the kitchen range later that evening, Molly realised that the house was cold. It was now July – surely the evenings should be warmer than this? As rain began to pound against the windows, she hoped that Margaret had reached home safely without being drenched. The thought made her shiver and she decided it was time to go up to bed, adding an extra blanket on top of the summer quilt as she did so.

She slept well for the first time in days, waking to dark skies. She lay in bed longer than usual, for she had no great need to get up and the chill in the room told her it was still unseasonably cold. Finally, with some reluctance, she left the warmth of her bed and went downstairs to heat water to wash, discovering to her surprise that it was already mid-morning.

Molly had just finished getting dressed when the rumbling of carriage wheels outside made her turn to the window. It was rare to see anything other than farm carts along the lane. To her surprise, the carriage drew to a halt outside the house, the door opened and Sally stepped down.

Molly flew downstairs in a hurry, hair still uncombed and unpinned, to open the door.

'Sally! Is everything all right? The children? Luke?' Molly struggled to make sense of her daughter's unexpected arrival, and in a carriage, too.

Sally frowned. 'Did I catch you unawares, Ma?'

Molly stood back to let her daughter in. 'Come in, do. I wasn't expecting you, it's true. But you haven't answered me: is everything well with the family?'

'Yes, yes,' Sally said. She was busy setting the kettle to boil on the stove. 'I might ask the same of you, though.' She surveyed her mother. 'Did I wake you?'

'No!' Molly protested. 'Although I confess I haven't long been up. I haven't slept well of late but last night I slept deeply and I'm a little behind this morning.'

Sally gave her mother a critical look. 'Do you want to finish getting dressed? Then you can tell me what's been happening.'

Molly went back upstairs to finish pinning up her hair, trying to shake off the sense that she was being chastised.

208

She wondered whether her daughter had come to lecture her and began to feel yesterday's resolve slipping away. But when she returned to the kitchen, Sally had set out cups and saucers, sliced the bread and taken butter and preserves from the pantry.

'Ma, you look as though you haven't been eating properly.'

Molly sniffed the aroma of the coffee as it brewed and suddenly realised she was very hungry. She evaded Sally's remark: 'Well, I haven't had breakfast because I got up so late. So this is very welcome, thank you.'

While her mother ate and drank, Sally talked of general matters such as the unusual weather for the time of year and the lack of potatoes and vegetables in the market, before moving on to the topic that Molly was half dreading.

'So, Ma, what's going on? Luke's parents said they'd seen Pa walking with a young woman on the path by the sea at Westgate. They kept it from me at first but they must have mentioned it to someone, because I hear it's quite a story in Margate. That's when they decided they'd better tell me.' Sally paused to sip her coffee. 'They lent me their carriage today so I could come and see you. Perhaps they're hoping I'll bring more gossip back with me.' Sally pursed her lips.

'Oh, Sally, I'm sorry you had to find out in that way. I'm afraid there's quite a bit more to the story. I should have told you before, but . . .' Molly took a deep breath.

'You heard Hannah say that George looked just like his father at Aunt Jane's house. I haven't seen you since then, but afterwards Harriet told George, and Charlie, that Hannah was referring to Nicholas.' Molly paused.

'You mean – Aunt Jane's son, Nicholas?' Sally asked.

'Yes. Of course you never knew him – he'd left the country long before you were born. George was furious with me for

209

keeping the truth from him. And it was a shock to your pa. He took it very badly.' Molly went on to describe how it had created a rift between them and how this had grown following the Assembly Rooms ball.

Sally heard Molly out in silence. Then she leant across the table and took her mother's hand. 'Ma, I'm sitting here listening to you apologise and I don't know why. You did what you thought was for the best at the time. I can't see why George has reacted in the way that he has and as for Pa!' Sally's brows drew together in a frown. 'Has he lost his mind? And Harriet, after you welcomed her and did your best to bring her back into the family – what can she be thinking of?'

Molly shook her head. 'Anyway, she's lost her job over her behaviour, left Margate and moved to Ramsgate, thank goodness.'

'Do you think Pa is—Do you think he'll come home now?'

'You mean, is he still seeing Harriet?' Molly shrugged. 'It's hard to know how he'd find the time to get to Ramsgate, what with all the work to be done to prepare the gardens for the open day.' She pushed to the back of her mind the fact that Charlie had absented himself from George and Judith's house the previous afternoon, when Margaret had paid them a visit. 'But in any case, he's angry with me over keeping another secret, that Nicholas was George's father. He doesn't want to talk to me.'

'I'm sure he'll come around in the end.'

Molly wondered whether Sally's words were those of a daughter wanting reassurance that all would be well again with her parents; a daughter who didn't want her own world to begin to crumble.

'We'll be laughing about it by Christmas, I expect,' Molly said, having no expectation of any such thing. 'And Luke's parents have lent you their carriage in vain. You won't return bearing interesting tittle-tattle.'

Sally laughed. 'I'd happily have walked over. It's not far, and on a summer's day it's lovely. But it doesn't feel like summer today – the weather is getting worse, not better.'

She recounted tales she'd heard from her husband about rioting in London over food shortages, and by the time she was getting ready to leave, Molly's spirits had sunk quite low. The weather seemed an echo of her own state of mind – cold and gloomy. Like her marriage, perhaps. She thought back to the sunny days in Faversham and wondered whether that was to be their only glimpse of summer that year.

But she put on a bright face for Sally's departure, promising her daughter she would eat properly. She told her of her plan to visit Agnes, and Sally waited while Molly penned a hasty note for her to post. Unless she heard back by return, she wrote, she hoped Agnes would be able to meet her in Ramsgate off the ten o'clock stage coach from Margate on Wednesday.

Molly had never been to Ramsgate before. As she waved Sally on her way, she reflected that it was another adventure to be had in a life that was, of late, proving to be full of surprises.

CHAPTER FORTY-ONE

When Molly set out the following morning, it was chilly enough for her to need a warm woollen shawl, even though she wore her spencer tightly buttoned over her printed cotton dress. She looked anxiously at the leaden skies and hoped it wouldn't rain while she walked to the carrier's office in Margate, for the Ramsgate coach. She had imagined the brisk walk would warm her but she arrived pinched with cold and discovered the weather to be the main topic of conversation among those waiting at the office.

'Tis more like a winter's day than a summer's one,' grumbled one of the women waiting in line to buy a ticket. Molly nodded in agreement and hoped she would be able to purchase one to sit inside the coach. If not, she would have to wait for the next, an hour later, for she wasn't dressed warmly enough to consider sitting on top. Luck was with her, for she managed to buy the sixth and final ticket for an inside seat. The remaining tickets were sold to hardier, and more warmly clad, gentlemen.

Molly, squashed between a large lady and gentleman, was unable to take in much of the view as the coach creaked and rumbled out of Margate shortly after ten. It proceeded at a stately pace until it reached a straight road cutting across the fields, when the horses picked up speed to a smart trot.

The large lady wasted no time in asking, in a friendly enough fashion, why she was going to Ramsgate. Molly's reply that it was to see her daughter led to further questioning. When the lady asked whether her daughter was married and received the answer, no, she was an artist, she was temporarily silenced.

'An artist,' she repeated at last. Apparently unsure how to pursue this line of enquiry, she tried another. 'And do you live in Margate?' she asked.

Molly feared that before they reached Ramsgate, she would be exposed as the wife of Charles Dawson, who had been causing such a stir in town, so she replied, 'No, but I used to and my sisters still live there.' Then, to head off further questions, she decided to pose a few herself.

The lady was on her way to visit her own sister in Ramsgate, it transpired; they met once a month and dined at the Harbour Hotel, before she made the return journey later that day.

Molly's heart sank. Was she to suffer the same company on her return trip? For now, though, they were winding down the hill into the town, the sparkle of water in the harbour telling Molly that she would soon be relieved of the discomfort of being quizzed and crushed.

She was glad to step down from the coach, shake out her skirts and pat her bonnet back into shape. She had worn her second-best dress for the trip, keen to look as presentable as possible. Agnes had mentioned in one of her letters that Ramsgate was becoming quite fashionable and attracting a good many visitors from London.

She watched the large lady greet another of very similar girth, presumably her sister, and they walked away arm-in-arm up the hill.

Molly could see from the clock by the harbour they had arrived earlier than she had expected. She didn't like to move away from her position outside the carrier's office, where the coach had left them, but she felt conspicuous. Did it look as though she had been let down, that whoever was supposed to meet her had failed to appear? Just as she was starting to feel uncomfortable, she saw Agnes hurrying towards her.

'Ma, am I late? I'm so sorry. I was just leaving and Mrs Townley called me in to see her—' Agnes broke off, out of breath. Molly noticed that her attention had been caught by something or someone behind her.

'Isn't that Harriet?' Agnes asked. She looked puzzled. 'Did she come up on the coach with you?'

'Harriet?' Molly's heart contracted painfully and she swung around to find Harriet almost upon them. There was no time to draw Agnes away: they had been seen.

'Agnes, I thought it was you. And Molly. What a surprise. Are you visiting for the day?'

Molly could find no words but Agnes, unaware of any difficulty, was ready with information.

'I'm staying here for the summer, working for the architect Mary Townley. Have you heard of her?'

Agnes looked proud, Molly thought. She and Harriet conversed while Molly stood in silence, examining Harriet's appearance. Harriet was wearing a muslin gown rather too lightweight for the chill of the day, which was exacerbated by the breeze off the sea. There was a freshness about her and she had a lively air; she looked barely older than Agnes.

'Well, it was lovely to come across you, Agnes. We must be sure to meet up again. I plan to be here for a while.' This last was said with a glance at Molly, before Harriet moved on, taking one of the side streets leading away into the town.

214

'Are you all right, Ma?' Agnes looked concerned. 'You didn't say a word to Harriet and you're very pale. Was it the coach journey? Do you feel unwell?'

Molly found it hard to catch her breath. She felt as though her heart was being squeezed by an unseen hand and she wanted to sit down. Agnes, by now very anxious, took her arm and guided her to a row of benches facing the harbour. They were occupied by passengers waiting to board the stage to London, their bags around their feet. A gentleman obligingly stood up as soon as he saw Molly, white and tight-lipped, being supported by Agnes.

'Whatever is the matter, Ma?' Agnes reached for her mother's hand. 'You're cold. We should go somewhere warm indoors.'

Molly shook her head. She couldn't face the possibility of running into Harriet again, before she'd been able to share the reason for her anguish with Agnes. Speaking in low tones, so that Agnes had to bend forward to catch her words, she recounted the tale she had come to Ramsgate to share with her.

She told her how Hannah, Aunt Jane's cook, had recognised George as Nicholas's son, exposing the truth Molly had kept hidden for over twenty-five years. She told her daughter how George and Charlie had reacted badly to her having kept such a secret, how George had barred her from his house and only the kindness of Judith had allowed her to visit her grandson in secret. When she explained that Charlie had moved out, Molly thought Agnes was going to cry. When she went on to describe how Harriet had caused a minor scandal in Margate by her behaviour, dancing through the evening with Charlie at the ball and then walking with him by the sea, Agnes's tears were replaced by two high spots of colour on her cheeks.

'How could she?' she exclaimed. 'And then to stand here and talk to us as if nothing had happened. No wonder you couldn't speak. To think I thought you were being rude to her, your lost sister. She's nothing but a brazen hussy. I should find her and give her a piece of my mind.' Agnes looked about her, as if determined to set off that instant.

'No, no.' Molly seized Agnes's arm. 'It would do no good. She's shameless, I think.'

The two women lapsed into silence, then Molly began to shiver uncontrollably.

'Come on,' Agnes, said, standing up. 'There's a hotel not far from here where we can get you some brandy.'

Molly, already on her feet, pulled away from Agnes, shocked. 'We can't do that!'

'Do what? Go into a hotel bar?' Agnes laughed at her mother's expression. 'It's perfectly all right.'

Molly was still reluctant but Agnes steered her firmly along the busy street and across the road, then up the hill to Nelson's Terrace and a row of Georgian villas overlooking the sea. 'The Harbour Hotel' was painted in discreet letters above the door of one of the villas. Molly remembered, too late, that her companion from the coach journey was dining here with her sister. She had no wish to be drawn into further conversation with her but fortuitously it was the sister who was facing out into the dining room as they passed through it and beyond, to a snug table set into a window overlooking the sea.

Agnes seemed to know one or two of the staff, for they greeted her as they went by.

'Have you been here before?' Molly was bewildered.

'Mrs Townley likes to conduct meetings here sometimes,' Agnes answered. 'I've accompanied her and got to know the place. You can relax, Ma. It's perfectly all right for two unaccompanied ladies to be in a hotel like this, having a drink.'

The drinks arrived at the table as she spoke and Agnes encouraged her mother to take several sips. 'It's good for shock,' she said firmly.

Molly discovered that her daughter was right: her trembling stopped once the liquid began to warm her veins. They sat in silence and Molly took in her surroundings: the polished dark wood tables; rugs covering the floorboards; a fire burning in the grate; and glasses at the bar sparkling as they caught the light cast by the flames.

Then, gazing out over the harbour, Molly said, 'There's something else I need to tell you. George has a half-sister. She's called Margaret and she's living in Margate, and working there. She's Nicholas's daughter, from the West Indies.'

CHAPTER FORTY-TWO

Agnes stared at her mother in silence: Molly could see her struggling to comprehend this latest piece of news.

'So who is the mother of this Margaret?' she asked, finally.

'I'm not sure,' Molly admitted. 'She still lives in the West Indies. Margaret came here to work, at the Royal Sea Bathing Hospital. She discovered her link to the area quite by chance, when she mentioned Nicholas Goodchild to Harriet.'

'Does Aunt Jane know?' Agnes asked.

Molly sighed. 'She does. It has all been rather a shock.'

A waiter came over to enquire whether they would like to eat and Molly sat back while Agnes ordered. It was a relief to let someone else make the decisions. Agnes was very much at home in this situation and Molly began to wonder whether her own years in the country, bringing up her family, had left her unable to manage out in the wider world. Yet years ago she had journeyed to London and worked there when she was younger than Agnes. It was as if she was thinking of a different person: the Molly of those years was undaunted by hardships and adversity. Had she lost that adventurous spirit with the passage of time? Or had she just been naive in her youth?

Molly realised that Agnes was asking questions and she needed to pay heed.

'Ma, why have you kept all this from me? I haven't been at home, I know, but you never mentioned it in your letters.'

Molly wasn't entirely sure. She tried to explain her hope that the situation would resolve itself, that both George and Charlie would become less angry as time passed. Her sisters had encouraged her trip to Faversham, thinking Charlie would miss her. Instead, Harriet had stepped in, seemingly casting a spell over Charlie, and now it felt as though everything had got out of hand.

'I'm coming back with you,' Agnes said firmly. 'I'm going to talk to Pa. He needs to see that he's making a mistake over Harriet. And that it's silly for him and George to be upset over Nicholas. What difference does it make to either of them?' She sounded exasperated.

Molly was alarmed. She wasn't sure that Charlie, normally so easy-going, would take well to a lecture from Agnes. The arrival of the food at that moment put paid to further conversation. The delicious aroma of the chops made Molly realise just how hungry she was after her early start and they ate in silence at first, until Molly stopped to take a sip of the wine Agnes had ordered. She judged it a good time to turn the focus of the conversation onto her daughter and her work.

'Tell me more about your employer, Mrs Townley,' Molly said. 'I can't believe there can be many lady architects.' It had seemed odd enough to have a daughter who was an artist; to discover that she was working for a woman who designed houses and instructed others on how to build them was another thing entirely.

'I suppose she is unusual,' Agnes replied, 'but she is the loveliest lady you could hope to meet. She is well-connected – she knew the artist Sir Joshua Reynolds, and even royalty, I'm told – but you would never know it. She is so involved in her work and has plans to build a great hotel in Ramsgate, after her success with Townley House, which is much admired. I hope you will see it next time you come to visit. It's very grand. It has a curved frontage set with pillars and statues, and stands high on the edge of town, with views out over rooftops to the sea.'

Agnes frowned, her enthusiasm momentarily dimmed. 'But, of course, I forgot. I'm going to come back with you. After we have finished eating I must go and tell Mrs Townley and pack a bag so I can return with you on the coach.'

'No, it's not necessary.' Molly hoped she sounded firmer than she felt. She would love nothing more than for Agnes to come back and stay with her, to make the empty cottage feel more like a home once more. But she couldn't take her daughter away from doing something she so clearly loved: it was an opportunity that might never come her way again.

'In fact,' she said, struck by a sudden idea, 'it would be more sensible for you to stay here and keep an eye on Harriet. It can't be too hard to discover where she is living.' Molly's impression of Ramsgate was that it was smaller than Margate, with most of the housing huddled around the harbour. Since Agnes was so enterprising, she felt sure she would discover Harriet's lodgings easily enough.

'And you might keep an eye open for your father, too. I have a feeling he might make his way here on a Sunday.'

It hurt Molly a great deal to utter those words and the effect on Agnes was instant. She had just lifted a spoon to her lips, to taste the flummery that had replaced the chops on the table, but laid it down at once. 'He wouldn't do such a thing, surely.'

Molly hesitated. 'I'm not certain. I think perhaps he was

here last Sunday. He wasn't at George and Judith's house when Margaret visited and they seemed unsure where he had gone. And Harriet said she intended to be here for some time. She clearly isn't working. So could your father be . . .?' Molly couldn't finish the sentence.

'Keeping her, do you mean?' Agnes looked bewildered. 'Oh, Ma, has he gone mad? Why would he do such a thing? She's barely older than Sally, surely? You must be imagining it – he wouldn't, would he?'

They both stared at the dessert in the centre of the table, without speaking. Molly took up her spoon and tried to eat but she was struggling to hold back tears and her throat felt constricted. Seeing Harriet had brought home the awful truth of her situation.

A voice Molly recognised broke in on them.

'This must be your daughter. You didn't tell me you would be dining here, too.'

The large lady from the coach was beaming down on them. Her gaze took in the dessert, virtually untouched. 'Good heavens, you haven't eaten your flummery. My sister and I almost fought over the last mouthful. It's quite delicious – they are well known for their desserts here.'

She came to a halt and looked expectantly at Molly, who felt obliged to introduce her to Agnes as her companion from the coach journey, even though she couldn't offer her name.

'Mrs Eliza Basset,' the large lady supplied helpfully. 'And this is my sister, Mrs Thornhill.'

She beckoned to her sister, and Agnes and Molly contrived to make polite small-talk until Mrs Basset announced, to Molly's great relief, that she was due to take the next stage back to Margate and would have to hurry.

They parted, with Molly uttering insincere regrets that they wouldn't be able to share the journey home. Once the pair had left, it suddenly seemed very quiet.

Agnes raised her eyebrows. 'How did you cope with Mrs Basset all the way here? No wonder I thought you looked pale when I first caught sight of you.'

They both laughed and Molly was almost glad of the garrulous Mrs Basset and her sister: they had lifted the gloom that had settled between mother and daughter. They each managed a few spoonfuls of the flummery; hopefully sufficient to satisfy the cook when the plate returned to the kitchen.

'I still think I should return with you,' Agnes said, dabbing her mouth with a napkin.

'No, it really isn't necessary. You can write to me at once if you learn anything. You must stay and do your work with Mrs Townley, and I hope to be introduced to her on my next visit.'

It cost Molly a great deal to maintain this stance. Agnes's suggestion of returning with her had raised hope in her heart but it wasn't fair. She tried to contemplate the journey home with equanimity: the coach to Margate followed by a walk through the countryside to Woodchurch Manor. On what should have been a lovely summer's evening she would have enjoyed such a walk, but looking out of the window she could see that the sun had deserted them once more and the water in the harbour reflected the grey of the sky.

She and Agnes turned to safer topics, such as how Joseph and all her nieces and nephews were getting on. Agnes asked more questions about Margaret although Molly could tell her little other than that she thought she had a young man – Henry Sayer – a friend of Lewis.

'I need to come home soon,' Agnes said. 'Too much has been happening while I've been away.'

'Why don't you wait until the garden party, in August?' Molly said. 'You'll be able to see everyone there.'

She thought Agnes looked relieved. She was clearly torn between her love of what she was doing in Ramsgate and her wish to see her family.

'And you and Pa?' Agnes looked stricken. 'What will you do at the garden party? Mr Powell always thanks the pair of you in public.'

'I don't know,' Molly murmured. 'I really don't know. I suppose we will have to wait and see.'

PART FIVE

HARRIET

CHAPTER FORTY-THREE

I was smiling to myself all the way back to my room in Rose Hill after my encounter with Molly and her daughter. It was clear to me that Agnes knew nothing of the situation – she was friendliness itself and I think we might have been able to enjoy some pleasant times together in Ramsgate, if it wasn't for her mother. Molly didn't speak; she looked unwell, I thought.

I was tempted to ask after Charlie but thought better of it. I wasn't sure I would have been able to hold in my laughter. I was certain that I had seen him more recently than either his wife or his daughter.

My landlady, Mrs Garrett, was less than happy when she came across Charlie as he left my room on Sunday. He didn't acquit himself well – blushing and stammering – but I hope I put her at ease by introducing him as my elder brother, in town by chance but considering taking lodgings here for the summer.

Charlie looked positively bewildered and opened his mouth to demur but I was quick to step in.

'If he does, Mrs Garrett, I will of course move out to be with him but, in the meantime, I trust you will be happy enough for him to visit on a Sunday afternoon, when he can spare the time?'

She looked unconvinced, I must say, but I know the rent she charges me is too valuable to lose, since she was widowed last year, so she kept any displeasure to herself, nodded to us and went on down the stairs. She normally visited her sister after church on a Sunday: we were unlucky to have been caught out.

Today when I entered the hallway – a lovely part of the building which I much admired, light streaming in from the fanlight over the door, prints hung on the pale painted walls, quite the most elegant part of the house – she was clearly waiting for me. My heart sank as she stepped out from behind the parlour door as I set foot on the stairs.

'Miss Dixon.'

I turned, ready with a smile, hoping she hadn't had second thoughts and was about to ask me to leave.

'Your brother was here.'

I was taken aback. It was the middle of the week. Surely Charlie would be at work.

'Your other brother.' Mrs Garrett paused, her lips pursed. 'Quite a different kind of gentleman, if I may say so. He said his name was John Goodchild.'

I started, then recovered myself. I thought she would surely enquire why we went by different names, but she didn't.

'He said he would wait for you in the Boatman's Inn.' Her lips were now so pinched I was surprised she could speak. 'It's down towards the harbour in one of the passages off York Street, in case you aren't familiar with it.'

I had been in Ramsgate only a short time but I was already aware of which streets were best avoided by lone women, and this was one of them.

'Thank you,' I said. 'Quite a surprise. I haven't seen John in a long time and had no expectation of seeing him here. I will go in search of him at once.'

I stood, smiling, at the bottom of the stairs until she withdrew into her room, then I hurried up to mine, on the top floor. I was breathless when I opened the door, from the speed of my ascent and from agitation. What did John want with me? And how had he tracked me down? As far as I knew, only Charlie knew of my whereabouts. And Molly and Agnes, I supposed, although I hadn't given them my actual address.

I dismissed this line of thought with impatience. I was wasting time when I needed to focus on what to do about John. He'd be looking for money from me, doubtless. It made me angry to think of it, but I would have to part with some of my precious nest-egg in order to be rid of him. I had hidden my collection, wrapping it in a handkerchief placed inside the gloves I had worn to the ball, now tucked into my chest of drawers. I extracted a ring from the little parcel, choosing one that fitted nicely on my finger. I would slip it off as if it was my own when the time came to give it to John. It wouldn't do to let him suspect that there might be more where this came from.

I could delay no longer. I was sure that Mrs Garrett was poised behind her door, ready to come upstairs and chide me if I didn't make haste. She would be keen to avoid John reappearing on her doorstep. He looked disreputable at the best of times and since I assumed he'd only recently left Maidstone gaol, I didn't imagine his appearance had improved.

I was light on my feet – I was down the stairs, across the hall and out of the front door before Mrs Garrett could accost me again. I didn't glance back as I walked down Rose Hill towards the harbour and I made a point of looking as though I was in no great hurry, even though my heart was hammering in my breast.

I glanced down, admiring the ring on my finger. The stones sparkled as they caught a shaft of sunlight, causing me a pang of regret. It was hard to part with it, but I needed John gone. He would doubtless work his way quickly through whatever he got for it, spending the money on drink. Then he'd be back for more, and I needed to have left Ramsgate by then. I had hoped to move away in any case, once the wretched garden party was done with, so that Charlie and I could be together somewhere. I favoured London, or overseas. He envisaged staying in the area, foolishly imagining that in time his family would come to accept the situation and we would all be reconciled. I allowed him his dream – it didn't concern me over much. But my feckless brother couldn't be allowed to spoil my plans for the future.

CHAPTER FORTY-FOUR

I couldn't help but reel back as I entered the Boatman's Inn. A potent mix of tobacco, wood smoke, sweat and unwashed bodies assailed my nostrils. Although it was barely one o'clock it was dark inside, which I put down to the small windows and the layers of grime upon them. A fire burnt in the grate and the dog stretched in front of it wasn't the only one to look up at my entrance. It seemed I was to be the focus of attention of the whole inn.

I held my nerve and looked around the room, taking my time, although it was an effort to do so. I had never seen such a collection of men: unkempt in appearance with stubbled faces, caps pulled low, shoulders hunched over their drinks. Some gave me bold, insolent stares. Others looked, then half turned away, muttering. I was beginning to wonder how I was to find John when a figure detached himself from a group at the bar and stepped towards me.

'So, sister, you got my message.'

Imprisonment had not improved my brother. He appeared to have lost teeth and weight since I'd last seen him, and his hair was grizzled now, more grey than brown. He carried a tankard of ale, so he'd found money somewhere.

John followed my eyes. 'A drink for you? A nip of gin? Come and meet my friends.'

I shuddered. I wanted to be away from this place as soon as possible.

'When did you get out of gaol?' I demanded. 'And how did you know to find me here, in Ramsgate?'

'A fine welcome, sister, after so many months away.' John adopted a hurt expression. 'I've been free a week or more. I journeyed to find you in Margate, at the hospital where you worked. Your friend Margaret, a lovely lass, was kind enough to tell me you'd moved on and could be found here in this town, although she didn't know where.'

John cocked his head to one side and regarded me. 'A bit of trouble, was there, in Margate?'

'No,' I said shortly. 'I was ready for a change.' I cursed Margaret for her freedom in describing my whereabouts. 'How did you find my lodgings in Ramsgate?' I asked.

John shrugged. 'It's a small enough place. I asked around. People notice who's coming, who's going, who's staying. Especially those giving themselves airs and graces.'

I didn't like the sound of this. I'd felt secure here, unnoticed up until now. I had no wish to be the subject of gossip. 'Well, what do you want with me?' I asked, eager to get our reunion over with.

'Sister, sister, such a lack of warmth for your beloved brother.'

I could tell John was putting on a performance for the benefit of his new-found friends. They were clustered behind him, taking a keen interest in us both.

'If you've nothing to say, I'll take myself off.' I was irritated and wanted to be gone from that place before it contaminated me. I began to move away but John grabbed my arm, as I knew he would.

He drew me aside and whispered in my ear, 'Can you see

your way to letting me have a bob or two? I've come out of gaol with barely a farthing to my name.'

'You mean you've drunk away what you had,' I snapped. 'And this money you want me to lend you – when will I see it back?'

'Just as soon as I find work, I promise.' He sensed victory and had adopted a wheedling tone.

'And does that promise include repaying the previous loans?' I asked.

He pretended to be hurt. 'Harriet, am I not a good brother to you? Would I try to take advantage?'

There was little point in answering. I moved on to the next stage of our game.

'I don't have any money with me. And you can't come to my lodgings again. The landlady won't allow it.'

'I'd like to see her try to stop me. But you must have something about your person. A few coins, a trinket?' His eyes roved over me, searching for a necklace, a brooch. I was unadorned, except for the ring. I made a move, as if to clasp my hands to hide it. He spotted it at once and snatched my hand.

'Now here's a pretty thing! This will do very well.' He began to twist it on my finger in an attempt to slide it over my knuckle.

I made to pull my hand away. 'I can't let you have this,' I said. 'It's the only thing of value I own.'

'A present from your fancy man?' he sneered.

I gave him a sharp look. I wondered just how much information Margaret had given him.

'Don't talk nonsense,' I said, but John had taken the ring and palmed it before anyone around us could see. I suppose it must have appeared to onlookers that we were tussling over him holding my hand.

He stepped back. 'You can go, sister. I won't trouble you no more. You've been more than generous.'

I turned on my heel and made my exit with as much dignity as I could. I heard laughter behind me but I didn't care. I'd accomplished what I'd set out to do.

I had to move, I thought again, as I turned my steps towards my lodgings. Perhaps away from Ramsgate altogether, now that John was here. Unless—I stopped so suddenly, struck by a thought, that a couple walking behind me were forced to step into the roadway. I called an apology after them as I made an abrupt turn. I was no longer heading for Rose Hill and Mrs Garrett's house. Instead, I plunged into the warren of streets at the back of the harbour, not far from the Boatman's Inn.

When I'd got lost early in my stay in Ramsgate, I'd seen the sign for a pawnbroker somewhere around there, the three balls suspended above the door, their golden lustre well-polished.

The pawnbroker looked up as I opened the door. I saw him take in my appearance – a cut above his regular customer, perhaps, although I was sure that ladies of reasonable means, fallen into temporary difficulty, must have visited him on occasion.

'What can I help you with?' he asked. 'You have a piece of jewellery to leave with me, perhaps? Just until circumstances change.'

I smiled – it was exactly as I'd thought. He had me down as one of his temporarily distressed customers, unused to being in such an establishment, and was keen to put me at my ease.

'I'm here on behalf of the Royal Sea Bathing Hospital in Margate,' I replied. 'One of our patients has reported a ring stolen from her – wrenched from her finger, no less. I'm visiting businesses such as yours in the area to alert them, in case the ruffian brings it here to pawn. We think he won't try to do it too close to the scene of the crime.'

The pawnbroker, who had been frowning, nodded.

'She described him quite clearly,' I continued. 'She got a good look at him as he attacked her, poor lady.' I went on to give the man a description of John, and of the ring. 'If he should come here, I would be most grateful if you could keep him here on some pretence, and send word to the watch.'

I wasn't at all sure that the pawnbroker, who was a slight man, would be able to keep John on the premises but, as my dear brother had said, Ramsgate was a small place. Once he'd been caught in the act of trying to offload stolen goods, I was sure he would be found out quickly. And even if he got away, I reasoned he'd be unlikely to return to the area in the near future.

I'd considered telling the pawnbroker something nearer the truth: that the ring had been stolen from me. But then I'd anticipated the likely outcome. When John was apprehended, I'd be called upon to identify him and he'd insist that I'd given him the ring, a present from a loving sister.

Adding the Royal Sea Bathing Hospital to the tale gave it weight, I felt. It certainly seemed to work. The pawnbroker was nodding and tutting about the scoundrel who would do such a thing and promising to make sure he was apprehended and the ring returned to its rightful owner.

We parted on very good terms. I reflected sadly that I was never likely to see the sparkle of a ruby and diamonds on my finger again, but if it would rid me of the inconvenient problem of John, it was a small price to pay.

CHAPTER FORTY-FIVE

I walked back to my lodgings feeling very pleased with myself. If I'd known then what my new-found relative Margaret was about just a few miles away, I might have felt less happy. As it was, I had Sunday and a visit from Charlie to look forward to. I smiled to myself, imagining how distracted he must have been as he worked in the gardens at Woodchurch Manor during that week. We had enjoyed a very pleasant interlude in my room the previous Sunday, although I'd stopped short of being too obliging. I was no fool. Charlie would have to wait for me until we were living together, man and wife as far as anyone else was concerned. In the meantime, there was no harm in teasing him with promises of the delights in store. Men were such fools. Did they really believe much younger women would happily tie themselves to them, all for the sake of love? It was a business transaction, like any other: for protection, for wealth, for security, for companionship. Rarely for love.

It was unfortunate, I suppose, that I'd been attracted to Charlie from the moment I saw him, before I discovered who he was. I needed to be careful: I'd found it too easy to enjoy my time with him, giddy and flushed by his attentions. Which worked to my advantage, of course. As long as he believed me as infatuated with him as he was with me, and as long as I kept a cool head, then all would be well. Molly's family would have reason to rue the day they had allowed my mother to take me from them, without speaking out against it.

I turned my mind to how best to entertain Charlie on his next visit. Mrs Garrett would undoubtedly be on guard and we would find it impossible to spend time in my room. If only the weather might be relied upon, we could find a sheltered spot somewhere along the cliffs to enjoy ourselves. This summer, though, was the worst I could remember. A hint of spring had been replaced by cold winds and regular showers. It felt as though we had moved from spring to autumn and forgotten to have summer at all.

There was no change in the weather by the time Sunday arrived. Mrs Garrett, as expected, had declared her intention of spending the afternoon at home, giving me quite a look as she made her announcement. So, I met Charlie by the harbour as planned and we took the coastal path northwards. Before too long, we both regretted it. The wind driving in off the sea and the leaden skies did nothing to raise our spirits. I began to shiver uncontrollably after we had been out for less than half an hour. I'd foolishly dressed to impress Charlie, in a light gown more suited to a true summer's day.

'We should turn back,' Charlie said, taking my hands in his and rubbing them to restore some warmth. I was touched by his concern, but also aware that few places would be open to us on a Sunday afternoon, when good folk were expected to be at home.

'Perhaps it would be more sheltered on the sand,' I said, trying to sound more hopeful than I felt.

We descended the steep path down to shore level and, at first, I thought there would be no respite from the elements. But the curve of the bay provided a spot in the lee of the cliff, tucked behind fallen boulders, where the wind didn't penetrate. We perched on the lowest of the boulders and I snuggled into Charlie's shoulder. My spirits had dipped: how long was I prepared to endure this situation? I had waited all week for the chance to spend a few hours with Charlie, only to find him morose and the weather matching his mood.

'Will you tell me what's wrong?' I asked, after several minutes' silence. He'd been monosyllabic on our walk and I'd put it down to the disappointment of being unable to spend time in my room, combined with having to endure this unpleasant weather.

He sighed. 'I think the garden party must be cancelled, or at least postponed.'

I almost laughed. I'd begun to suspect he was about to tell me that he could no longer see me, that he had reconciled with Molly. I waited for him to go on.

'There's not been a summer like this in my memory. It's hardly worthy of the name. The flowers are almost a season behind – they're struggling to open their blooms and who can blame them?' Charlie gestured to the grey skies. 'How often have we seen the sun this year? Hardly ever in the past month or so – just a glimmer here and there, barely enough to warm the earth. I've told Mr Powell we should call the whole thing off, but he's determined it will happen. He likes to invite friends down from London and he doesn't want to disappoint. So we've decided between us that it will take place at the end of August, now. Maybe the sun will decide to come out before then.'

He stared gloomily at the sky and my spirits sank even lower. I had been prepared to indulge Charlie's love of his work and all the garden talk that went with it. After all, I'd believed the garden party to be just over a month away, and once it was done, we could get on with our plans for a new life. Now, it looked as though there would be a further delay. And Charlie would be distracted and worried for all that time.

If only we'd been able to enjoy the comforts of my room in Rose Hill, I'm sure I would have been able to cajole Charlie out of his low mood. Here, in the open air under chilly grey skies, it was hard to feel any enthusiasm for romance. Nevertheless, I tried to kiss away the frown on Charlie's brow, caressing his face in the hope he would turn to me and forget his woes. He submitted for a while and did kiss me, but it was half-hearted, lacking any of the ardour he'd previously shown. I pulled away, offended.

'I'm sorry, Harriet,' he said. 'I'm not good company. I'm too taken up with worries. I shouldn't have come.'

I was at once alert to his words. 'Taken up with worries' – did he mean over the wretched garden party, or was there more? I wanted to ask about Molly, but couldn't think how to begin. Then he spoke abruptly.

'Margaret and George seem to have taken to each other. She visits George and Judith whenever she has time off.'

'That must be a good thing, surely, so they can get to know each other better?' I was impatient. I had no wish to waste time talking about anyone other than ourselves.

'Was she – is she a good friend of yours? Margaret, I mean?'

I was suddenly alert: had Margaret been gossiping about me? Charlie's expression was hard to read.

'Well . . .' I measured my words carefully '. . . I wouldn't say we were close. We worked together and I admired her skill with the patients.' I had decided to be generous. 'And I was pleased to be able to reunite her with her family, of course.' It didn't hurt to remind Charlie of her debt to me.

Charlie just nodded, then suggested we return to Ramsgate, for the sky had grown ever darker and now there was a real possibility of rain. I tried hard to think of light-hearted topics to discuss with Charlie on the walk back but my thoughts were pulled hither and thither. Was Margaret poisoning George's mind against me? If so, had George spoken to Charlie about it? They worked together every day, after all.

I was also conscious that my chance to bind Charlie ever closer to me – a precious once-a-week occurrence – was slipping through my fingers. Once we were back in Ramsgate we would have to avoid any displays of affection or risk causing offence.

I took his arm and pulled him close as we approached the town, but there was no answering response. His body was unyielding and, after a few steps, I relinquished my grip, annoyed.

As we descended towards the harbour, he stopped abruptly and turned towards me, his expression serious. 'I'm sorry, Harriet,' he began.

My heart skipped several beats and then began to race.

'I realise I've been poor company,' he went on. 'Can you forgive me? I promise I'll try harder next week.'

I looked at him, noting how the colour had faded from his cheeks, to be replaced by an unhealthy pallor with dark smudges beneath his eyes. He looked older than when I'd first met him.

'Of course,' I said. Despite my disappointment over the ruined day, a consequence of Charlie's mood and my landlady's stubborn refusal to leave the house, I waved him off, smiling prettily. As I walked back towards Rose Hill, I wondered how many more Sundays like this I could endure.

CHAPTER FORTY-SIX

I was feeling more than a little peevish as I returned to the house, and I was less than pleased to come across Mrs Garrett in the hallway when I let myself in. She had been hovering in the parlour, no doubt, waiting to hear my key in the lock. I scowled, expecting her to be triumphant that she had ruined my afternoon with Charlie by barring us from the house.

I was taken aback when she exclaimed, 'My dear, you look half frozen. You must come in and warm yourself – I've had a fire lit in the parlour to take the chill off this miserable afternoon.'

I was inclined to refuse but she drew me into the room and bade me sit by the fire, then stood over me, brow creased into a worried frown. I was puzzled by her concern but, after a moment or two, I realised I was shivering despite the heat from the fire.

'I think a nip of brandy might be beneficial,' Mrs Garrett said. 'I fear you have taken a chill, Miss Dixon.'

She rang the bell for Martha, the young girl who was a maid of all work. I listened to the rain lashing against the window pane and was grateful to have arrived back in time to escape a soaking, the thought of which set me shivering all over again.

Mrs Garrett administered the brandy, instructing me to take small sips. I would have preferred to be rid of it in a couple of gulps, having no liking for it, but I couldn't find it in myself to argue. After a quarter of an hour, during which I rested by the fire while Mrs Garrett took up her needle-work, glancing at me occasionally, I felt quite restored.

'I think I'll go up to my room,' I said, preparing to rise. 'You have been most kind. I mustn't take up any more of your afternoon.'

'Please rest a little longer,' Mrs Garrett said. 'I've asked the girl to light the fire in your room and to put a warming pan in your bed. I would welcome your company: Sundays are particularly lonely since my husband died. I try to see my sister whenever I can, but she was unwell today.'

My attention was caught by her last words. Perhaps she would go out to see her sister as usual the following Sunday, and I would be free to entertain Charlie at Rose Hill. I immediately began to feel better. It would do no harm to please the old lady by sitting at her fireside and conversing with her. In fact, it might well further my cause.

So, as afternoon faded into an evening prematurely dark as the rain beat down, I sat and talked with Mrs Garrett while the maid came in, stoked the fire and lit the lamps.

I'd intended to be careful in what I revealed about myself, for I was quite sure that my landlady was more interested in finding out about me than I was in knowing more of her. Perhaps the brandy loosened my tongue, or maybe it was the strangeness of my circumstances: sitting by the fire in a lady's parlour wasn't something I had experienced in many years. I found myself telling Mrs Garrett about my past and about my mother, who had moved us away from Margate into the depths of the countryside, only to abandon us there. I told her how I'd cared for my grandfather and how, after he'd died, I'd been taken on as a companion by a young lady who lived nearby in a crumbling manor house that had half terrified me. I'd been barely fifteen and thought myself grown-up until that point, but the house was filled with dark panelling, ill-fitting doors and shutters that creaked in the wind – a constant presence since it was set on a hill – and I became quite convinced that ghosts walked the floors at night.

I was only at ease in the library, the room where my mistress – Miss Freeman – spent most of her days. It had a fire that was kept alight all day, summer and winter, and it was the only warm room in the house, apart from the kitchen. The walls were lined from floor to ceiling with books: leather-bound volumes with tooled spines. They might just as well have been yet more panelling for all the interest they held for me. The wall over the fireplace was home to a portrait of a man of middle years, with a stern face and eyes that were always upon you, no matter where you were in the room. I learnt that he was Miss Freeman's father, who had died in his early fifties, bequeathing the house to her.

When I asked about her mother, she told me she couldn't remember her. She had died when Miss Freeman was barely two, while giving birth to her younger brother. The boy had outlived his mother by just a few hours and Miss Freeman had lived there with a father who barely acknowledged her presence throughout the next twenty years until he, too, died.

I could barely comprehend how lonely she must have been. I thought my childhood years were difficult, but to be closeted here, on this hill, with no company other than the servants must have been hard indeed.

I asked Miss Freeman whether she liked to walk, or perhaps ride, wondering how she had occupied herself through all the days. There was no evidence of the house being adorned by needlework – tapestries and the like – or flower paintings or even a piano, usually considered a necessity to while away the hours in a wealthy household.

She laughed and said, 'I spend little time outside. A walk around the gardens each day is enough for me.' She gestured to the walls of the room. 'Exploring the worlds within these pages takes me further beyond the confines of this house than I could ever hope to travel.'

And so Miss Freeman introduced me to a world that had been unknown to me until then. I could barely read and I confess I had adopted the plain speaking of my grandfather, with his country ways. Miss Freeman gave over her days to coaching me in my speech and giving me lessons. I was aware that I was hardly a companion to her; in effect, she was paying me as well as acting as my governess. When I raised this with her, awkwardly, one afternoon she laughed and said I was not to give it another thought, that she couldn't have been happier. I had given her a purpose in life, she said, and she woke each day full of plans for what we might do, all previous gloomy thoughts banished.

We went on like this for two years, but I should have known it couldn't last. That spring, our lives were to change for ever.

I had been gazing into the fire, lost in thought, throughout most of my tale. I looked up at this point and had to hide a smile. Mrs Garrett was transfixed. I stretched and yawned.

'But I have taken too much of your time. I must leave you to your supper.'

I saw that the maid had appeared and was waiting in the doorway.

'Martha, lay another place at the table,' Mrs Garrett said. 'Miss Dixon will dine with me tonight.' She turned to me. 'I hope I'm not being presumptuous? I can't let you go until I've heard the rest of your story.'

Chapter Forty-Seven

We moved through to the dining room, plainly furnished and not grand, but with the fire lit and the curtains closed against the rain it felt very welcoming. Mrs Garrett had dined earlier in the afternoon but I had missed a meal in favour of a walk with Charlie and now I found myself ravenous. It was an effort to restrain myself and not fall upon the array of cold meats and cheeses laid out on the sideboard.

Mrs Garrett, perhaps aware of this, suggested we pause the story to allow me to eat. She herself took only a few mouthfuls of her soup and touched little of the remaining spread. Her cook must have despaired of her efforts, I thought, if this scene was repeated each evening. I spooned up my soup more daintily than I might otherwise have done, and tried not to overload my plate. I could certainly have done far greater justice to the supper but, with Mrs Garrett waiting politely, it seemed rude to continue eating. So, regretfully, I began my tale again as Martha cleared away the plates.

'Miss Freeman received a visit from a distant cousin, Mr Malpas, in the summer of my eighteenth year. He was a good deal older than she was and there seemed nothing untoward in his visit. It was only natural that the family might feel concerned about Miss Freeman living alone in this remote spot and want to make sure that she was well cared for there.

Miss Freeman – whom by then I called by her Christian name, Rebecca – asked me to make sure that I spent as much time with her as I had before her visitor arrived. Although we were unable to continue our lessons, I sat with the pair in the library, took every meal with them and accompanied them on walks.

'One day, when the weather threatened rain, I was keen to stay in the library and continue reading a book I had discovered there, a novel, *Pamela*, by Samuel Richardson. Despite the weather, Mr Malpas was most insistent that Miss Freeman accompanied him on a walk as usual. For the first time I excused myself, pleading a headache.

'"Then a walk in the fresh air would do you good," Miss Freeman declared. I ignored her pleading look: Mr Malpas liked nothing better than the sound of his own voice and I had already made up my mind that an hour spent in the company of *Pamela* was far preferable. He was Rebecca's relative, after all: I had endured enough.

'I was lost in my reading and didn't hear them return, so I was startled and not a little annoyed when the library door was thrown open. They had surely been gone less than an hour. Mr Malpas came into the room, Rebecca trailing a few steps behind him. She was flushed and her eyes were downcast.

'"Well, Miss Dixon, you must congratulate us. Miss Freeman – Rebecca – has agreed to do me the honour of being my wife."

'I could barely have been more surprised than if Pamela herself had stepped from the pages of the novel and come into the library. The book slid off my lap onto the floor and I suppose I must have looked very foolish, my mouth agape in surprise, for Mr Malpas laughed and seized Rebecca's arm.

'"We have succeeded in shocking your little friend, my dear."

'I looked from one to the other. Mr Malpas, triumphant, with sparkling eyes; his prize, Miss Freeman, subdued and close to tears. I had had no inkling that she had feelings for him, this man who had so disrupted the harmony of our life with his pompous manner and determination to spend every moment of the day with us.

'At that moment, it dawned on me. The idyll of the last two years was over. There would be no place for me in the life of the new Mr and Mrs Malpas. It was only at the end of the week, when Mr Malpas had returned to London to deal with his business affairs, that Rebecca revealed to me the true nature of her betrothal.

'It had taken me that long to be able to offer her hesitant congratulations, once we'd waved Mr Malpas away in his carriage. The look she turned on me was full of bitterness.

'"There's nothing to congratulate me for, Harriet. I envy you. You are free to make your own way in the world, while I must play the part of loving wife to a man I can barely tolerate."

'I stared at her in astonishment, so that she shook her head and said, "All your book learning hasn't prepared you for the ways of the world, Harriet. Mr Malpas has status, but is short of funds for his business. I have money, but no one to protect me and my inheritance. It's my money Mr Malpas wants, not me."

'"Surely your money is your protection," I protested. "You can refuse Mr Malpas and carry on as you are, living here with me as your companion." I held on to a glimmer of hope that our life could go on as before.

'"No, Harriet. It won't be long before I can't manage here on my own. The house is crumbling, although the land has

248

value. I'm already of an age to be considered an old maid and I'm unlikely to find a husband for love. Mr Malpas needs a wife to help take care of his children, now that their mother is dead. I can't, in all honesty, refuse him."

'My head was still full of the novel I had so recently finished. "But Pamela . . ." I protested.

'Rebecca laughed. "That's a novel, Harriet, not real life."

'I knew that, I suppose. Marriage was a transaction: I'd learnt that at my mother's knee. Why had I thought it would be any different for Rebecca? Mr Malpas wanted Rebecca for practical reasons only. She would become a figurehead but in return she would have a house in London, fine clothes, society to mix in.

'"I will take the library with me to London, of course," she said.

'With these words I saw my world begin to change before my eyes. Rebecca had already made that leap, resigning herself to the course she must follow. I would have to make new plans for myself, sooner rather than later.'

I stopped to take a drink from my glass of cordial, my mouth parched from talking, my throat dry.

Mrs Garrett spoke. 'I must take issue with you, Miss Dixon. Marriage is not always a transaction. My own, with dear Mr Garrett, was a love match from the start. We met here in Ramsgate when I was just nineteen and he was a lowly seaman in the Royal Navy. He rose through the ranks to become captain on his ship and our fortunes rose with him. We were able to buy this lovely house shortly before he was lost at sea when his ship went down.' Her eyes filled with tears. 'We spent scarcely a year living here together. I can't bear to part with the house for it reminds me of him – all the rooms that we planned, the decisions we made. Every day I see him here, sitting across from me in the parlour in his chair, or at the table where you are now.'

I shivered at her words, less from imagining Mr Garrett's presence in the room, more from the realisation that I had begun to feel quite ill. My head ached and my throat was burning, and I couldn't begin to argue with Mrs Garrett. Instead, I thanked her for her kindness that afternoon, and for supper, and begged to be excused so I could go upstairs.

There, I fell into bed, blissfully warm due to the fire in the grate and the bed-warmer placed between the sheets, only to wake shivering a few hours later. For the rest of the night I was racked with fever. One minute I shook as though with the ague and couldn't warm myself, before falling into a restless sleep, only to wake and fling off my blankets as heat coursed through my body. I was glad to see the dawn and be rid of the demons that rode through my mind that night, torturing me with half-remembered moments from my past, all twisted into new, terrifyingly real scenarios.

It took me most of the following week to recover my wits and my strength, so when Charlie's visit was due, the following Sunday, I was still not myself.

Chapter Forty-Eight

Mrs Garrett had continued her kindness during the week, sending Martha up at regular intervals to check how I was. Sometimes she came bearing broth or hot chocolate or whatever Mrs Garrett thought might tempt my appetite or aid my recovery; always she came with a scowl.

I had the impression that, laid up in bed with all my defences stripped away, it was only too clear what and who I was. Martha could see right through me. As the week passed and I began to regain my strength, being well enough to get up and with no need of Martha's services, I tried to shake off this idea as a fanciful notion. But it never quite left me and I became wary of her.

When Sunday came, Mrs Garrett was insistent that I should make use of her parlour for Charlie's visit. 'You're not well enough to be out walking yet, even if the weather has improved a little.' We had met in the hallway. I was dressed to go out but in truth the effort had already exhausted me. I followed the line of her gaze through the window, where the sky was grey and a light drizzle was falling. 'I can send Martha to meet your brother and bring him back here. I'm going to visit my sister so you will have plenty of time to catch up on all his news.'

I didn't like the idea of Martha accompanying Charlie to the house, even though I wasn't sure I had the strength to walk to our regular meeting place by the harbour and back again.

'Thank you, Mrs Garrett, but I think some fresh air would do me good. I believe you are right, though, and I am not strong enough for a long walk in Ramsgate today. I am very grateful for your kind offer of the use of your parlour.'

I set off full of determination but I was already fatigued by the time I reached the harbour. Charlie was late, or perhaps I was early: either way, I was glad to sit on a bench, despite the drizzle. The sea had a gloomy, restless air, the waves rolling and roiling and never quite breaking. Charlie's voice in my ear broke into my contemplation and startled me.

'A penny for them, Harriet.'

I stood up swiftly and at once felt giddy so that I staggered. Charlie reached out and caught my arm.

'Harriet. Are you unwell?'

I could see the concern in his eyes. I suppose I must have lost weight during my week of illness. I was certainly aware that my dress seemed ill-fitting and my face had appeared deathly pale in the glass in the hall before I set out.

'I've been ill all week, Charlie,' I said. What I had intended as an answer to his question somehow came out as an accusation and a frown crossed his face.

'We can spend the afternoon at Rose Hill,' I said. 'Mrs Garrett has kindly loaned us the parlour while she visits her sister.'

I took his arm and we made slow progress up the hill to my lodgings. I told him a little more about how unwell I had been following our walk the previous Sunday; how kind Mrs Garrett had been. I realised I was irritated with Charlie, resentful, even. We had had no means of communicating all week and as usual I had had to bear the burden of deciding what to do that Sunday, as every Sunday.

'You should have written and put off my visit,' he said eventually.

'Oh, and where would I write?' I asked.

We'd reached the front door and I opened it, stepping in to see Martha at the end of the hallway. She gave me what I took to be an insolent look before descending the steps to the kitchen. Charlie was hesitating at the door with an expression on his face that made me think he was about to turn and leave. I reached out and put my hand on his arm.

'Let us not quarrel. I'm only peevish because I've been unwell. We shall sit down and I can rest while you tell me about your week.'

My attempt to resolve the chilliness that had developed between us didn't turn out as I had hoped. Charlie took up my invitation, and over the course of the next hour he regaled me with tales of woe about the wretched garden at Woodchurch Manor, in particular why this plant and that would never be in flower in time for the garden party. It was still six weeks away and I couldn't see why he was so worried.

Mrs Garrett had told me to ring for refreshments, but I had vowed not to do so, having developed such a dislike of Martha. I became so wearied hearing of Charlie's trials and tribulations that I was forced to break my resolve and reach for the bell-pull. When Martha appeared, I asked her to fetch lemonade and a glass of ale. I'd never commanded servants before, having usually played that role myself, but I thought I'd managed it well enough.

Martha, though, was less concerned with me than with Charlie. She was staring at him, while we both looked at her and wondered why she was delaying.

'Begging your pardon, sir,' she said to Charlie, 'but aren't you Mr Dawson? The head gardener at Woodchurch Manor?'

'Yes, I am,' Charlie said, ignoring my glare. 'And you are . . .?' He was regarding her, puzzled.

'I'm Martha, William Cobb's daughter. I used to play in the garden when I was little, when the Powells were away.' She gave a little bob and a nod and left the room, casting a glance in my direction as she left.

It was too late to tell Charlie that he should have denied his name. Martha was now in possession of a valuable piece of information. My gentleman visitor was not my brother at all.

'Who is William Cobb?' I demanded, as soon as the door closed behind her.

'He's one of my gardeners. He's worked with me almost as long as I've been at Woodchurch Manor,' Charlie said. He was oblivious to the damage his truthfulness had done so I enlightened him. Our afternoon had got off to a bad start, due to my ill-health and my irritation with Charlie. Now we were both thrown into gloom by the recognition of what Martha's revelation meant.

She came back into a silent room. I was trying to work out whether I could still pretend that Charlie was my brother. We were related, of course, although the difference in name presented a problem. But she would surely have access to too many facts about Charlie's life to make our pretence sustainable. Even if we could maintain it, why would he be visiting me here every Sunday? Why wasn't I travelling to be with him and his family?

Martha set down the drinks, gave me a small smile and went out, closing the door behind her.

Chapter Forty-Nine

It had been another wasted afternoon, I reflected, once Charlie had left – earlier than usual for we had been unable to move on from the unfortunate incident with Martha. I was preoccupied, trying to decide how best to resolve things so that she wouldn't tell Mrs Garrett. My time in Ramsgate was limited, since Charlie had confirmed that the garden party would take place on 31 August. I would prefer to stay in my lodgings until then, which meant I needed to find a way to keep Martha quiet. Appealing to her better nature would have no effect, I was sure. It would take money to persuade her to keep her mouth shut. I would have to pay another visit to the pawnbroker.

Charlie had been lost in his own thoughts, too, although I'm sure these concerned his beloved gardens. So when he left, I was unprepared for what he blurted out on the doorstep.

'Perhaps we should leave off meeting until the garden party has passed.'

I stared at him in shock – was this what had filled his thoughts during the remainder of his visit? I had never intended that we should spend our time together in my room, as we had done only two weeks before, although it felt like much longer than that. I was still not myself following my illness, and it would have felt like an abuse of Mrs Garrett's kindness.

'No!' I protested. 'I'm sorry about today. I'm still feeling weak after being unwell. And then Martha . . .' My mind was racing. If Charlie and I were apart for the next six weeks, I was quite sure I would fade from his memory. All my efforts would have been wasted, my plans ruined.

'I'll wait for you down by the harbour next Sunday, as usual. We'll find a way to enjoy ourselves,' I said. I filled my words with as much meaning as I could, slipping my hand into Charlie's as I spoke and gazing deep into his eyes until he flushed and looked away.

'I can't promise anything,' he said, and turned to go.

'I'll be waiting for you,' I said, keeping my tone as light as possible. My head was spinning. Did he mean he couldn't promise to be there? Or that he couldn't promise anything for our future together?

I watched him walk away down the road. He didn't turn to look back, so I mounted the stairs to my room with a heavy heart. I had to come up with a plan to draw Charlie back to me. And somehow to solve the problem of Martha. Despite my worries, I was seized by a great weariness and, within five minutes of being back in my room, I was asleep on the bed.

I was dimly aware of Mrs Garrett coming in to see me later that evening, when it was nearly dark. She tutted a bit, then tried to persuade me out of my clothes and into a nightgown. But I was resistant so she pulled the coverlet over me and left.

I woke the next morning with the birds. The room was bright – for once the sun was shining – and my spirits lifted. It was only temporary, though: they took a dive when I recalled the events of the previous afternoon. Then, as I began to make plans, they rose again and I lay with the coverlet pulled up to my chin, hiding the smile on my face.

I rested a while longer but I knew I felt better. The long sleep had restored me. I was unhappy that I had slept in my clothes – my dress would be in a sorry state – and I needed to get up and wash. That meant descending to the kitchen to ask Martha to bring water up earlier than usual. When she did, it would be a good opportunity to tell her how I planned to buy her silence, although of course I wouldn't put it quite like that.

The room had an early-morning chill, quite usual that summer, but I forced myself to rise and undress, getting into my nightgown. Martha glanced up as I entered the kitchen. She was on her knees, raking the ash out of the range. She looked surprised: it was unusual for anyone other than herself to be up so early.

'Could you bring up a jug of hot water?' I asked. 'And I think we need to have a talk.' I was brisk, determined to gain the upper hand. I wanted to remind her of her role in the house and to make her wonder what I was going to say. I left the room while she still knelt on the floor.

She appeared in my room fifteen minutes later, bearing a steaming ewer of water. She set it down on the washstand and gave me a look – of defiance, I suspected.

'Now, Martha,' I said, 'we both know that Mr Dawson isn't my brother. And that it isn't in my best interests for this to come to Mrs Garrett's attention. However, I wouldn't like Mrs Garrett to discover that a pair of her favourite pearl earrings has somehow found their way into your possession.'

I held up my hand as Martha began to protest.

'You work very hard in this house and Mrs Garrett values your services. You wouldn't want to give her cause to dismiss you. It would be hard, if not impossible, to find another position like this if you left here with a bad character.' I paused to let my words sink in.

'So, I propose instead that I make you a little gift. I will be here for just a few more weeks and I would like to remain as comfortable as I was before.' I hoped that my meaning was clear. 'I'm going to give you a little money. And, provided you remain discreet, there will be another gift for you when I leave.'

Martha's expression had changed. The defiance had gone, to be replaced by eagerness. She left the room with my promise to have the money for her by midday. I felt sure I had solved both my problems at the same time. I would be able to entertain Charlie the following Sunday as I wished. I could almost feel the pressure of his lips on mine as I devoted myself to washing and dressing.

I was out of the house by nine o'clock, hopeful that I would find the pawnbroker already open. He was just taking down the shutters as I approached his shop.

'I recognise you,' he said. 'The lady who reported the stolen ring. We got him, you'll be pleased to hear.'

'You did?' My plan to rid myself of John had gone quite out of my mind.

'Yes, he came in later that very same day, after you'd left. He'd spent the afternoon in the inn, I'd wager. Stinking of ale, he was, and barely able to walk in a straight line. He wasn't in a fit state to run away. We had him in front of the magistrate before he could come up with a decent explanation of how he came by such a piece of jewellery.'

'And where is he now?' I asked, as casually as I could.

'Maidstone gaol, I expect,' the pawnbroker replied. 'Not for long, though. It'll either be the gallows for him or a ship to New South Wales. I heard from the magistrate that this isn't the first time he's been caught thieving.'

I wondered what would happen when they approached the Royal Sea Bathing Hospital to return the missing ring.

Would they have to let him go when it became apparent they hadn't reported it? Or would he already be on the way to the other side of the world? I preferred to follow that line of thinking. I didn't like to consider that I might have sent my brother to the gallows.

The pawnbroker had finished with his shutters and realised, as I loitered still, that I wasn't a chance passer-by.

'Is there something I can help you with?' he enquired.

'There is,' I replied. 'I find myself waiting for my allowance to arrive from my dear father, and meanwhile the rent is due on my lodgings. I don't like to ask my landlady to wait, and it occurred to me after my visit here the other day that I could use this piece of jewellery to see me through my difficulties.' I fumbled in a little velvet bag that I carried at my wrist. 'I would never have thought of doing such a thing before.'

I glanced at him from under my lashes. I thought he seemed a little sceptical; perhaps I'd overdone my explanation. But his professional attention was caught by the drop earrings that I pulled from the bag.

'They belonged to my dear mother,' I said.

The earrings had tiny rubies set at either side of a central opal: not a fashionable design but then their previous owner, a patient at the Royal Sea Bathing Hospital, was in her sixties.

The pawnbroker went briskly to business: we had agreed a sum within five minutes; I was out of the shop with the money and my receipt within ten. I was glad to walk back by the harbour and enjoy the sunshine while it lasted. Clouds gathering out at sea told me the day would spoil itself before too long, but for now all was well with the world.

CHAPTER FIFTY

When I returned to Rose Hill, I went up to my room and laid the dress I had slept in on the bed, placing a pile of shillings beneath it. I put the crowns away with my secret hoard of jewellery and went downstairs to find Martha.

'I've left a dress on my bed – would you collect it and press it? It's very creased.'

She gave me an indignant look and I noticed Cook glance up from her work in the corner of the kitchen.

I murmured in a low voice, 'You'll find something else there, as arranged.' Then I turned to leave, saying in a more normal tone, for the benefit of Cook, 'I'd very much appreciate it.'

I had no wish to be in my room when Martha went up, and I was anxious to avoid Mrs Garrett and her inevitable questions about my afternoon with my brother. I was planning to abuse her good nature the following Sunday and I needed time to prepare my thoughts. I set out again from the house, but I'd failed to take my state of health into account. My mind was busy and impatient but, despite waking feeling refreshed after my sleep, I soon discovered that my vitality was low. I had to sit down as soon as I reached the harbour, and even after resting there, it cost me a great deal of effort to return to the house. It seemed unwise to stay out any longer: after half an hour the clouds were encroaching on the sun and the temperature was dropping.

Back at Rose Hill, I had to stand in the hall for a moment or two, daunted by the number of stairs I had to climb to reach my room. Mrs Garrett must have been listening out for me and she appeared in the hallway. Her smile was quickly replaced by concern. 'My dear Harriet, you are as white as sheet. Come in, come in and sit down.'

I was in no mood to be interrogated about the previous afternoon, but neither was I capable of shaking her off in my weakened state so I had meekly to submit. She let me sit in silence for a good few minutes, offering me brandy, which I refused. Finally, I felt recovered enough to make my excuses and go upstairs but first I knew her curiosity must be satisfied.

'Thank you for allowing me the use of your parlour yesterday,' I began.

Mrs Garrett held up her hand as if to dismiss my thanks, but I continued, 'We had a pleasant afternoon but my brother was worried by some business concerns. And I found I tired quickly. As soon as he left I fell asleep upstairs – I think you must have come in and covered me?' I looked at Mrs Garrett with a smile, my eyebrows raised.

She nodded, and I continued, 'I slept so well and for so long that I felt fully recovered this morning. Alas, it was an illusion so please forgive me. I fear I must go upstairs and rest.'

'You have been out twice already this morning,' Mrs Garrett scolded. 'You are still recovering and you should be careful for a few more days yet. I will send Martha to your room with a bowl of broth.'

I stood up, thanking her, although I would have preferred to manage without any further interactions with Martha.

'I wonder, may I borrow a book or two from your library?' I asked. I could see that Mrs Garrett would be watching me that week, determined to keep me at home. If I was to be back to my normal self in time for Charlie's visit I must submit, but I would go quite mad if I had nothing with which to occupy myself.

'I'll send something up with the broth,' Mrs Garrett said. She looked pleased at my request.

My enforced rest passed more pleasurably than I had expected. I was reminded of my days spent living with Rebecca, in the days before Mr Malpas arrived. I read morning and afternoon and would have continued into the evening if my eyes had allowed it. They were tired by then, though, and the words danced on the page in the lamplight.

Mrs Garrett sent meals up to me, delivered by Martha who deposited them and left, without a word. By Thursday, though, she was forced to speak, to deliver a message from Mrs Garrett.

'The mistress wants to know if you'd care to join her for some supper.'

The words were delivered with a stony glare into the distance.

I told Martha to pass on the message that I would be pleased to accept. The evenings alone in my room were dull and I'd been falling asleep very early for lack of anything else to occupy me.

That evening, as I descended to the ground floor, I was surprised at how shaky my legs were. I really should take some exercise the next day, I decided. I'd spent quite enough time as an invalid.

I enjoyed the evening in Mrs Garrett's company, being determined to hear more about her life than to focus on my own. She told me about her husband, their early married life together, and their disappointment in not having any children who had survived longer than a twelvemonth.

'Ramsgate has changed a great deal since we were married,' she said. 'We could never have imagined all the building that would go on around the harbour. They knocked down the fishermen's cottages that were here to build these grand terraces. I suppose the Navy's presence brought the gentry. Whatever it was, I wasn't sorry to see our old house coming down. It was cramped and unsanitary. If anyone took sick in those streets, there was no stopping the spread of it. I blamed it for the fact that none of our three boys survived. They were weak from birth – always coughing, never thriving.'

She stopped suddenly, tears welling at her memories. I murmured in a sympathetic way and turned the conversation to more recent, happier times, before her husband died, that is. I'd made a mental note of the loss of her family, though. If my planned future with Charlie didn't come to pass, I could do a lot worse than to stay here with Mrs Garrett. She seemed to like my company and I was not averse to being a paid companion again. It was far preferable to the sort of work I'd done at the Royal Sea Bathing Hospital.

Martha would have to go if I stayed, though. It wouldn't be difficult to carry out my threat to implicate her as light-fingered. Mrs Garrett's bedroom door was always unlocked, and when she went out it would be an easy matter to slip into her room to take some jewellery. Martha was busy downstairs all day and I could hide it in her room in the attic without raising suspicion.

I surfaced from my musings to discover Mrs Garrett gazing expectantly at me. She must have asked me a question but I had no idea what it was. She'd been talking about her husband when I'd drifted into my own thoughts.

I turned my head sharply. 'Did you hear that?'

'No.' Mrs Garrett looked alarmed. She was hard of hearing, I knew. I stood up and went over to the window, peering out into the gathering gloom.

'I thought I heard someone out there but I can't see anyone. It must have been the wind.'

I returned to my seat opposite my landlady. 'Now, where were we?' I asked.

Mrs Garrett, casting anxious glances towards the window, said, 'I asked you whether you had never had any wish to be married, Harriet. From our conversation before you fell ill, I gained the impression that you held a poor opinion of matrimony.'

'I've been happy in my work, Mrs Garrett,' I replied. 'The opportunity hasn't really arisen and I suppose now it never will.'

Mrs Garrett frowned. 'Don't say that, my dear. An attractive lady like yourself, I'm sure there will still be opportunities. A gentleman who has lost his wife, perhaps. But, then, you are very close to your family. Your brother, is he married?'

I didn't like to remind her of John by asking which brother she was referring to, so I replied, 'Yes, he is. But his wife is away a good deal, visiting her own mother who is too ill to leave her home. That's why he comes to visit so regularly. For company.'

The lies rolled off my tongue as Mrs Garrett nodded and smiled. It didn't hurt to paint myself in a good light. My sights were set on Charlie and I was determined to do everything in my power to bind him to me. But if I should fail, then it was as well to have something else to fall back on. Becoming a companion to Mrs Garrett wasn't how I saw my future at present, but there was no denying it would make for a comfortable existence.

CHAPTER FIFTY-ONE

Sunday found me awake early, warm in my bed and full of anticipation about the day ahead. I would allow nothing to spoil my afternoon with Charlie. Every Sunday that remained until the garden party would be devoted to drawing him ever closer to me – ever closer to my goal of having him all to myself.

I allowed myself to daydream a little about our future. I had already decided we would move away from the area and start afresh, under a new name. I tried out a few: Charles and Harriet Bayley. Charles and Harriet Freeman. Charles and Harriet Dixon. Perhaps it was best to avoid any surname that might be linked with me: Charles and Harriet Bayley had a nice solid ring to it. We could move north and Charlie could find a new garden to take on. Although I quickly realised that, under a different name, he wouldn't be able to take his reputation with him. I frowned. If we moved far enough away, he could keep his name without any taint of scandal. But I didn't want to become Harriet Dawson and be forever reminded of his real wife.

I sighed and allowed my thoughts to take me back to our walk by the sea, from Westgate to Westcliff. I remembered the ship I'd seen at sail. Could we travel further afield and start afresh where neither of us was known?

It was time to consider what to wear for the day ahead. Which dress would be most suitable? The muslin, I decided. The neck was low and I could wear a shawl around my shoulders to begin with, allowing it to fall away at a suitable moment. Mrs Garrett would have a fire lit in the parlour so, although the grey light told me another cool day was likely, I would at least be warm. And I had every intention that Charlie would be warm, too: uncomfortably warm.

I'd thought about entertaining him in my room but I couldn't be sure of Martha's discretion, despite my payment to her. And I preferred to keep on the right side of Mrs Garrett. There was time enough before the garden party to consider what further favours I might bestow on Charlie.

No sooner had I entertained this thought than I began to contemplate what those favours might be. I remembered the pressure of his lips on mind, the rough scratch of a trace of stubble on his cheek. I imagined his slim, tanned fingers finding the fastenings on my gown. My pulse raced at the delicious prospect of what would come next.

Martha knocked and flung open the door to deliver my jug of water for washing, causing me to start and utter an exclamation of surprise.

'Still abed?' she remarked, as she drew back the curtains to reveal the expected grey skies. 'It's Sunday. You'll be expecting a visitor, no doubt.'

I nodded, flushed, half convinced that she could read my mind and was party to my imaginings, all of them quite unsuitable for the Sabbath. She left the room with her usual curt nod and I focused on my preparations. I took my time, dressing my hair with more care than I normally would. When I was sure Mrs Garrett had gone to church, I went down to her library and put the books she had lent me on the table there, then selected

266

another from the shelves. I was no longer ill, but in need of something to occupy the hours until Charlie was due to arrive.

Mrs Garrett came up to my room at midday, to remind me that the parlour was mine for the afternoon, while she visited her sister. I thanked her, and apologised for taking a book from her library without permission, but she waved my apology away. I saw her eyes fall on the Bible, lying carelessly on the bed. I know she wondered why I didn't attend the service on a Sunday and I'd told her previously that I didn't like the preacher at St George's, having become used to my former church. It wouldn't hurt her to think that I'd spent the morning reading the Bible, even though I'd never opened it.

After she had gone, the house was very quiet. Cook had a half-day holiday and I wondered whether Martha had taken herself off somewhere, too. Did I have the house to myself after all? There was no time to consider what I might do with the freedom for I must go down to the harbour and meet Charlie.

I wrapped myself in my warmest shawl and set off, forcing myself to walk slowly so that I wouldn't arrive ahead of time. Charlie was rarely punctual so I had no expectation of seeing him when I reached the harbour. Even so, my heart beat faster whenever I saw a man of Charlie's build or hair colour, walking alone. But they were all intent on a destination – their home, their wife and family and a Sunday dinner table, I supposed, and none of them was Charlie.

I walked up and down for a while, then settled on a bench, only to stand up not five minutes later and walk some more. The air was cool, despite the glimmer of brightness through the clouds but, in any case, walking stilled the anxiety that was growing by the minute. I tried to keep my eyes from the clock on the Customs House, without success. Half an hour passed with no sign of Charlie.

I told myself that if I walked up and along Nelson Crescent and back down the harbour, he would arrive. I cast anxious glances towards our usual meeting place the whole time I walked, but to no avail. There was no sign of him. I walked up the hill to the north of the harbour, towards Albion Place, but then turned back, convinced he would arrive and leave again straight away if I wasn't there.

Perhaps I had missed him and he had gone to the house on Rose Hill. By the time this thought struck me it was three o'clock and he was an hour late. I cursed my stupidity in not thinking of this before and turned my back on the harbour, hurrying up the hill so that I was out of breath when I arrived on the doorstep.

I let myself in and Martha appeared at the end of the passageway. 'Has there been a message for me?' I asked.

'No, miss,' she said. I swear a smirk crossed her lips. 'Your brother . . .' she paused to give emphasis to her words '. . . he hasn't shown up, then?'

'I expect he's been delayed,' I said. 'He's very busy at the moment.'

'On a Sunday, miss?' she asked.

I didn't answer, but went instead into the parlour. I would wait there, I decided. If he didn't arrive, I would go once more to the harbour, but I was not hopeful.

My dreams of that morning were in tatters. I sat down and tried to compose myself, only to spring up and look out of the window, down the hill. There was no sign of anyone walking up from the harbour. I sat down again and tried to stay calm. If Charlie arrived, I would need to behave as though it was a minor inconvenience that he was late, and I would have to salvage what I could of my good intentions from the morning.

By the time I walked down to the harbour again at four o'clock, I knew it was a wasted journey. I didn't linger, turning for home after a cursory glance at the benches. I hurried back to Rose Hill, keen to be up in my room before Mrs Garrett returned from visiting her sister. My disappointment was too great to bear her sympathy: I would have a hard job shrugging off the ill manners of my 'brother'.

It was only later that evening, after a great deal of time spent staring out over the garden, a book unopened on my lap, that I began to wonder whether Martha had had a part to play in this. Could she have sent word to her father that Charlie Dawson was visiting a woman who lived in the very house she worked in, here in Ramsgate? And if she had, could that be the reason behind Charlie's behaviour?

I struggled to understand how it could be, but the idea had taken hold. It gave me a restless night, before the delivery of a note, midway through the following morning, caused me to rethink.

Dear Harriet,

I know you will be upset with me for failing to arrive for our meeting in Ramsgate yesterday. I can only apologise for being unable to get word to you until today.

Mr Powell has changed the date for the garden party yet again. Now it is to be 17 August, two weeks earlier than the most recent plan and a week after the original date. It has thrown all my preparations for readying the garden into disarray and I am having to work seven days a week to make up for lost time.

I hope you will understand. Once again, I can only say how sorry I am to have let you down.

I stared at the letter, then reread it, and reread it again, poring over every word and looking for hidden meanings. There was no mention of coming to Ramsgate again before 17 August, and although that gave me the date of the garden party, he hadn't included the words 'I hope I will see you there'. Nor had he done anything other than sign his name. There were no affectionate greetings, nothing I could retrieve to give me any hope. His final line chilled me. *I can only say how sorry I am to have let you down.* Was he talking about his failure to visit? Or was this a broader reference, a dashing of our plans for a life together?

I threw the letter to the floor in a fit of temper. Invited or not, on 17 August I would be at the garden party at Woodchurch Manor.

PART SIX

MOLLY

CHAPTER FIFTY-TWO

Molly's mood changed after her visit to Agnes in Ramsgate. She was angry with herself for standing silently by when they'd come across Harriet. She tried to shut out the memory of Harriet's expression – was it smug, or triumphant? She thought of all the things she now wished she had said and imagined herself seizing Harriet and shaking her. It didn't alter the fact that Harriet had captured Charlie's heart.

Molly's days felt very empty: how had she filled them before? She supposed, when Charlie had lived there, she had cooked and baked, cleaned the house, laundered and mended clothes. Now this burden must fall on Judith, who also had George and little Joseph to care for. So, once the weekend had passed, she said to Judith, 'You must let me help you in some way. I'm here alone with nothing to do, while you have all the extra work of my husband. Let me cook for you. Or at least,' when Judith looked doubtful, 'take in some of the washing.'

'It would be a help,' Judith admitted. 'Not the cooking, although I'd dearly love to say yes. I fear George and Charlie would notice if the food improved.' She laughed. 'I don't want them to suspect your daily visits. But laundry, and perhaps a bit of mending . . .'

So Molly took on the task of caring for Charlie and George's work clothes. Although prolonged sunshine was rare, it was often windy so at least the washing dried. She stoked up the range in the evenings to air the clothes and by day she patched and darned shirts and breeches where thorns and branches had caught and ripped the cloth. Before she washed Charlie's shirts, she clutched them to her, breathing in his scent. It was the closest she could get to her husband.

She told her daughter-in-law that keeping busy helped her to pass the time, which indeed it did. She persuaded Judith to allow her to look after Joseph for a couple of hours each day so she could attend to household jobs. At first, Molly did this at Judith's house, but as Joseph began watching for his mother as she passed through the room and setting up a wail when she moved out of view, it was decided he should be at his grandmother's house.

She would wrap him in her shawl and hurry the few paces between their homes, fearful of being spotted by George. Even though Charlie and George never came back from work during the day, she felt she must be careful.

One day, in the third week of July, Judith came rushing into Molly's house. Joseph was happy, lying on a blanket on the floor, and cried bitterly when his mother scooped him up.

'George came home.' Judith was gabbling. 'He got something in his eyes – fragments of bark blew in when they were cutting down a tree. He rubbed them and now they're red and streaming. I left him washing them in the kitchen but he'll realise Joseph isn't in the house. I must get back.'

She was half out of the door as she spoke and Molly could only watch, her own heart hammering, as Judith hurried away down the path. She felt a surge of pain even as she hoped their arrangement wouldn't be discovered.

She was Joseph's grandmother. Why on earth shouldn't she look after her grandson and help her daughter-in-law? Her thoughts went to the washing hanging in the garden. If George looked out of his kitchen window, would he see it? She almost stepped out to gather it in, then stopped. It was foolish. Maybe it would be a good thing if George learnt of her arrangement with Judith: it would force a discussion.

When Molly arrived on the doorstep to return the clean washing to Judith the following morning, she was met with an apology.

'I'm not sure George even noticed Joseph,' she said. 'He was in such pain. I hope he hasn't damaged his eyes for good. They were still red and painful this morning.'

'He must bathe them with boiled water, cooled and with a pinch of salt added,' Molly said. 'A tiny pinch, mind, or it will make them sorer still. And I will see whether I can find eyebright growing on the cliff top. If I can, I will make an extract for him to use.'

She handed over the washing and took Joseph in return, content that their arrangement could continue as before. She would walk out the following morning, she decided, in search of eyebright. It was Sunday but she was still avoiding church and it would keep her occupied. George would be at home with Judith and Joseph so she would be unable to see her daughter-in-law and grandson. Charlie would no doubt be going to Ramsgate, but she refused to allow her thoughts to travel in that direction.

The next day started brighter than any they had seen of late and Molly's spirits lifted as she set off towards the sea. It was no great distance – barely a mile – and provided she was successful in her quest, she would be able to collect the plant and return home in plenty of time to make the extract. She would have liked to be able to give it to George that night, for the sooner he used it the better, but she couldn't see how to bring that about.

Her mind was occupied with this problem and, at first, she paid little heed to the figure walking some way ahead of her on the chalky path that cut across the grassy downland towards the sea. She was just beginning to think that the person looked familiar when she realised it was Charlie.

She spun around to face the way she had come, then stood stock still, heart beating rapidly. It was important Charlie shouldn't think she was following him. As she gazed at the ground, biting her lip, she saw what she had come to find. The creeping stems of eyebright, tiny white flowers with throats of yellow tinged with red, were growing right by the path. Feeling thankful, Molly sank to her knees on the grass. She would gather them and pay no heed to Charlie. If he saw her, then so be it. She had a perfectly good reason to be there.

She moved away from the path in the direction of the sea, gathering as she went. A covert glance over her shoulder revealed that Charlie was no longer on the path but further away, standing on the grass near the cliff edge, gazing out over the water. He was too far distant to recognise her even if he saw her, she thought.

She stood up and gathered the plants together in a cloth she'd brought for the purpose, knotting the four corners together. Then she turned in the direction of home, a smile on her lips even though the brightness of the day had already passed and grey skies threatened. Charlie hadn't gone to Ramsgate and he wasn't spending the day with Harriet. That thought alone made Molly happy.

CHAPTER FIFTY-THREE

Molly set to work to make her eyebright extract as soon as she returned home. While the mixture was steeping and cooling, she decided she would make a cake. Eggs were accumulating in the larder: now that she was living alone she was surprised by how little food she needed. The familiar routine of weighing the ingredients, followed by the rhythmic beating of the mixture, was soothing and Molly felt happier than she had done in a while. The cake was out of the oven, cooling on the side while she finished the washing-up, when a knock at the door made her jump.

'Come in,' she called, her hands deep in suds.

Margaret poked her head around the door. 'Hello, Molly. I was visiting George and Judith again and I thought I'd call in as I went by. Is this a good moment?' She looked doubtfully at Molly, who hurriedly wiped her hands on her apron.

'Come in, do. Here, sit down.' She pulled a chair out from the table.

'Thank you. Something smells delicious!' Margaret sniffed the air.

'I made a cake. You must have a piece when it's cooled.' Molly was wiping surfaces and trying to restore order before she, too, sat down.

Margaret sighed and patted her belly. 'Thank you, but I couldn't. I've eaten far too much already.'

'How was George?' Molly asked. 'Judith said he'd hurt his eyes. I've been worried.'

'They looked sore,' Margaret said. 'He kept having to close them to rest them. I said I'd ask the doctor at the hospital whether he could recommend something.'

'I've made an eyebright extract.' Molly gestured to it, cooling on the side. 'It will have to wait, though, until I can give it to Judith tomorrow. I wish he could have it tonight – I'm sure it would help.'

'I'll take it round,' Margaret said.

'But where will you say it came from?'

'From you, of course,' Margaret said. She smiled at Molly. 'Don't look so anxious. He'd be a fool not to use it. And it won't hurt him to know that his mother is thinking of him.'

Molly was grateful but still nervous. George would wonder how she had heard of his accident. She didn't want to get Judith into trouble and expose their secret arrangement. But Margaret was speaking again.

'I've told George it's time he convinced Charlie to break free of Harriet. The hospital has discovered that she was stealing from the patients. It came to a light after a ring was reported stolen in Ramsgate and enquiries made about it at the hospital. It had belonged to one of Harriet's patients and now the hospital is suspicious about other pieces of jewellery that were thought to be lost.'

Molly was shocked. 'She's a thief?'

Margaret shrugged. 'I don't know. That's the gossip, anyway.'

The talk moved away from Harriet, and Molly was glad. She had tucked away the nugget of information and she could come back to it later, when Margaret had gone.

278

She cut Margaret a piece of cake, despite her protestations, telling her she could take it away with her to eat later that evening. Then she had an idea and wrapped half the cake in a tea-cloth.

'If you're sure you are happy to take the eyebright to George, then could you take this piece of cake, too? George can choose whether or not he eats it. It will only go to waste here.'

Molly felt braver with Margaret to act as her go-between. She didn't seem to have any qualms about jeopardising her new-found relationship with George. Molly wondered, not for the first time, whether managing her father through his illness had given her the quiet authority that was so effective.

Margaret's visit lasted an hour, then she stood up and said she needed to set off back to Margate.

'I'll deliver this to George and Judith first, though,' she said, picking up the wrapped cake.

'And this,' Molly said, handing her the bottle of eyebright extract. 'Tell George to add a few drops to a cup of water that has been boiled, then cooled, and use it to rinse his eyes now, and again before bed. Then once more in the morning and at least twice a day until they're better. And don't forget your cake, too,' she said, tucking a piece wrapped in paper under Margaret's arm.

Margaret, her hands full, set off down the path.

'I'll come and visit next week,' she said, turning at the gate. 'I've been lucky enough to be given two free Sunday afternoons in a row, although I fear I must pay the price next month.'

Molly nodded and waved, watching her as she made her way to George and Judith's house. Her smile faded: if only she could join them all at the table next Sunday, or even invite them to her house. How happy she would be!

Then she went back inside, scolding herself. It did no good to think in that way. Only time would tell whether her relationship with George could be repaired. She must be patient, and grateful to Judith and Margaret, who seemed to be determined that, in time, it would.

The following week brought a letter from Lizzie, asking Molly to come and visit:

> *Hannah has returned, and she is keen to see you. She's worried, as we all are, about how things stand between you and Charlie.*
>
> *And Sarah is back from Greenwich, with Constance. I know you won't welcome seeing her but I think you should. Remember – you did nothing wrong. The blame lies with Nicholas.*

The contents of the letter worried away at Molly throughout the day. Hannah's lack of learning had stopped Molly writing to her after she'd left Faversham. She'd wondered whether her mother had fully recovered and she was impatient now to catch up with her news. Sarah was another matter: she had told herself that Sarah would remain in Greenwich with Constance, to avoid the faintest likelihood of scandal, and now her hopes were dashed. She would have to face her, and the many questions that both mother and daughter would no doubt have.

She clung to Lizzie's words: *you did nothing wrong. The blame lies with Nicholas.* She had behaved badly, she knew. But not towards Sarah: after all, her marriage to Nicholas had taken place after Molly knew she was carrying his child.

The memory of how she had felt when she discovered Nicholas was engaged to Sarah struck her as forcefully as if all the years in between had never happened. She would go to Margate the next day, she decided. There was no point in putting it off. And she would try to hold on to that memory from the past when she spoke to Sarah: it was important she should understand the pain Molly had endured.

CHAPTER FIFTY-FOUR

Molly was prey to mixed emotions as she made the walk to Margate. She was looking forward to seeing her sisters and Hannah, but anxious at the thought of meeting Sarah now she was in possession of the truth about her husband. She hadn't seen Aunt Jane for some weeks, either, not since she'd been summoned to explain herself after the revelation about Nicholas, back in June.

She'd planned to see her sisters first when she arrived, then to visit Hannah, slipping down to the basement kitchen before she faced Sarah, Constance and Aunt Jane. But her plans were thwarted – no sooner had she turned into Princes Crescent than she saw Sarah stepping down from Uncle William's carriage, Constance already waiting outside the house. Molly froze, wondering whether she could slip away without being spotted, but it was too late. Constance said something to her mother and Sarah turned, so they were both looking straight at her.

Feeling unprepared, Molly walked on, wondering whether she could still stop at her sister's gate, but Sarah called her over.

'Molly – we'd hoped to see you. Will you join us inside and take some refreshment?'

Molly would have liked to refuse but there was little point.

She followed Sarah and Constance into Aunt Jane's house, casting a regretful glance at her sisters' door.

Sarah asked the maid for coffee to be brought up to the drawing room and they sat in uncomfortable silence until Elsie had brought in the tray. She cast sideways glances at Molly, who knew that Hannah would be made aware of her visit.

'Well, Molly,' Sarah said, as soon as the door closed behind Elsie, 'there have been some startling revelations since we last met.'

She looked at Molly, as though expecting her to fill the awkward pause, but Molly remained silent.

'It was a shock to discover that Constance has both a half-brother and a half-sister, after being an only child for all these years.'

Molly still didn't speak.

Sarah sighed. 'Molly, I'm not angry. What right have I? I confess I was at first, when my father-in-law made me aware of the situation. But I've had time to think since, and I've spoken to my mother-in-law, too. She's made me see that Nicholas was at fault, which wasn't easy for her.'

Sarah paused to sip her coffee and Molly noticed her hand trembling as she raised the cup to her lips. Constance still hadn't said a word.

'Molly, you were badly used. Both you and George have suffered in the years since Nicholas vanished from our lives. I hope that in future we can all get to know each other better.'

Sarah gave Molly a look of appeal.

'Thank you, Sarah,' Molly said. Her voice sounded strained to her ears and she cleared her throat. 'I'm grateful – I realise this has come as a shock. It has been difficult over the years . . .' She tailed off. 'I'm afraid George is unhappy with me over this business but I hope that eventually we can be reconciled. And that he and Constance will get to know each other.'

Constance nodded in acknowledgement although she didn't look enthusiastic.

'You must meet Margaret, too,' Molly added, addressing both women. 'You'll like her, I'm sure.'

Constance appeared unconvinced and left it to her mother to speak.

'I'm finding that prospect a little difficult,' Sarah said stiffly. 'It seems the reason Nicholas didn't return to us was because he had taken up with Margaret's mother.'

'I don't think so,' Molly said, surprised. 'I believe Nicholas met Margaret's mother a little while later. Margaret is four or five years younger than George and Constance.'

She bit her lip. Sarah didn't look happy. Molly had not only reminded her that George and Constance were born just a few weeks apart, but implied that Nicholas had simply chosen not to return.

Before she could attempt to make amends, the door opened and Aunt Jane entered, walking with the aid of a stick. 'There you are, Molly,' she said. 'I thought I could hear your voice. It's been a long time since we've seen you. Too long.' She cast a critical eye over her niece. 'You look thin – and tired. Have you been looking after yourself?'

'I'm well enough, Aunt,' Molly said. Her aunt's words instantly made her wish she'd made more of an effort with her appearance before setting out that morning. She was already feeling dowdy beside Sarah and Constance, who were always elegant in the latest London fashions.

Aunt Jane settled herself into her favourite chair, while Sarah poured coffee for her. 'It's a little cold,' Aunt Jane said, puckering her lips. Sarah reached for the bell-pull but Aunt

Jane waved her stick at her. 'It doesn't matter. Leave it,' she said.

'So, I hope you've had your discussion. About Nicholas,' she added, in case anyone was in doubt.

'Yes, we have,' Sarah said.

'And all is well between you?' Aunt Jane asked. This time she looked at Molly.

'Yes, Aunt Jane,' Molly said dutifully.

'You know, it hasn't been easy for me accepting that Nicholas was capable of such deceitful behaviour,' Aunt Jane's voice quavered, 'but I'm determined that some good will come of it. I have grandchildren, well grown, whom I know nothing about. And a great-grandchild, too.' She looked at Molly. 'I've remained in ignorance of this for far too long. We'll all meet up soon at the garden party, of course. And on the Sunday afterwards I want you to bring George and Judith here, with Joseph. And Charlie, too. We'll have a party, with Margaret. It will be quite a gathering.'

Pleased with herself, she looked from her niece to her daughter-in-law to her granddaughter.

Sarah spoke up. 'I'm afraid George and Molly are . . .' she paused '. . . having a difficult time at the moment.'

Aunt Jane frowned. 'Still? I'd heard something of the sort. Well, it won't do. You must sort it out, Molly.'

Molly suspected her aunt was more concerned that the party shouldn't be spoilt than she was for her niece's welfare.

'And Charlie?' Aunt Jane asked.

Molly shook her head.

'All because of Nicholas.' Her aunt spoke so sadly that tears sprang to Molly's eyes.

There were a few moments' silence. 'I'll speak to them both,' Aunt Jane said.

'No!' Molly exclaimed, then feared she had caused offence. 'No,' she repeated, with less vehemence. 'I will. You are right. All this has gone on for too long. It must be dealt with. Family is important.'

She looked between the women in the room. She meant what she said, but she didn't have them in mind. Charlie and George were the important ones. If they wouldn't come to her, she would have to go to them.

CHAPTER FIFTY-FIVE

Molly felt she had done enough to observe the social niceties and it wouldn't be seen as impolite to leave. She asked Aunt Jane whether she would mind if she went downstairs to see Hannah. 'I won't disturb her for long,' she promised. 'She'll have a lot to do now that you have Sarah and Constance here. But I haven't been able to speak to her since we were in Faversham together. I'd like to know how her mother is.'

Aunt Jane waved her away and Molly hurried downstairs. She was glad that the meeting with Sarah and Constance was done with. She'd been dreading it but, on the whole, it had gone better than expected. She couldn't imagine Constance getting on as well with George as Margaret apparently did. Perhaps Margaret had spoken the truth when she said that she and George had an affinity. Neither of them had Constance's airs and graces, of course.

She arrived in the kitchen to find Hannah hard at work, bent over the range and unaware of her arrival. Molly waited until she had finished turning the meat on the roasting rack, not wanting to startle her. Finally, she was able to say, 'Hello, Hannah. How are you? And your mother?'

Hannah dropped the cloth she was holding and rushed over to give Molly a hug. 'Oh, Molly, I've been worried about you, ever since you left in such a hurry. How is Charlie? And George?' Her brow creased into a worried frown.

'I asked first,' Molly teased, laughing. 'Is your mother better?'

'She is, thank you,' Hannah said. 'At least, she's well enough for me to leave her for now. But I won't be able to stay away from her over the winter.'

'What will you do?' Molly asked.

'I'll have to give notice,' Hannah said. 'Your aunt will have to manage without me. I'm getting far too old for this now.' She waved her hand around the kitchen, which was as spotless and orderly as it always was. 'She can engage someone younger to do the work.'

Molly opened her mouth to speak, then stopped. Aunt Jane wouldn't be happy about this. Hannah had worked for her for over thirty years, since Uncle William had borrowed her from the kitchens at Prospect House. Molly had thought Hannah old when she first knew her, although she realised now that she couldn't have been. She'd been grey-haired back then and now her hair was snow white. She was still as round as ever, but the lines on her face were deeply etched. She had to be in her late sixties, Molly thought, which made her mother in her late eighties. No wonder she wanted to leave to care for her.

'Aunt Jane and Uncle William will miss you very much,' Molly said. 'We all will. But I can understand why you want to go.'

'Now my mind is made up it's hard to be here.' Hannah sighed. 'And Sarah and Constance have arrived, so there's twice as much work. I won't be able to stop long to talk to you. You'd better tell me how things stand.'

She gave Molly a hard look, which had the effect of preventing her from uttering the half-truth she'd planned on telling.

'George still isn't speaking to me,' Molly said. 'Charlie is living at George and Judith's and I haven't seen him for weeks. Harriet has moved to Ramsgate and Charlie was visiting her there but I think he may have stopped.'

Hannah looked shocked. 'So your sister's letter – it wasn't all just a rumour. Charlie really has taken leave of his senses.' She flung some carrots she had cleaned onto the table and began chopping them with vicious strokes. Molly almost smiled at such a clear display of her feelings.

'Well, Molly,' Hannah said at last, when all the carrots were diced and ready for the pot. 'It's up to you to make him see what he must do. Men can be such fools, and proud with it. I dare say he wishes he'd never got involved with that woman, but doesn't know how to find his way back to you.'

'Do you think so?' Molly asked. She felt better for hearing it, even though part of her feared there was no way to save her marriage.

'I do,' Hannah said firmly. 'Now, I'll have to get on with this or there'll be no dinner on the table this afternoon. Unless you want to help me, that is?'

'Ah, no, my sisters are expecting me.' Molly gave Hannah a hug before she turned to leave. 'Thank you, Hannah,' she said. 'Your advice was similar to Aunt Jane's. Now I'll have to see what my sisters say. I'll come back when you're not so busy.'

Hannah sighed. 'I don't see that happening before Sarah and Constance go back to Greenwich.'

Molly left by the basement steps, feeling sorry for Hannah. Aunt Jane would have to engage a kitchen maid at the very least, if Hannah wasn't to be exhausted.

As soon as she arrived in the kitchen next door, her sisters fell on her with cries of delight. Despite Lizzie and Mary's efforts, the kitchen in their cottage was far removed from the orderly precision to be found in Hannah's, but Molly welcomed the chaos. It seemed a long time since they had been together, even though it was just over three weeks. She missed them and their support.

'Now, sit down,' Lizzie said. 'You'll have something to eat with us? And you're going to tell us, I hope, that all is well with you and Charlie now. And with George, too?'

Lizzie and Mary looked hopefully at her.

'Well,' Molly said, 'not exactly.'

By the time Molly began her journey home on foot, she had received the same advice from her sisters as from her aunt and Hannah. It was expressed in a different way, but the message was broadly the same.

'I never had Charlie down as a numbskull,' Mary had said, in exasperation, after Molly had retold her tale.

'I think you should try to make things right with George,' Lizzie said. 'Really, his father's name being kept secret isn't worth all this upset. Once things are settled with him, he might help you with Charlie. If you want him to, that is.'

Molly waited for her sister to go on.

'Well,' Lizzie said slowly, 'it's difficult to accept what Charlie has done, isn't it? Carrying on with Harriet in this fashion. Making a fool of himself and of you. It will be hard to forgive.'

These last words stayed with Molly as she trudged home. She was weary: all the conversations about her predicament had exhausted her. Or perhaps it was the recognition that she would have to be the one to solve the problem. Lizzie was right, though. It really was time to address the situation with George. Charlie was more of a concern. How did she feel about the possibility of a future together? She really wasn't sure.

CHAPTER FIFTY-SIX

Molly fell into bed that night not long after arriving home, stopping only to eat a piece of bread and splash water on her face. She slept deep and long, waking refreshed and with a sense of purpose. She would find a way to make things right with George: enough time had been wasted. Once that had been achieved, she could concern herself with Charlie.

It was Sunday and Molly, having failed to attend church for several weeks now, felt she couldn't allow this to continue. She wondered whether George and Charlie would be there. She hoped they would: she could acknowledge them and perhaps it would be the first step on the road to reconciliation.

She dressed with care in her Sunday best, a dress of printed cotton, indigo blue on a white background, which had seen little wear in the past weeks. It felt strange to be going to church on her own but she forced herself to keep her head up and walk at a normal pace, nodding to estate workers and their families when she arrived at the church gates. Her heart beat painfully when she entered the building. Where should she sit? Normally she would have shared a pew with Charlie, George and Judith. The dilemma brought her to a halt and she stood, uncertain, until she noticed Catherine, seated beside Francis, beckoning her.

'Sit with us, Ma,' she said, shifting along the pew to make space when Molly arrived beside her.

Molly, who had never sat on the Powells' side of the church before, felt this was only drawing attention to her plight. There was nothing to be done, however, so she sat down and looked straight ahead, willing the minister to start. Catherine squeezed her hand.

Molly was glad when the service was over and they were released back outside, into a sunny morning that was unusual for this year, even though it was the end of July. She lifted her head and closed her eyes, to enjoy the sensation of the sun on her face for a moment or two. She jumped, startled, when she felt a hand on her arm.

She opened her eyes to find George before her. Judith was standing a little way behind him: had she encouraged him to approach her?

'Molly,' he said tentatively, 'I wanted to thank you. For the eyebright,' he pressed on, seeing Molly's puzzlement.

'It eased all the redness and irritation within a day. I could scarcely believe it – I was ready to tear my eyes from my skull before then.'

He held out the empty phial to Molly. 'I brought this along, hoping I would see you to return it.' He paused. 'Will you come and eat with us? It would make Judith and Joseph very happy if you would join us.'

Molly noticed he didn't include himself, but perhaps it was too soon to hope for that. She wondered where Charlie was. There was no sign of him at the church and she didn't like to ask whether he would be present, too. Or had he already left for Ramsgate? Her heart sank at the thought.

'Charlie won't be joining us,' George said, as if reading her thoughts. He stared at his feet as he spoke. 'Do come. I think

293

you should.' He looked up again. 'Margaret will be with us too.'

Molly felt her heart lift. Margaret's presence would ease the situation, she was sure. 'Then I will,' she said.

Joseph provided the perfect distraction when they reached George and Judith's cottage. Molly devoted her attention to him, while Judith busied herself in the kitchen. George was awkward: he fidgeted in the parlour before going into the kitchen only to get in the way and be ushered out by Judith. Then he returned to the parlour and hovered until Molly was exasperated. She was saved by Margaret's arrival from speaking out of turn – never had two people been happier to see her.

Margaret was clearly taken aback, both by the warmth of her welcome and by seeing George and Molly in the same room. Molly returned to playing with Joseph, noticing how George relaxed as he talked with Margaret. She supposed Judith had put George up to the invitation, and although she wasn't sure that he was ready to make his peace with her, it wouldn't hurt him to see that she was still the same person as she had been before the revelation about his father.

Their afternoon was a mixture of lovely family moments and of awkwardness. Molly was delighted to see how at ease George and Margaret were with each other, and Margaret's genuine fondness for Judith and Joseph. Molly avoided addressing George directly, but she was at pains to cast grateful glances in Judith's direction at every opportunity.

As soon as they had eaten, Margaret announced that she would have to return to the hospital. 'I've been lucky to be able to visit two Sundays in a row, but I'm expected to be on duty this evening. And I don't suppose I will be able to visit next week. Even if I am invited,' she added, laughing. 'How long is it to the garden party? I must save up any time off I earn in the hope that I will be allowed to come.'

'Nearly three weeks.' The voice was a new one. Charlie had entered the room and Molly shrank back in her chair. Would he be angry when he noticed her there? She had just enough time to register how thin he was and how exhausted, with dark shadows under his eyes, before it seemed as though everyone was speaking at once.

'The seventeenth of August,' George said. 'That's the date.'

'I've saved your dinner for you. I'll fetch it.' Judith stood up.

'I'll be on my way,' Margaret said, already on her feet and fastening on her bonnet. 'The seventeenth of August. I'll remember that.'

'I'm just leaving too,' Molly said, depositing Joseph unceremoniously in his father's lap, causing him to wail. She closed her eyes briefly in embarrassment and caught Charlie looking at her again when she opened them. She couldn't read his expression: was it anger or sadness? The moment passed as Judith set Charlie's plate on the table.

'You're back early. Was *she* there?' she asked her father-in-law. It came out as a challenge.

'No,' Charlie said shortly. He sat down and began to eat, shovelling the food down in the way that Molly knew so well. Preoccupied, he wasn't tasting a mouthful.

She exchanged glances with Margaret and followed her out of the door into the lane, where they repeated their thanks to Judith. Margaret hurried away in the direction of Margate and Molly returned home, to pore over every detail of her brief encounter with Charlie and to consider what might be the next move to repair her relationship with George.

CHAPTER FIFTY-SEVEN

Molly had planned to visit Judith the following morning, to quiz her about how George had seemed after their dinner together, and whether Charlie had said anything about her presence in the house.

The weather, though, was against her. It was raining hard when she woke and continued to do so steadily for the rest of the day, making her reluctant to venture even such a short distance. Her thoughts turned to the Woodchurch Manor gardens and to Charlie and George working there. They would be mired in mud and worried about plants being flattened and spoilt before the big day. It was a concern she knew only too well from previous years, but never had there been such a miserable summer.

A watery sunshine broke through in the early evening – too late for her to consider visiting Judith. George and Charlie would be expected home and Joseph being put to bed. Molly was frustrated: she had longed to hear Judith's thoughts about the previous day but there was nothing to be done. Her questions would have to wait.

The following morning, though, she received an urgent message from her sisters. Aunt Jane had been taken ill and they thought she should come at once. Molly didn't hesitate: she threw a few items into a bag, took a quick glance round the kitchen, locked the door and left. She walked at great speed, having no choice but to take the roadway as the mud on the paths across the fields made them impassable. Even so, she despaired at the state of her boots while her gown was spattered a good foot beyond its hem before she was even halfway to Margate. Every passing carriage or cart splashed her with dirty water and she had given up expecting any to stop and offer her a lift; she feared she must be taken for a tramp.

She didn't even bother to look up as a cart slowed beside her, the horse reined in to walking pace.

'Where are you going in such a hurry?'

They were the first words Charlie had directed to her in many a week and Molly almost failed to register them as she plodded on, head down. When she grasped who was speaking, she stopped, amazed.

'Margate,' she said then, realising this hardly answered the question. 'To see Aunt Jane. She's very sick.'

'Climb up. I'll take you there.'

Charlie leant over and offered her his hand. Molly almost wept: the strength of his grip and the easy way in which he pulled her up to sit beside him reminded her of how much she missed him.

'Thank you,' she murmured, settling herself in as he shook the reins and urged the horses on.

He glanced down at her clothes. 'You look a sight, Molly. Hardly fit to sit beside a sick bed.'

He was right, Molly knew. She would have to change into her spare dress as soon as she arrived.

'Why didn't you ask for help?' Charlie asked. 'You could have been there by now and saved your dress and boots.'

Molly was at a loss as to how to respond. He was talking to her as though nothing had happened – as though they

297

hadn't been estranged for weeks. Possible replies ran through her head: I thought you'd be too busy in the gardens; I didn't like to bother you; we are hardly on speaking terms.

Had her appearance at George and Judith's just two days ago wrought this transformation in his attitude to her?

There was no time to find out – they were approaching the outskirts of Margate where the roads were congested with carts and carriages, the weather the previous day having, no doubt, prevented them going about their business. Charlie was concentrating on making a safe passage, calling to the barrow boys to move along and clicking instructions to the horse, so that Molly was forced to sit quietly. Before she could think to question him about the change in his demeanour towards her, they were outside her sisters' house. She climbed down and Charlie leant across with her bag.

'Wish your aunt well from me,' he said. He looked straight at her again and she found it hard to meet his eyes. 'Take care of yourself, Molly.' He shook the reins and the horse moved on. Then he was gone out of Princes Crescent without a backward glance.

Molly stood for a moment at the side of the road, then picked up her bag and opened her sisters' gate. She was no sooner through the kitchen door than they fell on her.

'Well?' Lizzie demanded.

'We saw Charlie,' Mary added. 'Is all well now?'

Molly shrugged. 'I don't think so. I don't know. He came upon me as I was walking to Margate.'

'Look at the state of you,' Lizzie broke in, as she took in Molly's dishevelled appearance. 'Have you got something else you can wear? And take off those boots – you're leaving mud everywhere.'

'How is Aunt Jane?' Molly asked, bending to unlace her boots.

'There's no change,' Mary said. 'I'm afraid the doctor thinks it's grave. Give me your boots and I'll clean them while you get changed. Then I think you should go and see her at once.'

Molly, attired in a clean dress, barely had time to lace her damp boots back onto her feet before her sisters were pushing her out of the door.

'We'll talk when you get back,' Lizzie promised.

Elsie answered the door and ushered Molly straight up to Aunt Jane's bedchamber. When the door closed behind her and her eyes had adjusted to the dim light – the curtains were still closed – she saw that Sarah and Constance were seated on either side of her aunt's bed, while Uncle William was standing by the fireplace, his back against the wall. In the quiet of the room, she could hear her aunt's laboured breathing and the regular tick of the clock on her dressing-table.

'Come and sit here, Molly.' Sarah stood up and indicated to Molly to take her seat. Aunt Jane turned her head.

'Is that Molly?' she wheezed.

'Yes, Aunt. I came as soon as I heard you were ill.' Molly went to stand at the head of the bed and took her aunt's hand.

'A lot of nonsense over nothing,' Aunt Jane croaked. 'A bit of a chill, nothing worse. I'll be perfectly well in time for the garden party.' She smiled at Molly, then closed her eyes, exhausted by the effort of talking.

'Of course you will.' Molly patted her aunt's hand and sat down. It was hard to imagine her aunt ever being well again: she looked so pale and shrunken beneath the tightly tucked sheet.

There was a knock at the door and Elsie entered, bearing a gently steaming bowl on a tray.

'Hannah made some beef broth,' she said.

'Shall I try to give her some?' Molly ventured, noting that no one else had reacted. She supposed they must all be tired, having been on watch all night. She smiled at Elsie and removed the bowl from the tray, then balanced it on her lap, waiting for it to cool a little.

'Why don't you all have a rest?' she suggested. 'I can ring for Elsie if I need anything.'

The family all looked relieved, Molly thought, although one by one they made a token protest before departing. Molly set the bowl on the night stand then went over to draw the curtains apart and open the window. The room was stuffy and she felt sure some fresh air would help her aunt to breathe more easily.

Returning to her seat she spoke softly: 'Aunt Jane, I have some of Hannah's broth here. Will you try a spoonful or two?'

Her aunt's eyes opened. 'Is that you, Molly? When did you get here?'

'I've just arrived, Aunt.' Molly's heart sank. Was her aunt becoming confused?

Aunt Jane yawned. 'I think I slipped into a doze. You were here before. Broth, did you say?'

Molly smiled. 'Yes, made by Hannah. I'm sure it will do you good. Shall I help you to sit up?'

'No need,' Aunt Jane said. She struggled to prop herself against the pillows and set off a coughing fit in the process.

'Now, are you going to tell me that all is well with that husband of yours?' Her voice came out in a hoarse whisper and Molly had to lean in to hear her words.

'Not quite, Aunt,' she said. 'But a little better, I hope. Now, try some broth before it gets cold.'

Her hope that she'd put her aunt off further enquiry was to no avail. Aunt Jane submitted to being fed a few spoonfuls of broth, then said, 'I'm expecting to hear that all is well by the time of the garden party. Just over two weeks away, isn't it?'

'Yes, Aunt,' Molly said. She hoped her doubtful expression didn't betray her. Then she devoted herself to persuading her aunt to take a little more broth before the old lady turned her head from the spoon, closed her eyes and drifted back to sleep.

Chapter Fifty-Eight

Molly and her sisters, along with Sarah and Constance, took it in turns to keep vigil at Aunt Jane's bedside. Uncle William was a more or less constant presence, too, unless he could be persuaded away to sleep or eat. The days drifted by, the hours spent in a darkened room adding to the air of unreality. As she sat and watched her aunt, listening to the rasping of her breath, Molly had plenty of time to think.

Aunt Jane continued to take a few mouthfuls of Hannah's broth at regular intervals and, as the week progressed, she was awake more frequently and her breathing grew easier. The doctor visited on Friday and declared himself astonished. 'She's far better than I dared hope,' he said. 'I think the credit must lie with the excellent care you have given her.'

As he spoke, he looked around the drawing room where the family had assembled to hear what he had to say. Uncle William appeared to be holding back tears as he drew the doctor away into the dining room to pour him a drink and settle his bill. The five women looked at each other, all of a sudden made weary as the anxiety eased. No one spoke, until Molly broke the silence. 'And credit must be given to Hannah and her broth, I feel.'

The others nodded agreement. Hannah was, at that very moment, watching over her mistress to allow them to hear what the doctor had to say. Molly felt relief that the worst seemed to have passed. She resolved to tell Hannah at once, and to thank her, for surely she had poured all her love and concern for her employer into that excellent broth.

She hurried up the stairs and cautiously opened the door to the bedroom. Aunt Jane was asleep but Hannah was watching over her as if she needed to see every rise and fall of breath to convince herself that all was well. Molly whispered, 'Hannah,' and beckoned to her as she turned. Taking care not to disturb Aunt Jane's peaceful sleep, Hannah came out onto the landing, pulling the door to behind her.

'Is everything all right? What did the doctor say?' She looked anxious as she spoke.

'She's doing very well. The doctor could hardly believe it and declared all credit must go to the excellent care she has been given here.' Molly saw tears start to Hannah's eyes and, on impulse, she pulled her into a hug. She felt the cook's shoulders shake with sobs as she did so.

'We all want to thank you, Hannah. Your broth has worked its magic, just as it did for your own mother.' The two women clung together for a minute or two longer. Then, as a door opened downstairs and Uncle William could be heard bidding the doctor goodbye, Hannah pushed Molly away to arm's length.

'Now, get yourself home, Molly Dawson, and sort things out with that husband of yours. You've been here long enough and there's matters needing attention at your own fireside.'

She didn't need to hear Hannah's words – Molly knew she was right. Now that Aunt Jane was on the mend, it was indeed time to return home. She remained with her sisters for the rest of the day, then set off early the following morning. Lizzie urged her to ask her uncle for use of the carriage but Molly said she preferred to walk.

'I've been long enough indoors. I'm in need of the fresh air and exercise,' she said.

She found her spirits lifting as she walked the familiar paths – so much overgrown due to all the rain they had experienced that a couple of times she missed her way and had to retrace her steps. There was, at least, some sunshine and while it lacked the warmth expected of an August day, it held promise, Molly thought. If it could remain fair for the next fortnight, then Mr Powell would have a successful garden party.

She had stayed away from the gardens since her unpleasant interview with Charlie and George in the glasshouse. Now she had a mind to see how it all looked. She risked coming across her husband or her son but she didn't care – she thought she might welcome it, in fact. She wondered whether her absence from home had been noted. Judith would have been puzzled that she hadn't visited, unless Charlie had told her he had come across Molly on the road to Margate.

Molly skirted the edge of the gardens, noting two or three men hard at work in the borders. The effect of the cold summer was obvious: it was a polite display of colour rather than the expected rich exuberance. She rounded the corner of the walled garden, intending to peek in to see who was there, only to walk straight into George as he came out through the gate.

'Molly!' he said, taking her arm to steady her as she almost dropped her bag in shock. 'I'm sorry if I startled you. I wasn't expecting to see you here. But I'm glad you're back. Can I come to visit you, after work? There's something I want to say.'

Molly was flustered by his words, and felt the need to explain her presence in the garden.

'Of course. I was just on my way back from Margate and had a fancy to see how the grounds looked, with the garden party so close.'

George shrugged. 'It's not as any of us would like, but if the weather holds up and we get some sunshine, there's still time for improvement.'

'I'll leave you to get on. And I'll see you later.' Molly was now in a hurry to be away, suddenly fearful in case Charlie should appear.

On her walk home from Margate, she'd remembered her plan to visit Judith the day after she had been invited to lunch. It felt like a long time ago, not just six days earlier. Now, as soon as she'd unpacked the few things from her bag and eaten a hasty midday meal, improvised from the few items that had remained fresh in the larder, she hurried the short distance to Judith's door. To her surprise, there was no reply to her knock.

Molly had expected Judith to be at home with Joseph, as usual, and couldn't think where she might be. She knocked once more, half wondering whether Judith might be avoiding her. Could what George had to say be in some way related to this? Had he discovered that Molly had been making secret visits and banned his wife from encouraging them?

Then she chided herself: George had been perfectly civil when she'd bumped into him earlier. She returned home and resigned herself to waiting out the hours until his promised visit.

Chapter Fifty-Nine

Molly was saved from too much deliberation over what George might have to say, for he arrived earlier than she had expected that evening. She'd assumed after his day in the garden he would go home to wash, eat and spend time with Judith and Joseph. Instead, he appeared on her doorstep two hours earlier than she had imagined, and still in his work clothes.

'Come in, sit down,' she said, opening the kitchen door wide to encourage him to step in.

'I'm not the cleanest,' he said, looking down at himself.

'No matter. It's a wooden chair I'm offering.' Molly smiled. 'Can I get you something? A glass of ale?' she asked.

'I wouldn't say no,' George said. 'It's been thirsty work today.'

Molly was impatient to hear what he had to say, and anxious too, but she knew her relationship with George was still fragile and she must wait until he was ready.

George took a draught of the ale she had poured, which seemed to give him the impetus he needed to get started.

'I had a letter from Margaret,' he began. 'What she said – about her father – got me thinking. She wanted me to understand that I hadn't missed out by not knowing him. I remembered the time I met him out in Martinique, when I didn't

306

know who he was. I had to deliver money to him on behalf of the captain and I thought then what a sorry state he was in. Not just because he'd been ill with yellow fever, but he'd clearly been drinking: there were bottles all around his room. Margaret told me that she and her mother had had to move out and leave him – they simply couldn't stay there. She didn't say much but I had the impression he might have been violent towards them.'

He took another long draught of ale. He hadn't looked at Molly while he'd been speaking, gazing at the table instead, but now he turned his eyes on her.

'Anyway, I don't know why I acted as I did when I heard my father named. Maybe I was embarrassed, certainly confused. And angry that it had been kept secret. Judith made me see why you did that, though, how if the truth had got out it would have caused problems in the family.

'So I want to say I'm sorry. We've lost enough time together, you and I, and I don't want to lose any more. Can you forgive me for the way I behaved?'

Molly could scarcely believe her ears. She'd never dared to hope that George would come around in this way. She opened her mouth to speak but he hadn't finished.

'If anyone has been a father figure to me, it's Charlie. He came to find me when I went off to Portsmouth and persuaded me to come back. He has been endlessly patient, teaching me all about the gardens. I spoke to him first to seek his advice when I wanted to marry Judith. And now I hate to see what has happened between you both.'

George turned his glass slowly on the table before lifting it to his lips to take another long draught. 'I feel somehow responsible for what has happened. It's all tied up with me, after all.' He held up his hand as Molly started to protest.

307

'And I don't approve of the carry-on with Harriet. I can't imagine what's got into him.'

He was so indignant that Molly almost laughed.

'I wanted you to know that I'm going to tell him so, and to persuade him he should return to you.'

Molly was taken aback. Although she had longed to hear these words, she wasn't sure that Charlie would be receptive to them. He was a fair and generous man, but he had a stubborn streak. Once a decision was made he was inclined to stick with it, as she knew only too well from their years together. George would have to take care not to push Charlie further down the road he had chosen to follow.

In addition, Molly was beginning to wonder whether Charlie hadn't come to his own decision, at least with regard to Harriet, if not herself. It might be unwise for anyone else to interfere at this stage. But she was grateful to George for his willingness to attempt to mend the breakdown in their relationship and for his loyalty to her over Charlie.

She stumbled over her words as she tried to express this and, to her horror, she began to weep. Once she had begun, it seemed as though she would never stop. Everything she had suppressed over the last few weeks – the hurt, the anger, the despair – welled up so she could no longer contain it.

George sprang to his feet and came around the table to hold her. He patted her back and murmured, 'Oh, Molly,' several times, which only inspired fresh tears.

Finally, she slowed to a hiccuping pause and could only say, somewhat incoherently, 'Aunt Jane.'

'Aunt Jane?' George was puzzled.

'Yes, Aunt Jane. I've spent the week with her. She was so unwell. I thought she might die. I was very worried.'

'I see,' said George, who clearly didn't.

'Thank you,' Molly said, when she was finally able to speak properly. 'Thank you for coming to see me. And for your words. They mean a lot to me. I don't want us to lose another moment of precious time, either.'

They hugged then and she added, speaking into his work jacket, 'But please take care with whatever you say to Charlie. He's a proud man.'

'Don't worry, I will,' George said. 'And now I'd better get going. He doesn't know where I am and we're fending for ourselves for dinner tonight.'

Seeing Molly's bewilderment he added, 'Judith has gone away, to visit her sister near Canterbury. So she can meet Joseph for the first time.'

That explained why the house had been empty, Molly thought, with a sense of relief. But she merely said, 'Oh, if only I'd known, I could have made dinner for you both.'

George laughed. 'That would have been welcome but then there'd be no hiding from Charlie where I'd been. And it won't do us any harm to make do, although likely as not Judith has left us well provided for.'

That was true, Molly thought, as she waved George away. Her daughter-in-law was not only well organised but thoughtful. She owed her a debt of gratitude for taking care of Charlie and for intervening with George in her patient way. If only she could draw on some reserves of patience for herself. After her discussion with George, she felt sad to think of her husband and son sitting down to eat together just a few doors away while she remained at home, alone. She longed for a change in all their circumstances.

Chapter Sixty

The following day being Sunday, Molly had fully intended to go to church and although she woke early, she fell back to sleep. When she roused again, she still felt tired. She supposed her days spent in Margate, keeping watch at Aunt Jane's bedside, were the cause. Perhaps the release of emotion brought on by George's visit had contributed to her tiredness, too. She allowed herself to lie in bed a little longer, feeling drowsy, before she made herself get up and think about the day ahead.

Once she was up and about, she regretted not attending church. With Judith away, she wondered whether George and Charlie would have gone; she could have offered them dinner at home afterwards. Then she scolded herself for letting her thoughts run on in this way. Her relationship with George might be on the mend but there was no indication of any improvement with Charlie. She must try to be patient. And, in any case, the larder was bare since she had been away most of the week.

Her own dinner was a scratch affair but she didn't mind. There was sunshine and she took her chair into a patch of shade in the garden, enjoying the warm breeze while she ate. She needed to make plans to fill her time: there was still a fortnight to be got through before the garden party. The event had developed significance in her mind that she was not sure it deserved. It would be an occasion when all her family got together and the lead-up to it had always been a strain, with the amount of hard work Charlie needed to put in. This year, she hadn't experienced any of the anxiety that plagued him in these weeks, but it had been replaced by a different worry of her own. Her sisters and her aunt, if she was well enough to come, were expecting to hear of her reconciliation with Charlie.

She thought back to the previous year: the party had been the usual happy affair. George and Judith had married just a few weeks previously and, after all her previous heartache over the loss of her son, she had felt such contentment with her life. Apart from Agnes, her family were all settled and she and Charlie had been happy. How had it all gone so wrong?

She allowed her thoughts to dwell on Harriet – something she rarely permitted. She had been glad to see her again and keen to re-establish their connection, inviting her to dinner and to Joseph's christening. At the time, she was saddened by how Harriet's life had turned out after she had left Margate but now – what did she feel? Anger at Harriet's deceit, she supposed, but there was more. Bewilderment, perhaps. How had she managed to worm her way into Charlie's affections? Should Molly have recognised what was going on and put a stop to it?

Molly gathered up her plate and glass to return them to the kitchen. She would keep busy in the days to come, she vowed. She would visit Sally and spend time with Catherine and Eleanor. She would write to Agnes to make sure she still planned to come to the garden party and she would make her room ready. No doubt Judith would arrive home later in the week and she could pay her a visit, too.

As Molly washed up it occurred to her that she should have a new outfit for the garden party. She didn't want to travel to Canterbury or Margate to see a dressmaker there but she could ask Sally when she visited her. She was a skilled seamstress, sharing the role with Mrs Rowe at the draper's shop in Margate. If she went to see her the following day, there would be time enough to complete the dress if she entrusted Sally with the choice of fabric.

Molly spent several minutes daydreaming over ideas for style and colour; it was a long time since she had treated herself in this way. Her future prospects might be uncertain and her savings diminishing but she was prepared to dip into them for this.

She was on the road the next day as soon as she had eaten breakfast. Sally was surprised when she arrived unannounced, but declared herself delighted to make a dress for her mother.

'I've got just the cloth for it in the shop. It's a chintz – not too showy – and it will suit you, Ma. I'll get rose-coloured ribbons to match for your bonnet, too.'

Sally refused to take the money that Molly pressed on her, saying, 'It's a gift from me. It's not often I get the chance to do something for you, while you've done plenty for me over the years.'

Molly walked home from Westgate with a spring in her step – she'd enjoyed spending time with Simon and Grace and she was looking forward to seeing the dress. Sally had promised to bring it in good time on the day of the garden party so that she could make any necessary adjustments. 'And I can spend time with you and Agnes before the party begins. It's rare for us to get time alone these days.'

She hadn't asked about her father or George, and Molly was relieved. It felt good to forget about that part of her life for a few hours. That evening, she wrote a note to Agnes, asking her when she planned to arrive. She hesitated before folding it, then added a final line, *By the way, have you seen anything more of Harriet?*

The following day Molly spent with Catherine, Eleanor providing a delightful distraction. Catherine, however, was more aware of how matters stood with her father and brother so once Eleanor had been settled for her nap she asked her mother outright about the situation.

Molly was pensive. 'Things are much improved with George, since Margaret and Judith brought their influence to bear on him. He has sworn to speak to Charlie and warn him off Harriet, which, I confess, makes me nervous. I fear it will only drive him further away.'

'Nonsense,' Catherine said briskly. 'I'm sure you misjudge him. I'll wager he's come to the realisation that she's nothing but a hussy and he's feeling foolish now.'

She wouldn't be drawn on whether she had this on good authority from anyone. Molly wondered whether it had come from her husband, Francis, who – as one of the estate managers – had regular dealings with Charlie.

She made her way home that afternoon feeling a flicker of hope. Catherine was sensible and not known for flights of fancy: her mother felt sure she wouldn't say such a thing without good reason.

The weather – windy and damp – kept Molly at home on the Wednesday but Thursday found her determined to pay a visit to Judith, who must surely be back at home. She was keen to thank her for being instrumental in persuading George to reconcile with her. She was still curious, though, as to whether Judith could offer any insight into Charlie's frame of mind.

313

CHAPTER SIXTY-ONE

On Thursday afternoon, when Molly knocked on her door, Judith had indeed returned from her visit. She hadn't seen her sister since before her marriage to George and they had clearly enjoyed the time they had spent together. Joseph had behaved impeccably, it seemed, and Molly listened patiently while Judith described what they had done each day in Canterbury.

'I'm glad to be back, though,' Judith said, as she finished her tale. 'The city is lovely for a visit, but I prefer the country-side. It's quieter and cleaner. Those streets, the smell . . .' She wrinkled her nose as she recalled it.

'I was pleased to see George, too,' Judith continued. 'It's the first time we've been apart since we were wed. I'm not entirely sure he noticed we were gone,' she laughed, 'although he was happy enough to see us back. He and Charlie had eaten their way through all the food I left for them.'

'And how was Charlie?' Molly asked, hoping that her enquiry sounded casual.

Judith frowned. 'Grumpy. He's working every daylight hour and dragging George along with him. He comes in, eats and goes straight to bed, without a word being said.' She looked at Molly. 'I get the impression he's missing home.'

It was Molly's turn to laugh. 'He's always like that at this time of year. Garden party fever, I used to call it.'

Judith's expression was serious. 'I think it's more than that, I really do. Don't forget you know him inside out. I'm sure he's feeling the lack of your company. When they come in, I'm busy telling George what Joseph has been up to, not asking them about their day.'

Molly shrugged, but she was secretly pleased.

Joseph had grabbed hold of a handful of Judith's hair and was tugging it, so she was looking down when she next spoke.

'What will you do, Molly? Charlie can't stay here for ever. Not that he isn't welcome, of course,' she added hastily, 'but it's been a while now and after the garden party . . .'

Judith was right: a decision of some sort had to be reached, Molly knew. They couldn't drift on like this.

'He's proud, you know.' Judith hadn't finished. 'I feel sure there are things he wants to say to you but he doesn't know where to begin.'

Molly frowned. 'I don't know what I'm supposed to do. I don't see him, and even if I did, I feel he owes it to me to start the conversation. He's the one who went off.' She grew hot with indignation at the thought.

'I know, I know.' Judith was quick to placate. 'Perhaps there will be time enough when the garden party is over.'

Ten more days, Molly thought. An agony of waiting – and for what? For a day that promised to be happy and uneasy in equal measure. She was looking forward to seeing her family, but not to them realising that she was still estranged from Charlie. And she didn't even know what resolution she sought. She missed Charlie, but she felt as though what they once had was destroyed, their years together erased by a

315

foolish infatuation. Or maybe Charlie didn't think of it as foolish – she had no way of knowing since they had barely spoken in weeks. It was hard to think back to how it had all started – was it just one chance remark by Hannah that had caused her world to unravel?

Molly sighed, then saw that Judith was watching her. She roused herself to take Joseph from her and devoted her attention to her grandson, resolutely pushing all thoughts of Charlie from her mind. The rest of her visit passed in play, and in discussion of the gowns that both women planned to wear for the garden party, Judith having used her time in Canterbury to visit the dressmaker there. Molly felt envious when Judith brought the dress downstairs to show her – it was a confection of cream and pale pink. Joseph's chubby fingers reached out for it – he was drawn to the delicate lace edging the sleeves.

'Let me keep it clean for a little longer.' Judith laughed, whisking it away just in time. 'It will be destroyed quickly enough on the day by your sticky hands, I'm sure.'

Molly was glad, then, of the cloth that Sally planned to use for her own gown. The deeper colour and the pattern should be proof against all her grandchildren – there would be three other under-fives who would be happy to clamber onto her lap that day.

Agnes wrote to say that she planned to take a holiday and spend it at home. She would arrive on the Tuesday before the event, which pleased her mother a great deal. There had been no more sightings of Harriet, she said, and Molly didn't enquire further once Agnes had arrived. She was just delighted to have her company. They took regular walks, Molly reminding Agnes of how, as a child, she had loved to collect things to draw and paint when they returned home.

'What will you do about your art?' she asked Agnes, as they strolled along paths lined with the white flowers of hedge parsley, threaded through with purple bush vetch. 'Have you quite given it up now that you are working?'

She asked the question without fully understanding what Agnes did to earn her living.

'Mrs Townley has employed me for my drawing skills,' Agnes said. 'I not only draw up plans for her – which are mainly straight lines and perfect dimensions, it is true – but I also paint pictures that help her clients imagine how their house might look in the road, or to illustrate the interiors. But I do long to paint again, just for myself.'

'You could paint something while you're here?' Molly suggested. 'You still have paints and paper in your room. We could pick some of these flowers to take home. Or collect something.' She cast around for the sort of pebbles and snail shells that had once fascinated Agnes.

'I don't really paint like that now, Ma.' Agnes was apologetic. 'I like to paint people – portraits.'

They talked no more on the subject until the Saturday morning, when Sally arrived with the new dress. Molly slipped it on so that Sally could check that the length was correct and the fit just right. Agnes came in and, after she had greeted Sally, both of them observing how well the other looked, she turned to Molly.

'Ma, stay there. I'm going to fetch my sketch pad. Don't move.'

Bemused, Molly did as she was told, looking out of the window and anxiously checking the sky. It looked promising – there were no dark clouds to be seen, and although the sun wasn't blazing down, it was bright and the gentle lifting of the leaves on the trees suggested a light breeze.

Molly wondered how long she would have to hold her pose while Agnes sketched her. It was already midday and she had planned they would eat a light meal together before the garden party began, since tea there would not be served until well after four o'clock.

Just as Molly decided she could stand at the window no longer, Agnes professed herself happy with the sketch. She refused to show either Sally or her mother. 'Let me work it up a little more,' she said. 'And add some colour. Then you can look.'

Until that point, neither Agnes nor Sally had directly referred to the challenge that lay ahead for their mother. They had been busy catching up on each other's news while Agnes sketched and Molly had listened without feeling the need to contribute. But now Agnes had finished, Sally took charge.

'Let's get you properly ready, shall we, Ma?' she said. 'You need to look your best today.'

Molly looked down, puzzled. 'But I am ready. I have your beautiful new gown to wear.'

Sally nodded. 'And it suits you well. I'm pleased. There'll be a lot of eyes on you today, so let's do something with your hair, too.'

Molly experienced a flash of anger. 'You mean, people will be looking at me and saying, "It's plain to see why her husband went off with a younger woman."'

Agnes, who had been upstairs to put her sketch safely away, came back into the room in time to catch her mother's words.

'No, Ma,' she protested. 'Sally didn't mean that at all. You're beautiful.'

Sally, who had flushed at her mother's attack, nodded. 'I just meant that if you look your best, you'll feel your best, too.'

Molly was only half pacified. 'So why didn't you wait to sketch me until I was all primped and prettified?' she demanded, turning to Agnes.

Agnes began to laugh. 'Ma, you look lovely as you are. And, anyway, I always prefer my portraits to look natural, as though they have captured a moment in time, not as though someone has dressed up and posed for them.'

Molly sighed. She wasn't sure why she had reacted as she did: Sally only had her best interests at heart, after all. 'I'm sorry, Sally,' she said, turning to her eldest daughter. 'I don't know what came over me. But I'll be happier as I am, rather than having to spend all afternoon worrying whether my curls have fallen out of place. By the time I've enjoyed the company of Grace and Simon and the babies, I'll have been pulled this way and that in any case. So, let's eat something now, then you two can dress and by then it will be time to leave.'

Imagining what lay ahead, Molly felt a nervous sliding sensation in the pit of her stomach. She laid out a selection of cheeses and cold cuts but discovered she could only pick at what she put onto her plate. Her heart was beating fast, her cheeks were flushed and she was distressed to see her hands trembling as she picked up her knife and fork. She just wanted to get the whole ordeal of the day over and done with and she was glad when Sally and Agnes went up to change. She'd refused their offers of help in clearing up, happy to have a few moments to herself to steady her nerves.

Why hadn't she gone to see Charlie during the week, to have a frank discussion? It would have made today easier:

319

they would have known where they stood with each other. She made a wry face as she washed and wiped the plates. She knew she had used the excuse of Agnes's arrival, and the knowledge that Charlie would be in the gardens until darkness fell, to avoid that conversation. If they didn't find time to talk today, the worst of all days to do so, perhaps it would never happen.

Sally came back into the kitchen, seized a drying cloth and flapped it at her mother. 'I'll finish this. You go and find your bonnet and shawl. I don't think we can count on sunshine all day. Then we must go – family will be arriving.'

Molly did as she was told, smiling to herself as she reflected on how the tables had turned. All the years she had spent reminding the girls to take bonnets and shawls and now they were doing the same to her.

She looked at herself in the glass in her bedroom as she tied on her bonnet, admiring the way the new ribbon picked out the deep rose in the dress. Sally had a good eye – an artistic talent not dissimilar to Agnes's, she supposed. Where had it come from? Neither she nor Charlie had ever picked up an artist's brush in their lives. Then she remembered how he could plan a border and weave colour through a garden and it struck her that perhaps he was an artist after all.

Her fingers were stilled as she tightened the bow securing her bonnet and she gazed into her own eyes in the glass, momentarily distracted by what she saw. She looked well, she thought. Her heightened colour suited her and her eyes sparkled. She remembered Sally's words: 'If you look your best, you'll feel your best.' There was something in it, she thought. She hadn't needed artifice, though: she was happy as she was. Today would be a good day, she decided. She would have her family around her and she would enjoy their company. Charlie would have to shift for himself.

She went downstairs to find Agnes and Sally waiting. As in so many past years, they linked arms and set off for the garden party.

CHAPTER SIXTY-TWO

Their route to the gardens was along the path Charlie followed to work each day, bringing them out beside the walled gardens at the distant edge of the party. The house presided over the lawns, which were already filled with people. Molly's fragile confidence ebbed away as they advanced towards the gathering. Sally broke their silent progress by pointing and saying, 'Look, there's Catherine. And Judith with her. Oh – what a beautiful dress. Where did she get that fabric?'

She guided her mother and sister towards their family group – Molly could see her own sisters as they drew closer. Her anxiety eased: it would be all right, here among her family. She reminded herself that Charlie was always busy on the day of the garden party, often until the moment it finished. Mr Powell liked him on hand to answer any questions his London guests might have about the roses, or the borders or the management of the woodland walk.

At that moment she saw him, listening politely as Mr Powell held forth to a small group, encompassing the entire gardens with expansive gestures of his hands. In the past, she would have caught Charlie's eye and a secret smile would have passed between them. Now, she was struck by how gaunt he looked and dismayed to see he hadn't paid

322

attention to whether he had dressed smartly enough for the occasion.

Then she was drawn into the heart of her family group, Grace and Simon vying for her attention while she asked Lizzie and Mary about Aunt Jane's health.

'She's much better, but not strong enough to come with us today. Uncle William has stayed at home with her,' Lizzie replied.

Molly raised her eyebrows. Uncle William liked nothing better than an event such as this: he loved the chance to play the part of someone of importance even though his local standing was much diminished by age.

Mary saw Molly's expression. 'He's still worried about Aunt Jane. He didn't like the thought of leaving her, in case she took a turn for the worse, even though Elsie and Hannah are both at home. Aunt Jane said to tell you she's still expecting to see you and Charlie next Sunday, though.' The look she gave Molly held a note of enquiry.

'Just the two of us? Or the girls as well?' Molly wasn't ready to be drawn on the subject.

'The whole family,' Lizzie joined in, with a frown. 'She's very insistent on it. I wondered whether she and Uncle William plan to make some sort of announcement.'

There was no time to speculate further, for the tea tables were declared open, leading to an unseemly rush by the waiting crowd. The family managed to secure two tables next to each other, the ladies seated while the men stood and the younger children sat on the grass or, in the case of the babies, were passed from lap to lap.

Molly looked up from tickling Joseph, delighting in his infectious chuckle, to see a familiar figure approaching. 'Here's Margaret,' she exclaimed. She noticed two things at the same time: Margaret was on the arm of a young man and she was drawing a mixture of curious and admiring looks as she moved through the crowd.

Even without her striking looks she would have stood out for her gown alone, Molly thought. She wondered whether she had brought the fabric with her from the West Indies: the colours were bolder than the pastel shades still in favour in England, although the style was very much in fashion.

Sally had spotted her and was beckoning her over. 'Margaret, it's perfect. You did well to insist on your fabric choice.'

So Sally had made Margaret's dress, too, Molly thought, as she no doubt had made several of the new gowns on display that day. The miserable weather that summer seemed to have made the ladies determined to put on a show, on a day when the sun almost shone through the clouds.

Lewis had been talking to his cousins but when he saw Margaret he came over. 'I'm going to steal Henry away, Margaret,' he said. 'Do you mind?'

'I need to introduce him to someone special first,' Margaret said, turning to smile at Molly. 'I don't believe the two of you have met before. Henry, this is Mrs Dawson, whom I've told you so much about. Molly, this is Henry.' She paused.

Henry laughed. 'And have you no description for me?'

Molly saw that Margaret, normally so serene and composed, appeared flustered.

She looked at the ground as she spoke again. 'This is Henry Sayer – my intended.'

'Goodness!' Molly said. 'What a surprise.' She registered the appeal in Margaret's eyes and added, 'A lovely surprise, of course. I'm delighted to meet you, Henry. I hope we will have the chance to get to know each other a great deal better. You are a very lucky man.'

'And I know it,' Henry said, momentarily solemn. 'I couldn't take my eyes off Margaret when I first saw her at the ball and I've been pinching myself ever since.'

'And have you set a date for the wedding?' Molly asked.

'As soon as possible,' Henry said firmly. 'But I must introduce Margaret to my mother first. She has been too unwell to travel here since my father passed away.' A shadow of worry crossed his countenance as he spoke.

'She will be delighted to give you her blessing,' Molly said, smiling 'No one could meet Margaret and not fall instantly in love.'

Margaret threw Molly a grateful glance before she and Henry were caught up in a wave of family congratulations. It must be hard for her, Molly thought. With her mother so far away, Margaret had no family she could turn to. Then she watched the easy and affectionate way that the young cousins – Helena, Susan and Lewis – drew her and Henry into their group and she realised Margaret was far from being alone. She had found her family in Margate – Harriet was owed thanks for that, at least.

Suddenly fearful that her half-sister might be somewhere among the crowd, intent on causing a scene, she took a look around. Her eyes fell on another pair of latecomers, Sarah and Constance, making their way towards the table. She arranged her features into a semblance of a welcoming smile, thinking as she did so that she must try to overcome her prejudice of many years. Sarah really didn't deserve it – and Constance even less.

Did Constance know of Margaret's engagement? It would hurt her, yet another reminder of how her own prospects had been diminished by her father's behaviour. She would have married well several years before, surely, if it hadn't been for the taint left by Nicholas's defection.

Margaret called Constance to her, and Molly was surprised to see how her face lit up as she left her mother's side and went to join the young people. She supposed they had all found time to get to know each other better over the past weeks, weeks in which she had been wrapped up in her own private misery.

Agnes broke in on her thoughts. 'Ma, I think Mr Powell is about to make his speech. Are you ready?' The look she gave her mother held no small measure of anxiety.

'Yes,' Molly said, surprising herself by how firm she sounded. She stood up and shook the crumbs deposited by Grace and Simon out of her skirts. Each year Mr Powell took to the bandstand to greet his guests and to thank Charlie and his team for all their hard work in getting the gardens looking their best. And he always liked to include thanks for Molly, for her support and for enduring her husband's long absences. This year would be no exception. Did he know the true situation? Molly wondered. Did he realise that she and Charlie were living apart on his estate?

She made her way through the crowd, murmuring, 'Excuse me,' as she pushed past those already clustered close to the bandstand. Mr Powell was mounting the steps, Mrs Powell following. Charlie was already standing on the makeshift stage, beside the small band who had been playing to entertain the crowd. He looked down at Molly and their eyes met for the first time that afternoon.

CHAPTER SIXTY-THREE

As she climbed the steps to the bandstand, Molly's legs trembled and she had to grasp the handrail to steady herself. She took her place at Charlie's side and looked at the crowd, a smile fixed to her face. Agnes and Catherine had followed her onto the lawn and now positioned themselves near the front of the crowd, to give her courage, she supposed. She barely heard a word that Mr Powell uttered, nodding and stretching her mouth into a forced smile when he turned towards her. She didn't look at Charlie, and she was sure it must be obvious to the whole crowd that she was standing stiffly at his side.

As soon as Mr and Mrs Powell made their way down the steps, she was on their heels. She hardly cared if she appeared to be hasty – she couldn't wait to escape back to the safety of her family. The band struck up behind her as she joined Agnes and Catherine and followed them back to their table. They didn't comment on how she had looked on stage and she didn't ask them, but Catherine squeezed her arm and gave her a sympathetic smile.

Molly had just settled back into her seat when she saw Charlie was not far behind her. He stopped to greet the male members of the family party before making his way over to her.

'I don't see Uncle William and Aunt Jane here,' he said, as he arrived at her side. 'Is your aunt still unwell?'

Molly was taken aback. He spoke as though the last few weeks had never happened, not quite as easily as if they had last parted company at the breakfast table that morning, it was true, but with no embarrassment and in a perfectly civil fashion.

Molly saw her daughters and Judith watching her.

'Not well enough to be here, I'm afraid. Uncle William has stayed at home with her.' She hesitated. Should she mention her aunt's expectations that they would both visit the following Sunday? She left it a moment too long, though, for Charlie turned to take a glass of ale that George had fetched before nodding at her and moving away.

He seemed perfectly relaxed as he chatted to George and the other menfolk. Molly saw her sisters looking at her and turned away, gazing out over the crowd of visitors while she regained her composure. When she turned back, Charlie had gone.

This was not how she had expected the afternoon to proceed. She had imagined the garden party as a turning point, she supposed. In her imagination, Charlie had begged her forgiveness and sworn never to see Harriet again, while she had prevaricated until he had pleaded to be allowed to come back.

Was it possible that Charlie didn't see things in the same way? She wondered, once more, whether Harriet was there. Had he invited her? Was he even now seeking her out in the crowd? She stood up to get a better view, peering out over the sea of heads. The tea tables were set on the terrace, affording a good view over the lawns. Her eyes ranged back and forth until they were arrested by the sight of Charlie, in conversation with a woman whose back was towards Molly. Her heart lurched and she almost cried out. Then in an instant, as the woman turned her head, she realised it was Agnes, petite in stature and easily obscured by everyone around her.

Molly felt foolish. She wished the afternoon was over so she could escape back to the cottage: she could feel a headache coming on. She now had no expectation that the day would result in any resolution of her predicament.

Judith came to stand beside her and drew her attention to the dark clouds gathering over the house.

'We've been lucky with the weather so far,' she said, 'but I think we should prepare to leave.'

It looked as though the other guests had had the same idea. Those travelling back to Margate were making hasty farewells and all around them visitors were rising to their feet, calling for children or looking anxiously out over the grounds in search of them.

A gust of wind swept across the terrace, making Molly shiver. She took her shawl from the back of her chair and looked up. The clouds were building and churning, moving ever closer.

Agnes had arrived back at the table and Molly called to her, 'Are you ready to go? It looks as though there will be a storm.'

Before they could make a move, they were swept up in a frenzy of goodbyes as Lizzie and Mary and their families, then Sally and hers, took their leave. Margaret was waiting to have a word with Molly, too.

'I will see you next week,' she said, as the first heavy drops of rain began to fall.

'You will?' Molly was surprised.

'Yes, at Aunt Jane's house,' Margaret said, then squealed in shock as a flash of lightning was followed at once by a clap of thunder. She ran, Henry pulling her along, as Agnes and Molly stood for a moment, indecisive.

'Over here,' Judith called. She had taken shelter with George and Joseph under the awning covering the long table, so recently serving tea and cakes.

'We'll have to wait until it passes,' Judith said, as they joined them. 'If we set off now we'll be drenched in an instant.'

Molly flinched as the lightning flashed again. The lawns had emptied very quickly. The Powells and their guests had taken refuge in the house, while everyone else was at the front, trying to find their carriages. Those who had arrived on foot would have no option but to take shelter where they could.

A voice in Molly's ear made her jump. It was Charlie. 'I remember another occasion when a storm almost destroyed a garden party.' He was unsmiling as he spoke. Molly knew immediately what he meant: his words took her back to when she was fourteen years old, standing in the gardens during a Prospect House garden party. Charlie had offered to show her round but they were interrupted by a cloudburst. It had been a significant moment – she knew he had been poised to say something of consequence but the rain had broken the spell. Now, as she shivered in another cold gust of wind that dashed rain into their faces, she noticed Agnes and Judith edging away, leaving her isolated with Charlie.

She hadn't answered and Charlie spoke again. 'Molly, there's something I need to talk to you about.'

She waited, unsure whether the shivering had turned to trembling. Was this it? Was this the start of an apology, a

330

plea to her to forgive what had happened? While she wasn't sure yet how she would respond, she felt a faint stirring of hope.

'I've been offered the post of head gardener by Lord Wilmslow at his place in Cheshire,' Charlie continued. 'I've worked here for twenty-eight years now, and Lord Wilmslow has asked me before. This is my chance to move on, to take on a new challenge. Perhaps my final one.' He sounded thoughtful.

Molly opened her mouth, then stopped. She didn't know how to respond. This wasn't what she had been expecting at all.

'With the way things are between us, it seems like the best thing to do. A fresh start, away from here.' Charlie paused. 'I know it's been difficult for you, having me living just a few doors away. This way, you can get on with your life.'

Molly turned to look at him, confused.

'It's only fair that I should go. My ties aren't so strong. You can stay here, with all your family around. I'll send money, of course.'

Thoughts crowded into Molly's mind. Charlie meant to leave her and move away, abandoning her, their daughters and grandchildren. How could he even think of doing so? Then it struck her like a hammer blow. Was he leaving with Harriet?

Chapter Sixty-Four

The change to the weather in the next ten minutes was as dramatic as the storm that had blown in. The clouds rolled away, the wind dropped and the sky was revealed as a vivid blue, washed and sparkling after all the rain. As Molly, Agnes and Judith picked their way home through the gardens, leaving George and Charlie behind to help clear up in the aftermath of the deluge, Judith turned to look back.

'Oh!' she exclaimed, coming to a halt.

The skies were still dark in the distance, beyond Woodchurch Manor, as the storm ran along the coast. A double rainbow cast its arc over the roof of the house, the colours in one of the bows so vivid they almost hurt the eyes.

'How beautiful,' Judith said. 'A message from the heavens.' She cast a sideways glance at Molly, who had been silent since they set off. Charlie had delivered his news, then moved away to leave her alone, lost in thought, as she stared at the sheets of rain blowing across the lawn.

Agnes squeezed Molly's arm. 'Come on, Ma, let's get you home. You're pale. I hope you haven't taken a chill.'

They turned their backs on the rainbow and continued on their way, Joseph snuffling sleepily in Judith's arms. A thought ran through Molly's head on a repeated loop: the hems of their gowns would be ruined by the damp grass of the gardens and the mud of the path. It filled her mind so there was no room for anything else.

Judith hurried away to put Joseph to bed after Agnes and Molly had reached their gate. Once through the front door, Molly announced she had a headache and was going straight upstairs. It was inconceivable that she might have to spend the evening going over the events of the garden party with Agnes, let alone telling her about Charlie's announcement just before they left.

She thought she would lie awake, racked by her thoughts. Instead, she had barely removed her dress, leaving it in a crumpled heap on the floor and replacing it with her night-gown, before she climbed under the covers and fell into a deep sleep.

She opened her eyes much later, to find herself in total darkness. The house was silent; Molly supposed it to be not long past midnight, since she had fallen asleep around seven o'clock. She lay there awhile, willing sleep to return, but thirst and the need to relieve herself couldn't be denied. In addition, Charlie's words had returned to her and they were insistent, demanding attention.

She left the warmth of her bed, first to use the chamber pot and then, throwing a shawl around her shoulders, to go down to the kitchen. She quenched her thirst, then took her glass to the window to peer out into the darkness. There was nothing to be seen, although a gradual greying of the light told her the night was more advanced than she had thought. Resigning herself to spending troubled and restless hours before it was time to begin the day, she turned away from the window to go back upstairs. As she passed the table, her eye fell on the paints and paper laid out there. Agnes must have been at work while she slept, Molly thought.

The light in the room was too dim to make out the detail, so Molly lit a candle and held it over the painting. Now she could just make out the figure of a woman – herself – half turned away from the viewer as she gazed out over the garden. Agnes had captured her well; she could see it even in this half-finished state. It was the emotion of the still figure that held her attention. Wistful, resigned, expectant, afraid? All of this and more, Molly thought.

She blew out the candle and trod slowly back up the stairs, hoping the creaking wouldn't disturb Agnes. Then she slid back between the sheets and, over the next hour or so, watched through her open curtains as the dawn broke, to reveal a day much brighter than the one that had gone before.

Molly must have drifted back into sleep, for she woke from a tangled dream to hear sounds from the kitchen below. She stumbled from her bed and down the stairs, feeling far more tired than she had on her earlier visit.

'Morning, Ma.' Agnes was seated at the table, a cup steaming gently beside her, a shawl over her nightgown and her paintbrush already in her hand. 'Did you sleep well?'

'I did,' Molly said. 'I got up in the early hours and came down for a drink, then went back to bed. I never expected to go back to sleep.' She yawned and rubbed her eyes. 'What time is it?' She answered her own question by looking at the clock. 'Seven. Not late.'

Agnes was absorbed in her work again so Molly picked up the teapot from the range and poured herself a cup, then took up the seat opposite her daughter.

Agnes dipped her brush into a jar of water, took a dab of colour from one of the mixtures on her palette and brushed it lightly onto the dress in the painting. She scrutinised it and, happy with the effect, carried on adding a little more of the shade here and there.

'Pa was here last night,' she said.

She uttered the words so casually that Molly barely took them in, before hastily swallowing the mouthful of tea she had just taken. She registered it was too hot and winced.

'He was? What time? Why? You should have woken me.'

Agnes glanced up at her, then leant back in her chair. 'Ma, why didn't you tell me what he said at the end of the afternoon?' She waited barely a second, then added, 'No matter. He told me himself. He came to see how you were.'

'How did he imagine I was?' Molly grimaced. 'He'd just told me he was leaving the area – leaving all of us – to go and live hundreds of miles away. And with that hussy, for all we know.'

Agnes gave her a level look. 'I don't believe Harriet is part of this. The thing is, Pa was worried. He thought he hadn't expressed himself well, that he'd left you confused.'

Molly raised her eyebrows.

Agnes continued. 'Actually, I think it's Pa that's confused. He's convinced himself that this is the right thing to do, that it's best for everyone. I hope I made him see that he needs to talk to you, not present you with a decision already made.'

Agnes had been studying her painting as she spoke. She picked up her brush, added another dab of colour to her mixture and carried on working, while Molly digested her words.

'What do *you* want, Ma?' When Agnes spoke again, it made Molly jump. 'Have you thought about it? What if you went with him? A new start, away from here.'

'The family,' Molly said faintly. Then, in a firmer voice, 'All my family are here. You, Sally, Catherine, Judith, George, the babies, my sisters, Aunt Jane, Uncle William.'

Agnes nodded and carried on working. 'It would be a big decision.'

'And what if it was the wrong one?' Molly burst out. 'What if I went all that way and we were unhappy? I don't even know how I feel about him any more. Or how he feels about me.'

She subsided. Until Agnes had put the thought into her head, she had never even considered going to Cheshire. It was a preposterous idea, surely.

'You could just come back,' Agnes said.

Molly gave a wry smile. Once, many years ago, she, too, had believed nothing was impossible. You simply went ahead and did something, then dealt with the consequences, whatever they were.

'I would say he still likes you, by the way,' Agnes said. 'More than that, he's still in love with you.' She washed her paintbrush and looked at her mother. 'He's asked me if he can have this painting to take with him. I said I'd have to speak to you first.'

Chapter Sixty-Five

Agnes carried on painting, leaving Molly to sit, her tea cooling, while she thought over what her daughter had said. After a long silence – at least twenty minutes, during which Agnes glanced up occasionally but did not speak – Molly stood up.

'It's time to get ready. We're going to church,' she said. 'And after church, we're going to ask George, Judith, Joseph and your pa to eat here.' She was struck by sudden doubt. 'I'm not sure we have enough to offer them, though.' She went over to the larder, opened the door and stared in.

Agnes rinsed her paintbrush and stood up. 'Good idea, Ma. Don't worry about the food. I'll speak to Judith: we can share what we have.'

Molly washed and dressed with a sense of determination she hadn't felt in many weeks. All the women in her family had offered the same advice. It was up to her to talk to Charlie and sort things out. If he was going away, they needed to discuss how he would stay in touch with the family. Her heart contracted. Charlie loved his daughters and grandchildren. The gardens had always come first but, nevertheless, he was a good family man.

Molly shook her head over Agnes's entreaties to eat some breakfast before they left. She was impatient, pacing up and down the kitchen while she waited for her daughter to get ready. The painting still lay on the table and she began to gather up the paints and clear away, in preparation for laying the table for dinner on their return, when her hands were stilled. Perhaps it did no harm for the portrait to be left where Charlie could see it.

The morning was fresh and bright, with a promise of warmth later. Agnes took a firm grip on her mother's arm, restraining her from marching at great speed along the lane to the church, so they managed to enter in a calm and collected manner.

They were among the first of the congregation to arrive. Molly was glad: it meant she didn't have to endure the glances and whispers of those already there. She sat with her hands in her lap, her eyes fixed forwards, her heart beating fast. Agnes glanced back at the sound of familiar voices, speaking in hushed tones. A moment later, Judith and George slid into the pew alongside Agnes. There was no sign of Charlie, and Molly's certainty faltered. She observed Agnes and Judith conversing in low tones then, just as the minister stepped forward to begin, Charlie slipped into the space at the end of the pew, causing them all to shift up slightly. He carried a sleeping Joseph in his arms, passing him carefully along to Judith, who smiled her thanks.

Molly heard her whisper to Agnes, 'He was so fractious – thank goodness he's asleep now,' before they all rose and the service began.

Molly's thoughts were elsewhere and she would have been unable to recount anything about the service, despite murmuring, 'A most interesting sermon. Thank you,' to the minister as they all filed out.

They stopped in the sunshine to exchange a few words. Charlie sought to catch Mr Powell's eye and she guessed he was intent on discussing the garden party. Hastily, cutting across George and Agnes's conversation, she said, 'I'd like you all to come to dinner. Charlie, too.' She added the last bit more loudly to get his attention.

Judith spoke up. 'We'd love to.' She glanced at Charlie. 'George and I will go home and collect a few things to bring along. Charlie, you take Joseph for me and we'll meet you there.'

She deposited the still-sleeping infant in Charlie's arms and set off, walking briskly arm-in-arm with George. Molly found it hard to suppress a smile at the way Charlie had been out-manoeuvred by the women in his family.

'Thank you,' she said to Agnes, as they walked back, for her daughter had clearly prepared Judith for the invitation. Charlie lingered, talking to Mr Powell, but Molly wasn't worried. The need to reunite Joseph with his mother meant he would have to join them.

In fact, Charlie, with his longer strides, caught up with them as they walked up the path to the cottage door. They all went into the kitchen together, and as Molly moved to the larder to fetch the vegetables to prepare, Charlie stood by the kitchen table.

'You've done more work on it than when I last saw it, Agnes,' he said. 'And that was only a few hours ago.' His head was bent over the painting. He spoke again without looking up. 'I rather like it as it is. With some of the colours only lightly sketched in. Would you consider leaving it like that?'

Agnes was quick to respond. 'That's a question for Ma. It's her painting, after all. If you want it, you must ask her for it.'

There was a silence in the room, which stretched until it was broken by a sudden shriek from Joseph, who awoke and discovered he was hungry all in the same moment.

The door opened and George and Judith entered, George bearing a plate on which lay a joint of meat, Judith carrying a pie and a jug of cream.

'It looks as though I've arrived just in time,' Judith said, laughing. She swapped her pie for Joseph, then carried him off into the parlour.

Molly took the pie from Charlie, looking up at him as she did so.

'I'd like to talk to you, Charlie. Now, in the garden. Agnes can get the dinner under way.' She spoke to Charlie in an undertone, but raised her voice for the final sentence. Agnes, who was showing George the portrait, nodded at her mother.

Molly stepped through the door and took the path into the garden, Charlie following. She stopped by the apple tree, now heavy with fruit although she noted, in a detached way, that the apples were smaller and greener than she would have expected at this time of year. As she turned to her husband, she had a memory of looking out of the kitchen window and seeing him seated on the grass under this very tree, talking to Harriet. It had been at Joseph's christening, in the spring. Only a few months ago, yet so much had happened since.

Molly took a deep breath and prepared to begin. She had no plan in mind. She would see where her words took her.

Chapter Sixty-Six

If the family were watching from the kitchen, Molly thought, they would see how awkwardly she and Charlie stood together. Not really together at all, in fact. He was half turned away from her, looking down the garden, and she had clasped her hands so tightly in front of her that the knuckles were white. She tried to keep her voice steady as she spoke.

'Charlie, I was very surprised by what you told me yesterday, of your plans to go and work in Cheshire. Is it because of . . .' She could hardly bring herself to say the name. Agnes had assured her yesterday that Harriet wasn't a part of this but she needed to hear it from Charlie. 'Is it because of Harriet?'

He didn't reply so she pressed on. 'Either way, have you considered how far you will be from us all? From the girls, from your grandchildren? Everyone will miss you.'

She waited, determined to make him break his silence.

He turned even further away from her, dug his hands into his pockets and put his head down. 'I chose it because it's far away. I'm ashamed of what has happened, Molly. It's an effort to look you all in the eye. I can't explain my actions. It's as though they are those of another man, a stranger to me.'

He turned towards his wife. 'If I go, you can all get on with your lives. I can send money regularly, you won't want for anything. None of you. But I can't stay here and be reminded of what I've done every day.'

He held up his hand as Molly made to speak. 'The thing is, I still don't know why it happened so I don't feel safe. Until I know that, until I can come to terms with it, I don't feel I can be around you all.'

Molly was confused. Charlie had sounded as though his mind was made up about leaving. Yet his last words implied a degree of uncertainty. She stayed silent while she tried to work it out. Then, weighing her words, she spoke. 'Charlie, I don't know what has happened, or why it happened. I don't know why Harriet came back into our lives and managed to cause such havoc. I was away in Faversham when the Assembly Rooms ball took place. I didn't witness what happened there, or when you were spotted as you walked together by the sea at Westgate.'

Charlie winced and turned away from her again but Molly pressed on. It was hurting her to relive what little she knew but he needed to hear it.

'I don't know what went on when Harriet moved to Ramsgate. I know that you didn't go to see her one weekend because I saw you walking by the sea, close to home.'

Charlie glanced at her. It seemed he hadn't noticed her that Sunday morning as she gathered eyebright.

'I'd hoped that it was over between you and Harriet. That we might talk, even though things were still difficult with both you and George.' It was an effort for Molly to recall the events and the order in which they had happened, how one thing might have led to another.

'Charlie, I'm sorry that I didn't tell you about Nicholas. Or about George. I know that I upset you. It was wrong of me and I think – I hope – I've explained why.

'I've been angry and sad about what has happened. It's made me very unhappy over these last few weeks and, if I'm honest, I'm not even sure what I want any more. But we've been through a lot together, brought up three lovely daughters, been reunited with my son. We have strong family bonds, still, and I don't want any of that to be thrown away.'

Molly's throat was dry. Despite all her words, she was still nowhere near saying everything she wanted to say or asking what she wanted to know.

She took a deep breath. 'Are you still seeing Harriet? I know you went back to Ramsgate again, the Sunday after I saw you by the sea. The day when Judith invited me for dinner.'

It was a while before Charlie spoke. Molly felt he was deciding whether or not to tell her the truth.

'I did,' he said at last, in a voice so low she had to strain to hear. Her face must have betrayed her feelings for he added hastily, 'But I only wanted to see her to warn her, to tell her—'

Molly cut him off. 'I don't want to know what did or didn't happen with Harriet. That's a secret you must bear alone if we are to move forward.'

Was it wrong of her, she wondered, to want him to feel something of the agony she had endured over the years of having to keep her own secret?

Charlie gave her a look of anguish. 'But it's important you should know.'

'Hush.' Molly said. She held out her hand to Charlie and he hesitated, then took it. The feel of his strong fingers brought a rush of tears to her eyes. It was so long since she had felt his touch. They stood for several long moments at a distance, linked only by their hands. Then Charlie drew her slowly in until she laid her head against his chest. She could feel and hear the beat of his heart, strong and regular, a little quickened. She drew a long, shuddering sigh.

She and Charlie had taken a long journey, apart rather than together. For Molly, it had been a hard and lonely road. Her soul felt scarred by the unhappiness. They could never return to how things had been before. This time, Charlie must carry a burden and feel the consequences of it.

Their love had been a quiet love, constancy. She had never wanted it to have to weather such storms: the revelations over her foundling son; Charlie's passion for Harriet. But they would be the better for it, she felt. She couldn't know what lay in the future, but she hoped they would support each other, love their family, enjoy their grandchildren. And love each other, in their own quiet way, as before.

A thought came to Molly, totally unexpected and unbidden. 'If you are set on going to Cheshire, then I will go with you,' she said.

She felt Charlie start and the beat of his heart quicken a little, then return to its regular rhythm.

'You would leave the family?' he asked. He held her away from him, so that he could look into her face.

'I would,' Molly said, nodding. She bit her lip. It would be a hard decision to take, but her daughters were well grown and happily settled, even Agnes. A pang struck her at the thought of the grandchildren. How quickly they changed as they grew: she would miss a great deal if they weren't close by.

'At least if I was with you, I could make sure that we visited the family each year,' she said, hoping she sounded braver about the prospect than she felt. 'And in any case, if you went to Cheshire and I stayed behind, I would have to leave this place.' She looked around at the cottage and the garden. 'It goes with your work and Mr Powell would need it for the new head gardener.'

She couldn't read Charlie's expression but a wave of weariness overtook her. She couldn't say another word on the subject. A final resolution would have to wait for another day.

'I feel quite faint with hunger,' Molly said. It wasn't true. She still felt too overwrought to have an appetite, but she was keen to go back indoors.

'Let's go and see whether Agnes and Judith have dinner on the table.' She turned towards the house as she spoke and caught a glimpse of someone – George, perhaps – moving sharply away from the window.

She smiled to herself and drew Charlie's arm into hers as they walked along the path. There was still much to be settled but she hoped they had taken the first tentative steps towards a solution to their unhappiness.

CHAPTER SIXTY-SEVEN

A nd so Molly and Charlie's marriage moved on to a new and final phase. In accordance with Aunt Jane's wishes, and to compensate for her having been unable to attend the garden party, the family gathered at her house in Princes Crescent the following weekend. And, also in accordance with her wishes, Molly and Charlie were there together. They did not hang off each other's words. Neither were they endlessly entertained by each other's cleverness, as they might have been had they been a young couple newly in love. Nor were they entirely separate, for they arrived and left together but spent the interval in between mostly apart, as might be expected of a couple married for nearly twenty-five years.

And yet, when Molly sat and talked with her sisters and Aunt Jane, her eyes strayed to Charlie in his usual spot, standing with the other men around the hearth. His attention was not totally engaged by the tale Uncle William was telling and his gaze, in turn, wandered to the end of the room where his wife sat. Occasionally, their eyes met and Aunt Jane was not the only one in the room whose heart rejoiced when she witnessed the look that passed between them.

Sally and Catherine were watching them closely, while trying very hard to appear unconcerned. They were seated at the other end of the room, by the window overlooking

Princes Crescent. It wasn't long before Molly joined them there, unable to resist the sight of all her grandchildren playing together, Grace and Simon attempting to keep their set of wooden bricks away from Eleanor's clumsy fingers, while Joseph's eyes followed their every move.

Not five minutes later, Charlie drifted away from the mantelpiece and joined the group by the window, standing behind his wife and resting his hands lightly on her shoulders for a moment, before getting down on his knees to play with Grace and Simon. Judith exchanged a smile with Molly over Charlie's head, and if anyone noticed that Molly's eyes were brimming with tears – happy ones, judging by the smile on her lips – no one said a word.

In any case the arrival of Margaret and Henry, coming as it did in the midst of a downpour, caused a distraction. Rain had been a feature of each day since the garden party, causing every person in the room to stop at some point during the week and say, 'Imagine if the weather had been like this on Saturday. The whole day would have been ruined.'

When Margaret and Henry had shaken off the rain, apologising for their dampness and lateness, they followed the example of most of the couples in the room and separated. Henry took up Charlie's place by the mantel, where his breeches began to steam gently in the heat from the low fire, lit to keep the unseasonal chill at bay. Margaret sought out Judith and, after a few minutes' conversation, scooped up Joseph to 'give him a little squeeze'.

The family tableau was complete: Sarah and Constance were at Aunt Jane's side with Lizzie and Mary; Helena and Susan were standing slightly apart, discussing the arrival of a new gentleman in town who had, unfortunately, caught the eye of both.

George was now holding the floor instead of Uncle William, who had grown tired. He was telling tales of his seafaring days to Lizzie and Mary's husbands, along with Luke, Francis and Henry. Into this now rather crowded drawing room came Hannah, to announce that food was laid out in the dining room, ready for everyone to help themselves.

After she had withdrawn to the kitchen and the guests had filled their plates and re-grouped between the two rooms, Molly slipped away to join Hannah downstairs. She found her with Elsie, tidying up in preparation to deal with the washing-up generated by the gathering. Molly hardly needed to reassure Hannah that all was well again, for the sparkle in her eyes and the flush on her cheeks spoke of something beyond the wine at the party and the warmth in the upstairs rooms. They embraced and exchanged a few words before Molly mounted the stairs, returned to the drawing room and sought out Charlie, tucking her hand into his. He folded his fingers around hers and absent-mindedly kissed the top of her head, causing those around them to smile – not in a patronising way but with joy that a balance had been restored at the heart of the family.

And so the party drew to a close as, not long afterwards, did the stories of some of those in the room. Aunt Jane lived on for another few months, but she hadn't recovered her strength enough to see out another winter. One night in December, she fell asleep but didn't wake in the morning. Uncle William was consumed with grief and the family rallied round to make sure he was never alone for long, yet he, too, slipped into everlasting sleep the following February. Although not before learning that Sarah – whose marriage had been a bitter experience, thanks to his son – had found new happiness and was to be married in the spring to a widower, a well-to-do gentleman: a neighbour of hers in Greenwich, where Constance, too, had found a suitor. The house in Princes Crescent was put up for sale and Hannah, who had been left a generous bequest in Aunt Jane's will, was at last able to retire and care for her mother in her final years in Faversham.

Constance and Sarah, it turned out, were not the only beneficiaries of Uncle William's will. He had become reconciled to the idea of having three grandchildren, leaving sufficient money to George and Margaret, too, to ensure that, with prudent management, they would be comfortably off for the rest of their lives.

Agnes, who had had to return to Ramsgate before Aunt Jane's party, had surprised Molly by also finding a husband within the year: a widower, somewhat older than herself with no children, who was delighted by his new bride and a ready champion of her artistic talent. They remained in Ramsgate in a charming residence in Liverpool Lawn where Agnes, taking the drawing room overlooking the green as her studio, became a portrait painter of more than local renown.

Her portrait of Molly joined the family group she had painted two or three years earlier, which hung over the fireplace in Molly and Charlie's parlour. Charlie had spent a good deal of time deliberating over where to place the new portrait: above the samplers stitched by his daughters and Molly? Or on the other side of the mantel? In the end, he had hung it near the door, saying that the sight of it each time he entered or left the room gladdened his heart.

Molly's brave offer to accompany Charlie to Cheshire was never put to the test. Francis heard of the job offer through Catherine and was quick to inform his father discreetly that he was in danger of losing his head gardener. Mr Powell acted at once: he raised Charlie's salary, offered him an area of the garden to develop as he wished, and increased his budget for his plant-buying trips to London. He also mentioned the possibility of travelling to foreign lands to search out unusual specimens there for the gardens.

Charlie was happy – and quite possibly relieved – to accept all that was on offer, apart from the suggestion of travel abroad. He told Mr Powell that George would be a better candidate for such a role, being an experienced traveller already. He himself was happy to stay as he was, and where he was.

And content he was, indeed. He and Molly had weathered the storm and emerged at the other side – not quite different people but certainly not unmarked by their experiences. They were careful around each other at first, but slowly found their old rhythm of life. Charlie devoted less time to the garden – leaving some of the management to George – and spent more time with his wife. And so the years rolled by, as they do in any family, with marriages and births, comings and goings, sadness and happiness. Molly and Charlie were never tested in the same way again and, if life was sometimes quiet in the years that lay ahead, they were never heard to complain.

PART SEVEN

HARRIET

Sydney, New South Wales
December, 1825

*A*s I write these lines, I am sitting at a desk overlooking what I suppose I must call a forest – but not the sort of forest you will be familiar with. This is a forest of what are known here as gum trees, with a scent that rises to fill the air on the hot afternoons we suffer at this time of year, and with bark that peels off in strips, exposing a trunk as smooth as paper. Peculiar things they are, as are the birds filling the air with their calls: parrots and cockatoos – far more exotic than those you might see in the trees in your parks and gardens. The animals, too, are of the kind I suppose you would be more likely to find in the zoological gardens.

But I digress. I am a respectable widowed lady here, living quietly with my brother, in a little house with a view over Sydney Cove, where we strive to create a thriving new community of souls. We have no murderers among us – at least, not that I'm aware – but we have those who sought to steal and offer violence. Now violence can be turned into the energy required to clear the land for planting. As for stealing – what would be the point, in such a small settlement? It would be uncovered in an instant. Our pastor instils into us what is right every Sunday, and I have become a helper in the church. As far as everyone here is concerned,

I have an unblemished record, unlike the other souls in our tiny congregation. They do not know that I also sought to steal something – and someone – that didn't belong to me.

That seems a lifetime ago, and I would like you to know that I have suffered. The sea journey that brought me here should have been the death of me. It certainly took the lives of many on board, through illness contracted on the journey, such was the overcrowding. In my case, it was terror that was nearly my undoing – I never, in all those long months, became used to the lurching of the ship, the cracking of the sails and creaking of the masts as the wind changed direction, the heart-stopping moments as we crested waves and plunged down again into the depths. Depths that I thought would take us to the bottom of the ocean, only to find us still afloat and ready to crest another wave. Each day, I thought I must surely die and I devoted myself to caring for those who were suffering on board, hoping that I would contract what they had and be carried away myself, my body cast overboard far out to sea.

My life was spared, for whatever reason, and I arrived in Sydney to find John waiting for me on the dock, helping me onto land on legs that refused to do my bidding. I found that I had earned myself a new reputation among the hopeful settlers who had shared my ordeal, as a godly woman, one who had selflessly cared for others on the endless journey from the port of London.

I have come to realise, in the years that have passed since I worked at the Royal Sea Bathing Hospital, that I am more like my mother than I care to recognise. Let us just say I am resourceful. I can be what you want me to be, while also getting what I want to have.

I had planned to stay awhile with Mrs Garrett in Ramsgate, once it became apparent that Charlie had given me up to return to the comforts of his family life. He would have thrived here, with his knowledge of plants and growing seasons. A man with his skills could do very well for himself, very well indeed. But he wasn't the adventuring sort, in the end. And my plan to lead John into the arms of the magistrate worked very well, but caused my downfall, too. The Royal Sea Bathing Hospital had been aware of the loss of valuable items of jewellery. When they received a report of a ring – apparently stolen from one of their patients – having been found in Ramsgate, they made enquiries. It was but a small step from quizzing the pawnbroker to discovering my address on the receipt for the earrings.

I left Rose Hill in a hurry, although I managed to take my little nest-egg with me. Martha never did get the second part of her bribe. I suppose it wouldn't have hurt Mrs Garrett to learn that she should be more careful whom she trusted in the future. I wonder whether Charlie came looking for me again, after he failed to appear on the Sunday when I was expecting him. No matter: if he had done Mrs Garrett would have told him what she'd learnt. If he hadn't already heard something of the sort from the gossips in Margate, I suppose.

As it happens, I went looking for him. I couldn't stop myself. I made my way to the Woodchurch Manor garden party, choosing to follow a route through fields and woods to avoid being spotted by anyone who might recognise me. I loitered a little distance away from the guests, hidden from view among the trees. I suppose I thought I might see Charlie looking forlorn and then I would have stepped out and surprised him. But he was hard to find, busy among the crowds, and in the few glimpses I caught of him, he was smiling. Molly was there, too, walking with George, Margaret not far behind on the arm of someone I took to be her beau. I felt bitter then. I was the one who had convinced her to go the ball, helped her find her family and a place in society. It was as if I had never existed. I thought about making my presence known, imagining the shock on all their faces. It would have been almost worth the risk of being apprehended to see their expressions. Instead, I turned and left the way I had arrived.

355

John was magnanimous when I wrote to him. After all, it turned out I'd done him a favour by getting him sent to Sydney. As soon as he had arrived, he had made himself useful to the officers. He had an eye for an opportunity and had his pardon within two years of landing. This place is full of those who are no longer the same people they once were; it is a positive virtue. We work hard, John and I, and I suppose we are what counts for prosperous around here. My brother will take a bride, I am sure. He is over forty now, but that matters little for a man.

I see the sails of a ship across the bay. New arrivals from England: I will go down to the wharf to see what assistance I can offer. Perhaps there will be someone whom I can take under my wing. It is amazing how trusting people can be, weakened by the length of their journey, made uncertain by the strangeness of the land in which they find themselves. They confide in me, grateful for the encouragement and support I give them, the doors I can open. All these little bits of information, so useful. Perhaps not now, but I store them carefully, writing them down for a time when I may have need of them. Very few in the colony can read and write. I intend to turn my skill to my advantage.

My ambitions have increased over the last few months. I hear the governor's wife is interested to meet me, hearing of my kindness in helping new arrivals find their feet. That would be something worth sharing with my relatives, who have no doubt never given another thought to my whereabouts or wellbeing since I left. I may write to them – or, at least, to Margaret. I would like her to know that she owes whatever happiness she has found to me. For now, I must ready myself: dress in my dark blue silk gown, which suggests refinement and prosperity without being showy, and go down to the wharf to introduce myself. I am Molly Goodchild and who is to say otherwise?

HISTORICAL NOTE

This novel is a fictionalisation of a period in history and although every effort has been made to retain historical accuracy, some liberties have been taken with the setting and historical events of the time.

The Royal Sea Bathing Hospital is a real place and the building still exists today, although converted into apartments. Dr Lettsom is also a historical figure, but the way the hospital was run and the acceptance of private patients is down to my imagination.

The location of Woodchurch Manor and its estate is loosely based on that of Quex House, with the garden descriptions influenced both by the gardens there and at Goodnestone (where Jane Austen visited and walked).

The references to the unseasonal weather are a nod to 1816 being referred to as The Year Without a Summer, a result of a volcanic eruption in Indonesia causing changes high in the atmosphere and affecting weather patterns around the world. Crops failed in Britain, as a result of the unusually cold summer weather and volume of rain, leading to food shortages. It would have been a very difficult time in a country still recovering from the costs (in men and money) of the Napoleonic Wars.

Historical Note

ACKNOWLEDGEMENTS

Thank you, as always, to my agent Kiran, at Kean Kataria for her unfailing words of wisdom and support, and to my editor, Eleanor Russell, at Piatkus for her encouragement and enthusiasm. Thank you to Francesca Banks (and the rest of the team) for getting the word out about the series. Thanks also to Hazel Orme for bringing clarity to *The Lost Sister* with her skilful copy-editing.

The Tuesday Writers – Alison, Helen, Jane, Jess, Keith, Sarah, Simon and Sindy – were a weekly dose of uplifting energy online throughout the isolating months of the pandemic in 2020, when much of this book was written. And my family and friends never failed to be a reminder of how important relationships – real or fictional – truly are.